UNDENIABLE SPIRIT

UNDENIABLE SPIRIT

Michelle Gillen

authorHOUSE®

AuthorHouse™ LLC
1663 Liberty Drive
Bloomington, IN 47403
www.authorhouse.com
Phone: 1-800-839-8640

Published by AuthorHouse 12/18/2013

ISBN: 978-1-4918-3749-8 (sc)
ISBN: 978-1-4918-3748-1 (e)

Library of Congress Control Number: 2013921520

I would like to dedicate this book to my mother, for all her efforts in helping me get my voice out there, and my family for their unending support in me.

Sayuri
August 12th, 1945

"Sayuri-chan. Sayuri . . ." Her voice floats into my troubled and hazy mind, causing me to lift my head from my arms. I found myself huddled in a corner. My mother crouched in front of me, holding a dirtied plastic cup, pitiful despite its size, of water to my face. Giving her a grateful look I took it, raising the cup to my lips to take a much needed drink, then spat out the liquid. The water tasted of oil, rot, and saliva, making me scrunch my face.

"You must drink it. It's good water . . ." My mother's admonish trailed off, her tone fatigued. We both knew this wasn't the time for arguing over how water tasted.

"Not good water . . . No." I shook my head, my throat dry and parched. Trying to burrow into myself, to disappear out of this wretched place, never worked. This was here and now.

Three days had passed after the atomic bomb dropped from the U.S. air forces on Nagasaki, the place where I lived. My mother and I were the only survivors of our family after the explosion. We both knew if we didn't find enough food or water we would meet the same fate as the rest of our village.

It's hard to survive in a catastrophe. Images of disaster similar to the ones I saw in the textbooks in school haunted me and darkened my heart. They helped me understand how people felt in those situations in the agony and pain, faces twisted, thoughts all the same. My eyes watered, but I refused to cry. *Being strong in more ways than one shows true spirit,* my mother once said. The tears dried and left me. They held no purpose.

My mother's black hair once shined in its effulgence and fullness. Her complexion matched the women in magazines I used to browse through when I had nothing to read. Now she looked half crazed and emaciated as she gave up cajoling me to drink, downing the whole cup's contents in a single gulp. Gurgling and clutching her stomach she lay herself on a ripped straw rug, her breaths ripping into my ears in a disjointed beat.

Her quivering body showcased ribs and veins; my mother was a shell of what she had represented to me. It broke my heart.

My fingers ran through the strands of my matted, dirty hair. If I owned a mirror I knew I'd recoil from my appearance in a different situation. Now I didn't care how I looked. I knew we'd both die soon enough.

The thought of my father and Baunsu, my dear sweet brother, entered my brain. Their bodies hadn't been found in the rubble, adding to the numbers of the dead. I remembered them in great detail, just memories now. Memories of life that would never return.

My mother's leg twitched, her face twisted. She flipped over and over, trying to find a comfortable position she could sleep in. It deepened the rift in me and I pushed on my temples, trying to find some ground to balance on in my shaky reality.

I pushed away the blanket of hopelessness, not wanting its darkness. Too much of it existed in me now. Too much of it clogging me.

Standing on shaking weak limbs and walking outside the crude impression of our home, which had become annihilated, I looked for sustenance. The dismal dark clouds cloyed the sky and leered down on me. My jaw set, my worn and punctured shoes crunched on gravel, glass, wood, and other bits and pieces underfoot. All my hopes and happiness vanished. The cold biting wind whipped my frail body, its intent to divert my path. I continued, looking this way and that for anything of nourishment.

Cockroaches scuttled from my path, fat antennae waving in the wind. The more unfortunate ones crushed under my footsteps, adding to the loud crunches of fibers under me. Broken rubble, destroyed statues, and uprooted trees were the remains of the small village I lived in for most of my life.

Pawing at the pieces of house and wood, even if I knew it wouldn't do good, a part of me, a small part, hoped to find something to change everything in this moment. I gasped as the prick of a splinter entered my pinkie finger. The tiniest drop of blood fell and splattered on the inky soil as I clutched my hand close to my bosom. Another breeze buffeted my body, my hair undulating in its wake. If I became any lighter I'd believe my body could fade into the darkness altogether.

Musk, soot, and smog filled the air, blanketing the sky. It seemed hazardous to even breathe the air and live. Feeling lightheaded after a few coughs I returned back to what resembled my home for now, my lips pressed into a line.

Plopping to the soiled tatami mats once more made me sigh. My mother rolled over on the mat and gazed at me, eyes half glazed over, expression chilling. Something looked wrong about the way she slept. Her body lay motionless, like a rock.

"Mother?" My body shook as I crawled over to rouse her. No response elected at my touch. I knew why even as my mind refused to face reality: My mother had just died on me.

I lay beside her, deriving warmth from her body, agony reigning in my heart, the dark chains binding my organ tighter in its grip. Then came the next painful realization: I was now the only one left in the village. The only girl who survived.

Dear gods above, why must this happen to me? I'm just seventeen years old!

When night fell I trembled like a frightened child under a tattered blanket, my body curled into a fetal position, my eyes scrunched shut. I tried to sleep. It felt impossible. My mind tossed and turned over and over, adding to my discomfort. I heard the sounds of reluctant life, of scavengers creeping back to the place they once called home. They squeaked, chattered their teeth, and scuttled across the ground.

I sneezed once, then again and again, my chest wrenching with each olfactory explosion. The night grew cold, my outlook becoming the same temperature. I wrapped the blanket tighter and felt the prick of an object below my body. As I moved, in the gloom, a long thin blade shone like the arrogant eyes of a winner.

A frown furled my lips downward as I took the handle in my grip and placed it on the other side of me. I knew it could help me now more than ever.

I had survived the test of survival, but the road to proving it to others had just begun.

Sayuri
Middle March 1947

I walked outside, breathing the air that smelled cleaner and cleaner as each day passed. A tombstone jutted a ways away from my shelter for my mother. The small flowers I could find now lay around it, serving their purpose to embroider the dismal slab of stone. They were sweet peas, my mother's favorite flower.

The wind buffeted my body with a gentle touch and the sensation of my long matted hair, streaming behind me, rushed into my senses.

"Mother? Do you see our village from my eyes? Do you approve of this slow renewal?" I asked the sky.

Two brown rats fought over crumbs of leftover soiled food at my feet, segmented tails erect and twitching as they bared their teeth at one another. After a moment I shooed them away with my foot. Numerous muffled squeaks told me that somewhere in this junk heap a rat family survived just like me.

To keep myself busy I decided to scavenge for more food. The sunlight pierced my ragged body for a moment after escaping the clouds, causing me to stop for a second to think. The rays lay on my skin like warm fingers.

The sun shied away again and the darkness returned to its rightful place. Something still gleamed in the soiled dirt and I crouched to pick up a small glittering object. A locket of some sort. Its gold color sparkled in my palm despite the gloom. I opened it to see the words: 'Wakai raibu ka shinu', pop at me and nothing else.

Eyes burned into my back. I turned and noticed someone sitting on the rocks near my shelter. A teen, just like me, sat cross-legged as he watched me, eyes intent. In all of the years I've spent living alone I figured I was the one survivor of this small village's utter demise. Feeding on shoots of grass and scant water was enough to make anyone go insane, let alone survive.

"Who are you?" I asked, tensing in place. Options came into my mind and I contemplated whether or not to wait for his answer or become defensive. My curiosity won over my wariness and I waited for him to speak. If worst came to worst I still had another means of escaping trouble. The sharpened dagger at my side awaited its use.

"My name's Akio and I'm here to help you," the guy said as he stood, leaping off the rocks.

"Help?!" A startled laugh bubbled from my lips. "In this wretched place there's no way you can help me! I've lost all I ever loved. Nothing can bring them or my happiness back to me. You seem quite at ease around someone you don't know, Akio."

He walked over to me, a strange look in his eyes. Upon a closer inspection I could see a slight scar slashed across his dark eyebrow. His golden-brown eyes breathed a certain life I didn't have. It made me scowl.

"I've lost everything as well. You can see I'm harmless so you can ditch the caution," he said, his tone gruff. Tensity rose in me. He was perceptive. Such a person would have no trouble finding weaknesses in a person.

"I also have the feeling that it's better if we stuck together. One person living alone is kinda pitiful and lonely, don't you think? I can tell you've lived alone for a long time. Don't you miss human company?"

His question irritated me but he looked ready to continue speaking so I let him, sealing my lips.

"Teamwork's needed now more than ever. You never know what lives beyond the borders." Akio looked pleased, as if he thought he sounded smart to me. I didn't buy it for a second.

"That's why I'm armed," I said, narrowing my eyes. He looked at me and burst into a laugh. His chuckle faltered as I took out my dagger, holding it at the ready in his vision to show him. Akio's mouth flattened and he advanced over to me, one eye on my weapon. All traces of his previous emotion disappeared.

"You're a fool, a real fool. You think you can wait until people come save you without perishing? You believe you can find hope in flying solo? Well hear me out. Other surviving people like you around here won't feel as considerate as me. Those few people, their hearts will have turned from lack of faith, lack of mental stability even. They'll do anything to survive, even kill if given the chance!" Akio's voice rose as he grabbed my shoulders. "Don't you understand?"

"Now why would you want to pair with me, a pathetic girl who can't even save her own mother." I leered at him as I pulled my dagger from the broken tree limb it pierced when Akio grabbed me.

"For survival purposes. Now give me your answer." Akio stood straight, looking like an authoritative person.

My eyes narrowed again as thoughts ran through my mind.

Akio seemed like a valuable ally, notwithstanding my concern for him being a total stranger. His strange mature personality could come in handy. To consider me as someone to trust made me want to laugh, but not in jest.

"Fine. I'll join beside you. Don't even think of trying anything stupid, Akio." I sheathed my dagger in my dirty kimono pocket.

Akio nodded. "What's your name, if you remember it."

I stood still, for a whisper snaked into my mind. *Sayuri . . . Sayuri remember who you are.*

"It's Sayuri," I said.

"It fits you." A faraway gleam entered his eyes. I felt bemused, but shook it off, not wanting to ask.

"That's where you live now?" Akio gestured to my dingy shelter. "In this structure?"

"Yes."

"Hmm, better than what mine used to look like before it caved in on itself. Shall we go inside for the day?" he suggested, stepping foot into the crude impression of my home. His bold action made me grit my teeth, but I knew I couldn't say anything. I didn't own the destroyed establishment.

"What happened to you when the atomic bomb dropped?" I asked as he turned around, eyes looking at me in question.

"That terrible day . . ." Akio trailed off, pain entering the hardness in his eyes. I just looked at him, waiting for him to continue.

"I remember the day being normal. I had been lazing around the house, my mother asking my father if he watered the bonsai plants outside on the porch. A large boom sounded after she spoke and it escalated the longer it lasted. My family didn't know what to do or where to go as the whole house shook. Our possessions—everything—fell off the walls and shelves, shattering on the floor.

"Everything went white to my vision as a rush of smoke, flames, and destroyed establishments crashed into our house. When I could see again I saw my family still standing and alive. The look in their eyes and the soot and dust staining their clothes horrified me. My mother stood over a cracked picture of her sister and she wept, crumpling to the floor.

"After we consoled each other and made sure we were fine my father left the house to check outside for help. My mother and I huddled in the farthest corner of the house, the least destroyed part, waiting for him and the help he said he would find for us. We clung to the hope that everything would turn for the better. My father never returned.

"Wailing and groaning became our ambiance, the sounds coming from people with missing limbs and destroyed families. If it felt impossible to sleep it felt even more impossible to stay asleep. My mother prayed to the gods often, pleading them to send protection for us and all the families in the village. The gods never answered her prayer.

"My family and I were lucky to have survived the first night and we all knew it. However, the next day, my mother never made it. She died from radiation poisoning," he said and pressed on his palm with his thumb.

I felt confused by his gesture but his eyes looked cold once he finished, his expression free of pain.

"What about you?" Akio asked and I felt my guard come up again. I knew I still couldn't trust him to hear my story. It made me wonder why he felt so open around me.

So I settled on telling him something shortened. "My whole family perished just like the rest of my village's people and every other one in Nagasaki had. I couldn't save my family or even myself from what the Americans did to us. I don't know why the gods decided to let something terrible like this happen to us." I shook my head. "I'm surprised I'm not dead yet."

We fell silent, just sitting on the soiled tatami mats, looking anywhere but at each other. My dagger's tip poked into my side and I shifted in position.

"You do realize we can't stay here. We have to go on to find another place," Akio said and I turned to look at him as he continued, "I don't have a map or anything to help steer us in the right direction but once we leave we can head to a nearby village, if one exists."

I sensed he would take charge of our survival by himself.

"We set off tomorrow so why don't we rest?" He looked at me. I sighed and nodded.

Sayuri
Middle March 1947

The sound of voices woke me and I leaped to my feet, dagger in hand.

Akio's eyes blinked open. He looked at me, eyes narrowed, until the voices sounded again. He rose to his feet as well.

"I hear people outside, Akio!" I said in a low tone.

"So do I. Perhaps they're rescuers for any survivors," he said. He sounded cautious.

"Why would any search parties for survivors come here?" I asked, giving him a look. "The destruction happened well over a year and a half ago."

"Maybe other people survived like us."

I peered outside alongside Akio, seeing strange outfitted men trudge through the broken wasteland, kicking away rubble and anything else in the way of their spiked boots.

"Why does something about those men unnerve me?" Akio said the question under his breath. After his words a loud crash sounded as the walls to my fragile shelter collapsed. I flinched along with Akio. Six men stood in the light as the dust cleared, looking at us. Adrenaline rushed through my senses. They looked ready to kill to me.

"I told you survivors still lived in this rotten dump!" one of the men said in triumph to one of the others. They didn't notice our stares as they glared at one another.

"How's Yuki supposed to know? What do you think he has psychic powers or something?" a sarcastic voice said in reply to the first man who spoke.

"Who are you people?" I asked, trying to sound calm and collected. The men faced me at my words, chuckling at my attempt at intimidation.

"Why would two children still hang around this dump? Don't you know there's no life here?" one of the men asked and, as he shifted a foot in anticipation, I saw a long sword sheathed to his belt. It made my forehead scrunch. It's rare to see a man with a sword in Nagasaki or anywhere else in Japan. Were these men stuck in time? They also wore the strangest get up I've ever seen. Black armor shone on them from head to toe.

"You're loitering Jaakuna lands!" said a voice. An even larger man entered the scene, armored as well, a scowl on his square face.

"I don't know who or what the Jaakuna are, but I can tell you guys don't realize that armored men only exist in stories now," I said. Akio and I gave each other a smooth cursory look. His face held impassiveness and calm, but I could see the anger behind it. We both knew the men outnumbered us.

"People undergo changes in destruction. They revert back to their roots and remain in the same way until they feel it's safe," the large man said, a grin on his face. "So too bad. As long as it helps us with our plunder I don't care how my men or I look. This little village we stand in now? It's ours and so are the other lands we can capture."

The other men bared toothy smiles at his words.

"We didn't know you guys own this land now. We planned to leave today and didn't know you all would appear," Akio spoke, butting into the conversation. The armored men looked at each other, unspoken words passing through them.

"We can use them, right leader?" asked one of the Jaakuna to the leader in an undertone. The larger man's eyes alighted on the dagger in my hand, noting it. No emotion flared onto the leader's face at this observation.

"Hmm . . . They look too weak to serve any purpose," another Jaakuna man said.

"I disagree." The leader turned to him. "Every potential victim of destruction we find will look the same way. We do need more hands to help rebuild our own village. Wasn't that the point of this whole mission? To find slaves? Don't question me about capturing them, guard. Bind them."

My teeth gritted. *How dare they call us weak!* The leader's words made my grip tighten on my dagger.

No one noticed the movement as my dagger flew into the air and embedded itself into the armor of one of the strange men. The man I struck didn't flinch at the impact or look pained. All men now drew their swords.

"Feisty, eh? I guess you want to prove something to us?" the leader asked as he brandished his blade.

"That was poor, Sayuri," Akio said to me under his breath. I looked at him, set my jaw, and turned back to the men. The dagger still stuck in the man's armor and he pulled it out, inspected it, then tossed it into the rubble. As if it looked like a piece of rubbish.

Akio's hand rested on my shoulder and I contemplated whether or not to shrug it off until he grabbed me and fled, making the Jaakuna men flinch.

"Oh no you don't!" a Jaakuna man called out and dashed after us. Akio grimaced as his toe stubbed against broken plywood, but he still kept going, me in his arms.

"Don't let them escape!" the leader yelled as we made it out of the broken establishment. The Jaakuna men crashed through the destroyed house, hot on our trail.

The air outside smelled of charred skin and smoke, which confused me. Nothing had burned in the village since the day of the bombing. More of those Jaakuna men stalked through the rubble in the distance, burning objects in blazing fires. I saw a limb and then I knew: the men decided to burn the dead and emaciated bodies of people they saw, throwing the corpses into the flames and feeding the fire. It horrified me to see how heartless those Jaakuna men acted.

"So what's the plan?" I asked as we dashed out the village. "You can't carry me like this forever."

"You're right, I can't." He dropped me, making me grunt.

"What did you do that for, Akio?" I said as he turned right around and helped me to my feet, contradicting his rudeness.

"Use your legs. Run!" he said as the sound of tromping feet came closer. "I'll distract them from following you."

"Great. How am I supposed to find you again if this plan succeeds?"

"I'll think of something. Just go!" He waved me off and I dashed away, not waiting to hear him a third time.

Dead trees whizzed past in my vision, branches slapping my arms and legs, making them sting and itch. I continued on, breath huffing. I didn't want to waste any valuable time.

My chest heaved and burned, slowing me down, and anger for my weaknesses rose in me. Over and over I loped into a dash after slowing to a jog, trying to widen the distance between those Jaakuna men and me. The sky still glared down on me in the same charcoal gray color as yesterday. I ran through darkness.

A crow's raucous call ripped through the forest. I was alone, just as I had after my mother died. The feeling gave me a strange sense of discomfort. I sidled down a tree trunk and rubbed my temples, griping my head in my hands. Things had spiraled out of control and balance fast.

"Now how will Akio find me?" I asked aloud, as if the atmosphere held all the answers for me. Shaking my head I leaned against the trunk, sighing. *What a stupid plan . . .*

The sound of a fallen branch cracking made me tense. I lifted my head and stood, ready to run.

A sword embedded with a slick thud into the tree trunk inches above my head, making me to dash on impulse to escape my potential enemy's sight. A curse sounded as the Jaakuna man on my trail came after me.

My heart in my throat I looked around and spotted an uprooted tree trunk, brown roots sticking in the air like fingers. Without thinking of any consequences I leaped behind it and held my breath, trying to find my dagger. Spitting a small curse under my breath I remembered that the Jaakuna man threw it into the rubble.

Crawling under the tree's roots, breaths snatched and hiccuped-sounding, I tried to slow my heart beat and make every inch of my body disappear. The Jaakuna man's thundering footsteps crashed on the other side of the tree.

"Where did the girl get to?" He sounded frustrated and out of breath.

I pictured him gazing around like an idiot, expecting me to materialize from the air. I tensed and curled into a ball, straining my ears to hear. A footstep sounded close, too close, crunching on dried leaves and the soil near my arm. My eyes focused on the black spiked and belted boot, my breaths coming out hot and silent.

The feet lingered for a moment more then the man spat on the ground and left, sword gleaming in his hand. I lay on my back, safe for now.

I wiped sweat off my brow, feeling faint, and breathed in and out, in and out, willing myself to return to calm. I thought about where Akio went to and if his plan turned out successful.

The clouded sky darkened and I wondered if sunset loomed close. Instead a drop of rain fell, pattering the hungry soil and leaves. I turned over to my side and there, in the undergrowth, I saw eyes watching me.

After a blink the eyes disappeared, dread coursing in my veins. I knew I couldn't stay here and face capture by those strange men, but I knew this solitude of tangled roots was all I had now. Akio entered my brain again and I figured he'd come find me once the Jaakuna gave up their search.

Shivering, I felt stray droplets of rain slather themselves across my arms and feet, the cold making me flinch. I had just escaped certain peril today, I knew it as much, but the situation would still stay the same tomorrow. The men wouldn't stop trying to find me so quick.

In my pocket I felt a small circular object press against me: the locket I found yesterday. I didn't know what compelled me to take it and keep it, but that's where it'll stay.

By nighttime I began to feel worried for Akio despite myself. The woods seemed alive with the sounds of rats and hardy insects. *He should start to look for me now while he has the advantage of the night.*

A sound lashed into the air: a yelp. Then nothing. I blinked, jarred from my moment of reverie. The sound could have come from an animal, although a bad feeling stirred in my gut. My eyes closed and everything else faded away as exhaustion took over me. I couldn't stay awake anymore and contemplate Akio's whereabouts.

Following the next morning Akio still hadn't come for me. I sighed, stretched, and crawled from my shelter. The air smelled dewy and I peered around with a cursory movement. No Jaakuna lingered about, encouraging me to walk a few paces.

"I guess I have to go find you now, Akio, right?" I asked aloud as I picked up the pace, going back the way I had come. Sure it sounded dangerous to backtrack, but I didn't want to leave behind an ally, one who I had just started getting used to. A secret part of me blamed myself for getting Akio into this mess, but I waved it away and focused on the task. I'd worry about doubts and blames later.

The morning was solemn, which sounded good to me. The scenery looked the same the longer I traveled and the longer I looked for Akio. Familiar sights such as a broken signpost on the ground popped out to me, making me feel relief.

Trodden leaves and broken branches became more apparent sights as my path continued. When the sight of blood slathered on a tree trunk came into my vision a cold shiver ran through me.

The next sight made me flinch: a person looked right at me, limbs shackled to a tree trunk. It was Akio.

"Akio? What happened to you?" I called, going over to him. His expression looked dark.

He shook his head. "Don't come closer, Sayuri."

"Why? What's gotten into your head?"

"It's a trap."

I took one step closer. "What trap? For who?"

Akio didn't respond, his face twisting as I stepped nearer and stopped five feet away from him. I waited a moment, then snorted.

"Nothing happened, you see? Now let me help unshackle you-" My breath caught as what felt like a boot slammed into my back, knocking me to the ground. I couldn't move for a split second, my muscles tensing in shock. The boot lay planted on my back, pinning me down into the dirt. Rage filled me.

"Hmph! Seems this was too easy for us," a man said and I squirmed to see behind me. A Jaakuna man stood, one foot on top of me, sword gleaming at his side.

"I told you . . ." Akio trailed off as I swung to look at him, a glare on my face.

"You proved to us a challenge, brat. Your friend over there was much easier to capture and use for bait."

It all came to me and I wriggled with renewed vigor. The man pushed down harder, his foot digging into my back. I huffed, annoyed as my struggles became futile.

"You got her?" Another Jaakuna man entered the scene, who I remembered led these strange men.

"Yes, the plan proved successful, Yuki, sir."

"Good. We spent enough trouble trying to catch these two together. Bind them and bring them back to the village." Yuki nodded his head and left again. Another Jaakuna man came and held me down as the first man produced a rope, getting ready to bind my hands.

I went to try and squirm, but a second realization came to me. I had exhausted my body to its limit. If another chance came where I could escape I might not have the stamina to follow it through. My jaw set and I stole one glance at Akio, who had a blank and fatigued expression on his face.

"Just think, we're saving you from certain death if you let us take you without resistance," the Jaakuna man binding my hands said, a cruel laugh following his words.

"Listen up lass," the leader said, leering into my eyes, "you're now the property of the Jaakuna. If you betray us or try to escape, the penalty's merciless death. The same goes for your friend over there as well."

I licked my chapped lips as Yuki and the other Jaakuna guard lifted me to my feet and held me in iron grips. Another man stepped around the trees to unshackle Akio from the tree, holding him in a visor-grip, spitting on the ground.

"Let's go! March! We'll arrive at our village in forty minutes," Yuki said.

With a hasty 'sir yes sir', the men assembled, beginning to walk, forcing me to move my feet. I still contemplated punching at one of them, despite having my hands bound.

"This is for yours and our own good, girl," the man holding me said. "If you want people to regard you as trustworthy I'd suggest you follow every order and keep your mouth shut."

Blood blazed in my veins. I wanted to instill pain on him and all these arrogant Jaakuna in any way I could once I escaped.

We arrived at a crude version of a village. Haggard people lined the side of the dirt road, jeering as our group passed them. Some people who looked unfortunate gazed at us from shanty-looking houses. Sweat and grime left their stains on these people; I couldn't help but gawk.

The more fortunate houses, built in the traditional gassho-style, looked fine except they had no windows for light. Long sheets covered broken doorways, the linen material fluttering in the wind. A smell came from them, one I couldn't specify. Some houses had signs specifying what they represented.

"Keep moving!" a Jaakuna man said. I hastened my steps and stumbled as a man pushed me, a chuckle spreading throughout the people.

My breath caught when the smell of rotted flesh and bile blasted my nostrils, causing me to gag. Akio smelled it as well; his nose wrinkled.

"You'll get used to it, just as they have," the man holding me and Akio said, gesturing to the people in the street. He looked at me. "I'm your guardskeeper. Korudo's my name. Remember it."

The group parted and Korudo hastened our steps through the village. My gaze turned to the rundown houses, the dried blood, grime, and mud all about the area. It made me feel sick to know this could happen to a village over time, this desolation. I assumed the atomic bomb affected them more than any other village. In my village the people always looked clean and methodical. They never knew what it felt like to have poverty strike them.

We came to a stop before a half-destroyed building. "In here." Korudo led us alongside him. As we went inside I noticed desolate-looking people gazing at us from prison cells. Korudo chuckled at my horrified expression as we came to a stop in front of a vacant cell. He shoved me in and locked the cell door behind me.

My voice sounded shrill to my ears as I snarled and banged on the bars but Korudo just snorted over his shoulder, eyes flashing. He continued on, Akio looking back at me with his lips parted halfway as Korudo led him from me.

I slammed against the cell door until my shoulders screamed out their aches. "This is all your fault, Akio. If you tried harder to prevent the Jaakuna from capturing you we wouldn't have to deal with these Jaakuna guys," I said under my breath, gritting my teeth.

The cell smelled of a previous person's odor and splats of blood, dirt and other debris stained the floor. Cracks in the concrete ceiling showed some chunks of the sky behind them, as if to tease me.

The people in cells juxtaposed to mine watched me slam my body against the cell door, sympathy in their eyes. One man muttered the words, *"Oni no ie"* over and over, eyes closed, brow shiny. Another man rocked, his knees held into his chest, not speaking, eyes dead.

Exhausted, and out of breath, I collapsed to the ground, feeling frustrated. If only I wasn't so weak . . . My body thrummed in pain as I looked around to see if I could spot any weakness in the metal bars. Nothing jutted or jumped to my eyes.

With a huff I craned my neck to see if Akio's cell was anywhere near mine. My hands slid together, but they made no further movement to show they could slip free from their bondage. A small scream built in the back of my throat, hot and ready to release itself. I held it back, gritting my teeth. Again and again the vision of my carelessness back in the forest entered my mind, further angering me.

A shushing sound entered my ears and I turned, seeing the man who had been repeating his strange phrase looking at me, mouth moving without words, eyes darting to me and back to his cell door. I cocked my head at him, disturbed by his manner, and he beckoned me over, mouth still moving in a 'shhh'.

I blinked, then wriggled over as best as I could over to the boundary of our cells. Until he drew a knife, making me gasp.

"Shhh," he said over and over as he made a gesture for me to come closer, weapon gleaming in the weak electric light shining down on us. His eyes looked just as dead as the other man's, who now curled on the floor, groans coming from him as his legs twitched. The sight reminded me of my mother, who had slept in the same position two years ago after drinking the contaminated water and sealing her fate. I pushed it out my head, sickened to have let my insecure emotions free themselves inside me.

"Shhh." The strange slave's voice lowered as he saw me edge closer, his eyes watering, his hands shaking. I tensed, expecting any moment for him to reach out and slit my throat. However, no malice existed in his expression. If I looked closer I could see a desperation and deep sadness as the darkness in his eyes cleared. His breath sounded shallow as my back rested against the cell bars, my head sideways to watch him in close. For some reason I trusted this slave with whatever he would do to me.

I flinched as his knife slipped past the roping and cut it, cold and slick, freeing my hands. They dropped to my sides and I looked at the man.

He sheathed his knife and asked, voice hoarse in a whisper, "Okay?" His whole body trembled as he looked at me, eyes watering still. Pity rushed in me for this man. He had just wanted to help me, the only person he could help in the span of time he lived here behind bars. What right did I have to assume he wanted to harm me for any purpose?

I nodded my head. "Yes, I'm okay. Thank you . . . friend."

My words lifted a weight off his chest, for he sighed and closed his eyes as his fingers twitched. His rags for clothes rattled as he shifted position, his back turned to me, breath snatched and shuddered sounding.

I rubbed at my wrists, the slashed rope laying on the ground, frayed ends sticking in the air.

The man who groaned and twitched fell silent, body laying limp as he slept, his breaths hollow and soft.

A frown curled my lips. I crawled over to a nearby mat, the one thing barring my limbs and body from touching the grime making up the ground in my cell. The sky behind the ceiling showed the looming darkness as rain fell, pitter-pattering the ground next to me, and hitting my body. I shivered, closing my eyes, keeping true to the hope that tomorrow could host a way for me to escape.

"Wakey wakey," said a man, his tone menacing to my ears. Upon opening my eyes again I saw someone standing behind the cell door. It seemed I had closed my eyes to sleep for just a few seconds. I remembered the man's name, Korudo, as he leered at me, squinted eyes glinting.

"You slept long enough. Come along now. It's time for you to witness your future, should you cooperate and act like a good little slave," he said. A jangle of keys marred the somber air and my cell door opened with a shrill squeal. He sauntered over to me as I leaped to my feet, disgust rippling in me.

"Seems as though you somehow broke free of the roping." He glanced at the severed rope by the cell boundary. Korudo shook his head. "No matter, I have an extra means to keep you from trying to escape." He took out a chain and reached to grab my arm.

I tensed, readying myself to push him away until a small voice called, "Don't!"

Startled, I paused and turned to see the strange man who cut my hands free look back at me with a small subtle shake of his head. He gasped upon noticing the chain gleaming in a sparse glow of the afternoon sunlight in Korudo's hand. He recoiled, eyes dilating, and skittered from the cell boundary, shaking his head. "No, no no!"

With my attention deterred Korudo snapped the chain clamp on my arm, the cold metal burning my skin. With a rough gasp of my own I tried to free myself, but he held his end of the chain tighter.

"Come along now." Korudo tried to pull me with him from my cell. I refused to budge.

"Stubborn, eh?" He took a hold of my arm in one hand and squeezed, eyes boring into my own.

"No, no no!" the man cried out again and Korudo turned to him.

"Pipe down you insignificant thing. Or I'll feed you to the rats just as I had done to your brother!"

The man yelped, hiding his face behind two grime-stained hands.

Korudo shook his head in contempt and pulled me with both the chain and his strength. As much as I tried to fight him it proved too much for me. The metal bit into my forearm and the pressure against my skin worsened if I resisted. Knowing I needed my arm I gave up and let him pull me. Korudo's triumphant expression seared me.

"You put up a bit of a fight, I'll give you that," he said, leading me. I refused to respond, not wanting to speak to him.

"Spunk's the line drawn between a coward and an expendable person." He pulled harder, making me stumble. "The slave behind bars next to your cell is a coward. He deserves no recognition from anyone."

Korudo's words made my jaw set. *How dare he mock the man who helped me!* I set my teeth, hoping the Jaakuna man would stop talking.

"I'll wager he's the one who helped cut your hands free. It doesn't matter anyway. Guess I'll have to just keep a closer eye on you from now on."

The wind tore through the village as we walked, shoe steps echoing on the gravel and dirt roads. Village people peered out of houses, their eyes meeting mine. They withdrew, as if shamed to have made eye contact. All around a tense atmosphere took over the village. Goosebumps rose on my skin and I gazed around, expecting specters to leap out and attack.

Korudo chuckled at my concern and yanked me along. A dog barked thrice in the distance, then it yelped and fell silent. I swallowed, moving my feet and letting the Jaakuna guardskeeper drag me. My stomach started to flip the longer we walked.

The sight opened up to me like a book and made me gasp. People gathered around in a circle up ahead, some laughing, the sounds piercing my ears, while others just stood mute, watching. I squinted to see better and went rigid as the sight of people in chains, Jaakuna men lashing them with a whip, came to me. Korudo growled an order to a Jaakuna guard close by, who saluted and headed off to do as told.

"Welcome to the slave trade. Here's the event that changes lives," Korudo said, eyes gleaming. We entered the arena and people parted the way for us, some whistling and others just staring. The Jaakuna man dropped me to the mushy ground and held on tight to his end of the chain.

"Is that scrawny girl a part of this trade?" a man asked, licking his lips as he took out some yen.

"She's just here to see what her fate in the next slave trade is next time." Korudo shook his head. "Slaves need to see what they'll deal with in the coming months. Since she just arrived yesterday I wager Yuki would want to break her in first." His words didn't conceal the mean contempt and anticipation in them.

I shivered and turned away, bile rising in my throat. The slave trade dragged on and I remembered what my mother had told me about this kind of thing.

"*Sweetheart, in other countries they have what's called a slave trade. It's when people gather others and sell them to receive money. Often the sold men become slaves. Most of the people who buy them don't have a nice bone in their body. They don't care for the well-being of their new slave. Slave trade can also happen between people of other races. It's a cruel world we live in, my Kawaii.*"

"*Is there a slave trade here in Nagasaki, mother?*" *I had asked.*

"*Who knows, Sayuri-chan? People can do almost anything now without restraint . . .*"

Lost in my memories the jerk of the chain on my arm startled the wits out of me. Korudo yanked on the chain and said, "Get up. The trade just ended."

I sighed and stood, the Jaakuna man leading me back to the slave establishment, not a word said between us.

Once Korudo took the chain off my arm and locked me into the cell the strange man came alive again, rising from his fetal position on the ground.

"You hurt?" he asked, and I retrieved the notion he couldn't speak well. I shook my head no to reassure him, sitting down in a huff on the mat, rubbing the chaffed skin on my arm.

"Why did you tell me to stop before when Korudo came into the cell? I could have escaped," I asked, giving him a glare.

He just looked at me with a blank expression, then said, as if ridiculing me, "Korudo would have hurt you."

"So?"

"No . . . don't get hurt." He came over to the cell boundary. "You the first female slave."

"The first in this . . . Jaakuna village?"

"Yes."

"Why?" I prodded when he fell silent, eyes flittering about him. He looked down, eyes hooded.

"Jaakuna believe females don't work efficiently as slaves."

These words angered me. "Females work just as hard as males!"

"I know." He nodded. "Show them."

An idea spawned in me at this moment, making me pause. A heat began to blaze in me. *Maybe if I roped into the Jaakuna's plans and followed their orders their trust for me would rise and then—*

The man made a small grin as well, as if he knew he helped me formulate a plan.

"Okay?" he asked and I nodded.

"Yes." A question came to me and I looked at him. "What did Korudo mean by feeding your brother to the rats?

The man's smile faltered. "My brother . . . he did bad. Korudo came into his cell one day and threatened him. He said if he didn't shape up the rats would come. My brother told me he tried his best. One day my brother came back to the cell. He told me Korudo was on his way. Coming to kill. I tried to tell him . . . about escaping, but Korudo came. He opened cell door and wrapped a chain around my brother's neck." He looked as though he couldn't go on anymore as he covered his face.

"Bastard! He had no right to do that!" I said and the man flinched at my curse, looking at me.

"He did it."

We fell silent. Not wanting to hear the man's emotional gulps of breath, I asked, "What's your name?"

He looked at me, leaned closer to the boundary, and said in a tearful whisper, "Yowai."

"I'm Sayuri, Yowai-san" I said.

Yowai looked at me now and, in a hoarse voice, he said, "You're blessed . . . blessed."

His words made me cock my head, but once footsteps sounded in the establishment the slave's smile ran away. He crumpled to the floor, lip quivering as he watched his cell door. It made me wonder if he expected Korudo to come and kill him as well.

Instead a short stocky man with long greasy hair entered my vision, his squinty eyes gazing straight at me. I shuddered. Yowai sidled to a seated position and stared at the man, lips parted.

"Here you go, slave. Your lunch," the man said as he crouched down and pushed a bowl under the cell to me. I went over to it and saw my "lunch": Lumpy soup. Bits of floating green matter in the gruel made my lip curl. I took one whiff and, feeling my eyes water at the rank of the food, refused it.

"You gotta eat it or you'll waste away and what fortune would you give us Jaakuna?" The man stood, looking at the other slaves. "You don't see the other curs in this hellhole complaining." His expression flared as he looked at me. "Fine. Soon enough you'll start to feel like trying it, sweetie, I promise you." He shot me a glare as he waddled to another cell in a lurching gait. I shook my head, accepting his unspoken challenge.

"Okay slave. Here's what'll happen to you, starting now," Korudo said as he appeared and walked over to my cell. Yowai cringed and turned his face after seeing the chain at the Jaakuna man's side. I looked at Korudo, keeping my face blank, but open, following Yowai's advice to show him my strength and willingness to obey.

"In order for us Jaakuna to make a good deal and profit off selling you in the future, you have to prove yourself. What better way to do so than by helping us rebuild our village?" He leered at me. "A perfect opportunity, one you can't refuse."

"Whatever." I held back a sigh.

Korudo barked out a raucous laugh, as if he had a private joke. He opened my cell and clamped the metal band around my arm. Yowai trembled, but looked as though he tried fighting it. I shot him a cursory nod to ease him nerves while Korudo led me out, muttering to himself under his breath.

He told me I had to push heavy stones to the village for building, and that he'd keep a close eye on me. The Jaakuna man watched me with surprising alertness as he readied a whip, eyeing my every movement. Feeling insecure I focused more on the labor as I approached the stone, which looked in every way bigger than me.

"How will I push this?" I turned to him, arching a brow. "It's bigger than me."

"Shut your trap and push it to the warehouse shack over there." He sounded bored as he pointed to the warehouse, as if he received this question all the time from the other slaves.

I rolled my eyes and turned around, putting both hands on the stone and pushed.

"Push harder!" He glowered at me as I panted, feet slipping on the mud. The stone did move, but at a snail's pace.

"You who thinks you're so strong. If you don't even own true strength how can you prove it?"

I flinched as the crack of a whip lashed my back, knocking the wind from me. My blood boiled in the now inflamed area.

"Push!" Korudo said as he stalked over, hoisting me to my feet using one arm. Gritting my teeth I yanked my arm out his grip, proceeding to push until my legs gave away again. Then he whipped my back until I stood.

Once my body crumpled to the ground and refused to move after pushing it to the warehouse, Korudo stalked over to my side and spat saliva near me. "What a useless lump you are. I expected more of a fight from you."

I swallowed back a retort and tried to stand, my limbs quivering. Then I thought better of it and said, "Too bad. What you have's all you get."

"You will not talk back to me, slave," he said, his neck tightening as he raised his hand. The blow came in a flash and made me grunt, white lingering at the edges of my vision. My hand rose to feel the heat blooming on my cheek. Korudo laughed.

"Come on, get up off the ground now," he said as he hoisted me up, tired of watching me try to stand. "If you can't do anything productive without acting weak what's the use for you?"

I said nothing as he jerked the chain, taking me back to the other stones.

"You better shape up. If you don't I'll feed you to the rats and no one, I repeat, no one will care. Understand? Get to work on the other stones. You're not done yet."

I hadn't seen Akio since the day the Jaakuna captured us and I hoped he was all right as I proceeded to try and push the next stone. Although somehow I knew he was fine. In the short time we were together I knew Akio could face anything that came his way. I envied him for his strength . . . because I sure didn't have any.

The stench of the soup grew worse since the day before, but it still served as nourishment and it made my stomach growl. When my hand reached out to grab the plate on instinct I mentally smacked myself, trying to convince my hungry self that the gruel could have been poisoned.

"Pah! What a waste of food. Oh well, starve. Or you can have our special for today: fresh raw pig meat," the man who gave me the soup yesterday said, a bark of laughter following his words after seeing my twisted facial reaction.

His grimy hand reached in my cell and he grabbed he platter, guzzling it whilst smearing the juice off his face with the back of his hand.

"Mmm . . . tasty! My favorite!" He let loose a cackle, clutching his barreling belly and stumbling away. After he left I curled into a fetal position and rubbed my arms until sleep washed over me.

My dreams were dark; they caused my breath to catch. I couldn't scream or move as images of terror flashed over and over of the Jaakuna, the atomic bomb, and blood. Then nothing as the sensation of precipitation slathering my skin entered my senses, waking me.

The rain rushed down from the cracks in the ceiling. They felt like the tiny needle the doctor gives you, except in a larger multitude. I opened my eyes and watched as Korudo walked past my cell, then backtracked and peered in to look at me. I feigned sleep, keeping my breathing even and slow, not wanting to deal with him. Not after what he had said to me.

Korudo muttered under his breath, something about women being weak-hearted, and laughed. He walked out of the establishment, his head shaking.

Feeling miserable I rose to a seated position and picked at my nails, removing the gunk behind them. My hair fell like drapes down the sides of my face.

"Labor yesterday?" Yowai asked as he looked at me and I nodded.

"Hard work. Korudo whipped me when I couldn't continue."

His eyes darkened. "My brother. He said the same happened to him. Then the Jaakuna killed him."

"I guess I have to try harder, Yowai-sama."

"Only way."

"Yes . . . it's the only way."

"You came here alone?" he asked and I shook my head.

"No. I came with someone named Akio. A friend," I said and felt a frown tug on my lips. It seemed like a long time since I'd seen him last. Even if three days just passed. Yowai looked solemn.

"A friend." The way he repeated my words made it seem like they sounded foreign to him. As if he never had a friend or heard the word before in his life. Maybe he hadn't . . .

"Are we," he stumbled over his words, "friends?"

Yowai looked at me, eyes watering, and I knew the answer. Even if we met just a few days ago I knew I could trust him.

"Yes, Yowai-sama." I tried to make a smile, but one wouldn't come so I settled for nodding. The man's face bunched before he came over to the cell boundary, reaching his hand out for me. I came over and took his weathered and callused hand in mine.

"Blessed . . . Sayuri. You'll survive the *Demon House* many times over."

I nodded to his words, not knowing what he meant. He held my hand for a moment more then let go and went back to his mat, rocking his knees to his chest. A small smile lingered on his face. He looked so peaceful for a moment that not even Korudo entering the establishment tore at his mood.

"Time to work," Korudo said as he unlocked my cell, clamping the chain around my arm again. I rose to my feet as he led me out into the whipping wind and pelting rain. I looked forward to the labor, despite feeling wrung out after it ended. It was the one escape I had from the cell holding me caged like a wild animal from normal life.

Once again I pushed stones, seeing the Jaakuna men running around like busy ants, assisting one another with machinery which helped drag and pulverize the stones. So why did I have to push stones all the way over to them? Were they that lazy?

I saw other slaves outside today, their faces drawn, their limbs quaking, their eyes dilated and full of fright. I felt myself reach out to them, wanting to help them even if I knew I couldn't.

Korudo whipped me again and again as my legs slipped. It made anger blaze hotter in my blood, but I felt helpless. If I tried to fight back it would sever the slow trust the Jaakuna started to build with me. I had to show Korudo I wasn't looking to escape. Once his guard lowered I could break away and help Akio escape as well.

The Jaakuna guard's mouth hardened as he said, "Take a break."

I blinked, not sure if I heard him right. Yesterday he whipped me senseless if I even paused in my movements. Now he wanted me to rest? I decided to follow his suggestion and stood still, collecting my snatched breath. My work was almost done anyway, the last stone I had to push waited in front of me to reach the warehouse, which stood ten feet away from me.

All too soon Korudo snapped his whip in the air, indicating my break's end. I turned to the stone and pushed, willing my fatigued muscles to work and push. Someday I'd find a way to escape. Someday . . .

One of the slaves died in the night. The one who quivered and groaned to himself, his dead eyes seeing nothing. The one I compared to my mother. Korudo and three other Jaakuna guards came into the slave establishment and carried the slave's dead body out the establishment. Yowai and I watched, feeling remorseful. Even though we hadn't known him he still had been a fellow slave.

I sat in my cell once Yowai went back to sleep, picking at my nails without success. Flies darted to and fro in the air above me, the buzzing of their wings being the ambiance besides the chirping of birds. I could just imagine how I smelt.

Korudo came by as usual to drag me out to work, but this time something seemed different about him. He didn't look gruff and his rough demeanor appeared to have disappeared as he held out a hand to me instead of chaining my arm.

"Come along now!" he said, holding out his hand. I stared back at his face, which looked pinched. If this was a trap then I sure wasn't falling for it. His neck tightened the longer I refused to move.

"I can't wait all day," he said, his tone returning to its usual gruffness. I blinked and gave up trying to think of a reason why Korudo trusted me not to break free and run. I had to stifle a snort. I figured my plan must have worked. I had tricked him into thinking I wouldn't escape.

Sighing I heaved myself to my feet and gave him my hand, which he held in an iron grip before pulling me to the work field.

As I pushed stones I flinched when Yowai entered my vision, heading to a stone as well. He looked at me, pity in his expression, then began to push his stone, his face melting into concentration, his muscles straining.

I turned to my stone and pushed it as well, noting that it didn't feel as hard as it had in the beginning. It moved quicker each day I worked and soon the rocks moved enough where I felt tired after the last rock.

I didn't feel hungry anymore. The hunger pangs in my stomach faded, a lull replacing them. Yesterday the stocky man brought out some decent food for us and all the slaves, which we ate like savages. I had never felt so full since I lost my home but now the hunger felt horrible when it came back, still lingering around long after the initial pangs ended.

Being so intent on my thoughts I missed the feeling of a tiny stone pebble slide under my foot and I gasped, falling against the stone, my wrists scraping against the rock. I tensed as Korudo unsheathed a whip from his belt without hesitation and lashed me, the bite of the leather snapping against my skin.

"Leave her alone!" came a voice and I looked to see Yowai stop his stone pushing to look at Korudo.

"Shut your mouth you slow speaking idiot. I can do whatever I want to her. Trying to act like a hero now, you coward?"

"She slipped. No reason to whip her." Yowai defended himself and me and I felt saddened. He didn't have to to jump to my case. My slave friend stalked over, startling the guard watching him, and clamped a hand on Korudo's shoulder, who grimaced.

"She's been slipping since the first day. You wouldn't know about it anyway since you're too busy living in a dream world. Maybe you should wake and face reality. Your brother died because of the same reason." The Jaakuna man's voice had levels of disgust in it.

Those words made Yowai's face contort and his lips parted as the color drained from his face. He looked at me for a moment before he faced Korudo again. A new flame burst in his eyes, a realization had just come to him.

"Get this cur away from me." Korudo turned to Yowai's guard, shrugging the slave's hand off his shoulder, and the man nodded. Yowai's mouth uttered inaudible words as his guardskeeper dragged him to the slave establishment, his eyes watering.

"I want you to stay awake past the time the moon's high in the sky," Korudo said and I stood, glaring at him. After hearing what he had just said about Yowai there was no way I'd go anywhere with him. Despite that a strange confusion entered me.

"Just do it!" He glowered at me, impatience making him shift position several times. "Don't you think that's better than just sitting in your grimy cell and staring off into space like you do everyday? I have the key for your door anyway."

After a long moment I nodded, my curiosity taking over my wary feelings. Perhaps when Korudo wasn't looking tonight I could find a way to escape . . . .

The moon crawled higher to the middle of the sky behind the ceiling cracks. The spring night air felt cold enough to the point where I could see every exhale I made. The Jaakuna gave me a blanket for the night, but it probably harbored lice or any other parasite from the person who had it last. It warmed my body, despite the fibers making my skin crawl.

Soon a figure appeared, the clang of a key as it opened my lock reverberated through the night. Then silence—nothing, until a soft pop sounded as my cell door stood ajar. The sounds woke Yowai who looked at me, then at my cell door. Wariness took over his expression.

I stood, my legs wobbling, shifting towards the opening where Korudo waited. His arm stretched out to me. I wondered what happened to him that made him change his attitude. I took his hand, feeling curious as to why he gave it a healthy squeeze before dragging me along behind him.

Korudo led me out the slave establishment and I wondered where he would take me as we passed house after house, heading out the village. Did Korudo realize I should go free instead of being enslaved? Then what about Akio?

The night air felt brisk as we kept good pace. The moon shone through a cloud cover, its effulgence reduced.

A small dirt trail appeared and Korudo made a sharp turn for it. Had I not caught myself I would have fallen flat on my face. The path took us out the village, but not far. He said nothing to me the entire walk.

"Here," Korudo said as we stopped in front of a large oak tree, its gnarled branches and new growth shining in the gloom. It looked beautiful. In all the time I spent in the Jaakuna's village I've never seen anything like this. I knew I'd never forget it. The smell of flowers wafted in the air and I breathed in deep, missing the smell of them. They were sweet peas.

"This here . . . is my mother's grave." Korudo closed his eyes and opened them, looking off into the distance.

I looked, spotting the slight hump of dirt under the oak tree. It seemed like a beautiful setting to put a loved one in, I had to admit.

I gave him a look. "Why did you bring me out here? Do you trust me so much already?"

His expression flattened at my words; it looked as though he tried to struggle with it. A pained expression now replaced the previous one and that's when I realized I almost slipped in my words. If he ever found out about my tricking him into trusting me my plan would fail.

"You somehow remind me of my own mother. That's why I brought you out here. Despite acting weak you have the undeniable spirit my mother had. No one besides you and I know this place is in remembrance of her. Not even my own father." Korudo fell silent. I shifted position on my feet, unsure of how to respond or if I should respond to him at all.

I decided to speak. "But why bring me of all people, a slave, out here? That's what I don't understand."

He looked at me. "There's this weird feeling I have each time I see you. It's almost as if you're special in a way I can't explain." He turned from me, contemplating what he said, then he whirled and his eyes met mine. A coldness now existed in them. "You know what? I take that back. You're right. Why would I bring a weak slave like you out here to a place that means so much to me?"

"Maybe to tease the slave about escaping."

"Maybe. Well, we both know you can't escape now, not without your friend."

I gritted my teeth. Of course Korudo would know I couldn't leave a friend behind in the village. Maybe that's another reason why he felt at ease. He knew that my trying to save Akio would stall me and give him more of a chance to find me and catch me again, should I escape.

"Come on, we spent long enough here," Korudo said and grabbed my wrist without warning, wrenching me back to the village.

"Why did you spare me from the slave trade anyway?" I asked, my breath coming out in short huffs as I hurried to keep up the pace. Korudo sighed and glanced back at me, slowing his gait.

"Must you always question what I do or say?"

I had to snort. It seemed I had just frayed the last of his patience.

"Yeah, because what will I do instead? Just sit there and take everything you tell me? I'm not keen on just accepting what an enemy says to me."

"You'll listen to what I say and you won't say another word against it, got it?" Korudo said and I rolled my eyes, exasperated and done talking to him.

As he led me to my cell I saw that Yowai watched me, eyes solemn.

Once Korudo left after locking me in my slave friend spoke. "Sayuri. Bad news."

"What happened?" I asked, feeling tense.

"My guard not happy. He said I need to shape up. Or else the rats come."

"Why? All because you tried to defend me?"

He nodded his head.

"Oh Yowai-sama . . ." I trailed off, knowing he would sacrifice his life for the well-being of mine. "You shouldn't help me anymore. I don't want to feel responsible for your death . . ."

"I must help!" His voice sounded strong in this moment, as if he had just found hidden courage and wanted to express it. "You're my friend. Friends . . . help each other . . . right? Always there for each other. You're better than most, Sayuri-chan. You're someone worth saving. You're helping me. I must reciprocate your kindness."

His words made my throat thicken and I looked at him, seeing in his eyes the clarity of his words and the truth they held.

"You're all I have now. All—" He seemed to fumble with his words, "—all I need."

We fell silent and in the gloom I could see new lash marks on his skin, some bleeding, while others scabbed over and turned black. I looked no different, lash marks left their red bands on my skin as well.

"Why does your guard tell you to shape up, Yowai-sama? It's the first time you've done this," I said.

"No. it's not." He shook his head. "Before you came . . . I didn't do well. Jaakuna men captured my brother and me. We came here and they worked us. We worked in the fields, pushing stones. I was the weaker brother . . . and they forced me to do more because of it. My brother . . . felt shamed at times. He knew I wouldn't survive long if he didn't do something. He tried to escape. Tried to go back home for help. Jaakuna caught him and gave him one more chance, but he disobeyed them again. He knocked out his guard and tried to run. Again, they caught him. Relentless.

"Later that night . . . Korudo killed him. 'The rats were hungry' Korudo said. 'They needed food.' He took my brother away from me, killing him right in front of me. I'm next now . . . to join my brother."

"Don't say those things," I said, shaking my head. "You can always try again, to prove to the Jaakuna you can survive as well as any other slave."

He rocked, his knees to his chest. "I wish I . . . had strength. Your strength."

"I don't have strength." I looked away, lip curling. "I couldn't even save my mother two years ago when the Americans bombed us . . ."

"You did what you could." His voice came after a moment, making me look at him. "We all do. Don't lose faith, Sayuri."

"Thank you, Yowai-sama," I said, hearing emotion in my voice that never existed in it. He nodded and looked off into the distance, laying down, breaths coming out in a shudder.

In the morning it rained in sheets. Korudo never came for me. I figured that labor wouldn't call my name today. However the other slaves, including Yowai, worked outside in the downpour, making me wonder why I wasn't out there alongside them, working until my limbs gave way.

I watched as the trees whistled in the wind behind the cracks in the ceiling, letting my thoughts wander back to last night with Korudo and the oak tree. Scuffing the dirt with my foot, I stood, stretched, then plopped down again.

I heard the sound of village people chattering outside and narrowed my eyes. Korudo hoisted me to my feet after coming into the slave establishment in that moment, opening the cell door door and pulling me along with him.

"What's going on here?" I asked over the wind and the crowd's voices to Korudo as we took a spot in the circle. The place where the Jaakuna sold slaves. He ignored me as a strange sounding horn noise echoed in the air, silencing us all. Yuki stepped forward then, sheathing the horn on his belt after preening his hair with his fingers.

"People of my beloved village! You might wonder why we're all gathered here today despite the weather conditions," he said. People grumbled agreement and shifted around, not happy about standing in the rain, hair damp and dripping.

"Well," Yuki said, flinging his arms wide in a flourish, "there's a rumor, albeit a small one, that says below our village in this area, gems of many sizes and shapes lay in the walls. All of them said to be worth thousands in yen."

Everyone cheered except for me and the slaves, and the Jaakuna leader waved his hand for silence. I noticed an elder man standing next to him. His face harbored an expression of cold indifference. The man looked as though he knew something we didn't.

"Now I don't know how true this is but Kimu," here Yuki gestured to the old man, "has told me this. It must be true. Why? I'm glad you asked." His eyes swept over us. "Kimu's an excavator of jewels. He has researched this land we now stand on to find insurmountable wealth."

The crowd roared their approval again. The Jaakuna leader looked pleased at the prospect and the acclaim the idea received from his people. His eyes glittered.

"So when do we start excavating for these jewels?" Korudo asked, obvious excitement and anticipation in his voice.

"We start when the rain lets up so we can dig into mud without any trouble. Here's the plan. We'll tunnel underground to the jewels under us. I'm guessing the area near the big oak tree about a few minutes away from here will suffice as a starting point for reaching our goal."

A look of horror flushed on Korudo's face, then disappeared. His reaction didn't seem to affect the village people, who cheered all the louder at this spectacular news.

Once Yuki dismissed us, Korudo led me back to my cell and locked me in without a word. Rain dripped into my cell, making some parts of the ground mushy. The electrical light above crackled and flickered as rain fell near it.

Yowai stared off into the distance until Korudo came back and led me and him to the campsite outside the village where already many people gathered. The oak tree waved in the gusts of wind and looked weighed down as the raindrops slathered it.

"Choose your weapons; I've crafted them to the best of my ability!" a man standing on a mat of rusty shovels said. I rolled my eyes and hoisted one "weapon", a shovel, in my grip.

"That's right, even women will help us in this glorious attempt for plunder and money," Yuki said and feminine groans sounded.

I stifled a snort as one woman called out, "Who's gonna take care of my children? You men can't be trusted to even provide for a child!"

"Yuki, why do we have to start digging at this point? Isn't there a better place that's even closer to the village?" Korudo's voice reverberated and, from the look on Yuki's face, I could tell the question was foolish.

"The reason," the Jaakuna leader drew his words out, eyes darkened, "is because this place, right here, holds something special."

Korudo's face drained itself of color and Yuki laughed, turning with a flourish at us all.

"It seems Korudo has forgotten the rule not to question me. Right?" he leered at him. Korudo's throat tightened, his gaze training itself to the ground, not meeting Yuki's glare.

"Now my crew, start to dig! Don't show any hesitation or you'll have serious consequences to consider!" The Jaakuna leader brandished a whip, glaring at us. The slaves and village people thrust shovels into the sucking fresh mud.

A semi-large hole in the ground yawned into the day when Yuki stopped us for a short break. Once it ended, he ordered for us to continue digging in a diagonal this time, eyes gleaming in mad delight.

I felt tired and sluggish from repeating the same motions over and over again, not used to repetition of hard work. A painful whip crack across my back told me not to even think of stopping.

It felt like hours later when Yuki called out, "We stop here for now, my people. Tomorrow we'll start digging again, so don't get too comfortable at home. We should reach our goal in—" he paused, closed his hard dark eyes and opened them, "—in two to four days. So if you work hard, all of us will get a share in the rewards."

Everyone cheered, going their separate ways, throwing shovels down, rolling shoulders and cracking knuckles, relieving tension.

As Korudo led me back to my cell the old man, Kimu, stared at me, eyes narrowed, jaw tensed. Beside him the sweet peas lay, crushed in the mud.

Sayuri
Late March 1947

I almost recoiled when I spotted Akio walking around the slave establishment, sporting dinner platters for the slaves. As he walked over to my cell I wondered if he would speak to me.

"Sayuri! Are you all right?" Akio asked after making a cursory look around to make sure no Jaakuna guard watched us. He looked at me and most likely could see the cloying grime on my skin. Dark circles under his eyes jumped to his vision and grime made its own stain on him. I flinched as I noticed whip marks on his skin as well. The Jaakuna must have him do the pushing stones labor as well.

"I'm okay, Akio, but what about you? I felt uneasy when we separated the day the Jaakuna captured us," I said and Akio grimaced.

"I felt worried for you, Sayuri. I mean, it's all my fault we got caught up in this mess in the first place. I also worried about you being sold during the slave trade. Good thing Korudo made up the story about you having to watch what happens first. You'd now be a slave in an unfamiliar place without any way of escaping if it weren't for him."

A mysterious glint appeared in his eyes as he said this, but I shook it off as nothing, standing to come over closer to him. He set my platter in my cell and looked at me.

"Listen, we have to get out of here somehow. Together," I said, conviction in my words, and Akio nodded.

"Sayuri . . . you don't know how hard I've tried to think of a way we could escape undetected. Korudo seems to have his eyes on you all the time."

"What do you mean?"

"He's always around you when he lets you out of your cell for the stone pushing labor. I'm sometimes out of my cell at the same time as you, but I can never get to you because he's always there." Akio looked annoyed. "I come up empty every time I try to think of a potential plan. Something always comes up and changes my mind."

"We'll find a way out sooner or later. We should just let the Jaakuna's trust for us grow so we aren't suspected or kept a close eye on all the time."

"I think that's the best way, Sayuri." Akio nodded his head, then we both tensed as clumping heavy footsteps entered the jail.

"I'll try to find an easier way to keep in contact with you, all right? I don't want someone catching us now," he said in a low undertone as the footsteps came closer. "Promise you won't give up on me."

"I promise," I nodded, looking at him. All our hopes for escaping rested on him now. We both knew this.

"Sayuri . . ." His sentence faded as the footsteps paused. He hurried off, looking pained. I too felt pained, hoping I could see him again. He's the one person who could help me now. I needed him.

The stocky man who always carried dinner for the slaves now stood in front of my cell, a mean smile on his face. He thrust a bowl of what smelled like *Nikujaga* soup into my hands.

"It's a special order for you, girlie, from Korudo," the chef said, his eyes looking extra squinty today. "If you think the Jaakuna will trust you now because you haven't tried escaping, then you're wrong."

"Don't eat it all so quick now. You won't get the same gruel again." He laughed and waddled off to give the other slaves their share of food.

My mouth watered at every spoonful. I tried to drink it in a slow pace but all too soon it was gone. At least my stomach felt fuller than it had in days.

"Was that your friend before the chef appeared? The one you came here with, Sayuri-chan?" Yowai asked me as he finished his bowl of gruel. I felt terrible. He had to eat the gruel while I received the real deal.

"Yes. His name's Akio, Yowai-sama. He's someone I can rely on now for help."

My friend nodded, then fell silent. Yowai looked bedraggled and fatigued. His hands shook now more than ever and at night he seemed to have gripping nightmares that forced him to cry out and shake.

"Yowai, if Akio helps me escape, I'll help you escape too. We'll go together," I said, and this caused his head to turn.

"You'd do that? For me?" He looked at me now, a bottomless gratitude in his eyes.

"I will. No question about it."

A smile stretched on his face from ear to ear. I noticed since Yowai and I became friends he had become open and his sentences seemed to be getting longer. It made me wonder why he sounded clipped in the beginning when we first met.

Yowai stiffened as Korudo walked into the slave establishment, heading right for my cell. His eyes looked sunken and a frown lingered on his face. However, those beady eyes shone with purpose.

"Come!" he said in a ferocious whisper as he unlocked my cell, holding out his hand. I stood, feeling wary. He beckoned me closer, taking my hand into his, before whisking me out of the establishment, Yowai watching us go with worried eyes.

Korudo urged me on, pulling me, insistent to get somewhere. He glanced all around him, anger in his expression. The ferocity in his gaze took me aback somewhat. It was almost as if he wanted to exact vengeance on someone.

The village disappeared behind us and the digging site opened to my vision. Out of the corner of my eye, I could have sworn the massive oak tree looked ready to wilt and die. Even when the wind came the leaves stirred somewhat.

"We have to stop this before it all falls apart. Please tell me you will help me! I can't let Yuki destroy the one thing that means the most to me." Korudo turned to me and I just stared at him. What could I gain from helping the enemy? Did he trust me that much? After a moment of silence he looked at the tree, hands clenching and unclenching.

"How did your mother die?" I asked and Korudo whipped his head around to look at me. He sighed, walking over closer to me, eyes trained downward.

"It was five years ago," he said, looking hesitant but continuing, "my family and I used to live in a quaint village full of happiness and love. My father ruled over the clan, the Jaakuna, which you know now as the superior army in this village. Back then they were different. They didn't harbor slaves and they didn't live as poverty stricken as they do now. The Jaakuna men didn't believe in giving brutality to people lower than them. They wanted to protect those they lived among. They wanted acceptance and pride. A peaceful clan they were. The likes nobody in Nagasaki had ever seen before in their lives. People lived in hope, knowing the Jaakuna could solve any problem, feeling nothing but the lightest regard for them. However, the good times didn't last . . . but they never do in this life.

"My mother harbored a child who never survived outside the womb once she gave birth. The baby would have been my little sister. My mother didn't take this well; she started refusing food and became ill and mental. Her movements always looked jerky and twitchy. When I asked her once about our future she'd laugh and say, "There's no future for me or anyone else in this cursed plain of a village! My baby daughter's dead, you hear me? Dead! My only daughter!

"I would get frightened of my mother in these times, and I remember I'd cry at night, her words bouncing in my head. She made it seem as though it was my fault all along. Plus my father stayed away from home for longer hours so I didn't have another parent to confide in for comfort. I figured he knew what happened to my mother, so I respected his position to stay away and have some space.

"One day sunny day in May, something happened that I'll never forget." Korudo's voice sounded choked. "My mother couldn't take all the agony and sadness . . . so she killed herself. I walked into the kitchen after waking up for breakfast to find blood welling around my feet. I couldn't cry out, breathe, or move even as I saw my mother's unmoving body. I felt stuck in place, frozen and horrified at what my mother did. When word of my mother's death got around to my father something in him changed. He came into our village, glanced around, and ordered his army to take children and everyone hostage for slave labor. If the Jaakuna protested my father threatened them with a sickle-shaped sword.

"A strange look existed in his eyes and as I watched him through the window I felt the need to hide from his gaze. He saw me looking and stalked into the house, grabbing me by my wrist. 'Come on, Korudo-chan. We're going to a better place,' he had said, dragging me outside the house. 'What about momma?' I asked him and he shook his head, jaw tensing. 'She's gone now, Korudo. Dead. If she's not in this world alongside me, I'll never open my heart again.'

"The village people looked horrified and caught off guard at my father's request. They could do nothing but stare as their children were taken away, kicking and screaming, before they too were taken. My father warned that if anyone tried to escape blood would spill onto the soil. The Jaakuna took me and the other children to a place which looked too perfect to me. They continued to plead my father not to do this but he warned that he'd kill the next man who protested otherwise.

"Most of the children never survived long after being thrown in cells and I even thought I'd die next with each passing day. However, I wanted to survive. Life was all I had left to cleave to and keep despite its curse. I stole food from the other children in adjacent cells, but they never complained. They already given up their resolve to live after a few days of isolation from their parents. In time however, the dozen or so surviving kids and I weren't kept in prisons and my father allowed them to walk around the grounds of the Jaakuna village. I'd always wonder at night, laying on the grimy ground, why and how my father changed. As I grew older, I took on the tasks of serving the town and guarding people of interest. The village soon fell to poverty, people selling any and everything just to get by in life.

"The children became bullies when they reached their teen years. I've had more than a score of fights with them, showing them their place. Some even became my trusted advisers. Most of them hated my arrogance and determination. I always readied myself for the day those teens would gang up on me. Good thing that day never came.

"I never refused any of my father's orders and did all my duties, which earned me a place to stay close to his house in the village. I never once thought of escaping because I'd have no place to live if my plan succeeded. I remember repeating to myself at night over and over that my father was my only parent.

"My mother's body showed up in the village one day, handled by the Jaakuna. Unspeakable sadness existed in their eyes. I couldn't bear to look at her. It reminded me too much of the mania and pain. My father just tsked, telling the surgeons to wrap the body and keep it in storage, out of sight. To me, I felt my mother deserved better. So when night fell, I left my house and raced into the storage area, holding my mother's wrapped body in a gentle grip upon exiting. I carried her to one place my father or his guards would never find or check for a corpse."

"This place right?" I looked at him. It all came together now.

Korudo nodded, expression solemn as he looked at the withering oak tree and the moon shining on the leaves, turning them a greenish-white color in the luminescence.

"I would've never guessed my father would find this place . . . even if it isn't my mother's body he's searching for," he said after a moment, a dark look in his eyes.

In the spur of the moment I dared ask, "And your father . . . where is he now? Is he dead?"

Korudo shook his head, jaw set. "Yuki is my father."

As I started dozing, thoughts swirled in my head. I began to wonder why the Jaakuna now seemed so ruthless and quick to anger. How they whipped the slaves they watched, noting all mistakes. Korudo did mention about the children surviving alongside him and becoming bullies. Maybe those children were now full grown Jaakuna adults, exacting their anger on slaves and those of lesser value.

This also made me think about why Korudo seemed open and willing to tell about his mother's death and his past. How it all tumbled out him. No one trusts someone in as quick as a few days. It's human nature to feel wary.

My thoughts faded and the vision of a dream came to me, one of white flower petals dancing in the air. Three men stood in front of me, looking at me, their expressions solemn. The only person I recognized was Korudo. The other two people I had never seen before in my life: an old man who looked silhouetted in the light and the other who stood tall with authority. They continued to stare at me, even when my eyes opened to find a sunbeam flickering its radiance on my face.

Korudo rattled the door to my cell. "Get up! Time to dig."

I groaned, stood, and walked over to the door, allowing the Jaakuna man to take my wrist into his hand and lead me.

Yowai grimaced as his guard tugged him along as well, the familiar chain clamped around his wrist. I looked at my own and saw it free of any metal enclosure. Why did Korudo decide to take it easy on me?

As we reached the digging campsite his face twisted as he picked up a shovel and lurched over to the medium-sized ditch, taking his place. As I looked at Korudo and Yuki, I began to see the similarities between them. Their eyes were the same color and their faces had the same masculine square shape.

Everyone soon assembled themselves and when Yuki snapped his whip in the air we all planted our shovels in the dirt, scooping it up and repeating the motions. After a few dozen repetitions my arms shook and my legs burned from standing and handling the heavy shovel.

Deeper and deeper we dug, some of us feeling brave enough to venture into the ditch and continue digging in there, rather than widening the hole.

When the sun glared at the back of my head I noticed something glisten deep in the ditch. Yuki saw it as well, for a smile grew on his face. He held up a hand, jumping into the cavern and striding past the people standing around, sweat dripping down their faces. The Jaakuna leader came back above ground after a moment, holding a small piece of a shiny rock.

"Behold people! I have found a bit of silver, which means we're progressing," he said and we all cheered no matter how exhausted our voices sounded. More and more silver emerged into our sight as we continued to dig. I risked a glance backward to see Kimu, a dark hidden expression on his wrinkled face as he watched the digging progress.

I heard someone shuffle beside me and turned to see Yowai give me a shaky smile. My friend walked over to me, escaping the watch of his guard.

"Hey," I said, digging through the soil and hoisting it behind me.

"I'm not doing too good," he said in an undertone back as he tried to shovel, arms quivering.

"You're doing fine," I said, looking at him. He had an expression of dejection on his face. "If you haven't been whipped yet through all this, Yowai, then you have to be good."

He said nothing for a long while as we widened the chasm's entrance, more and more people going inside the carve out a path in the ditch. The wind gusted, then lay still, ruffling our clothes and hair.

"Anyway," I said to him in a low tone, tired of the silence, "it's better out here than being in a prison cell all day."

"True." He looked at me now, a small grin on his face.

"Faster!" Yuki said, making Yowai flinch and stumble, his shovel clanging against mine. An accident, one that didn't escape Korudo's vision.

"Why did you fall?" he asked, looking straight at my slave friend. I felt the need to protect Yowai and readied myself to speak.

"Don't," Yowai said, as if he knew what I wanted to do, his eyes downcast, "it's all my fault."

I grimaced, looking at Korudo and my friend, seeing the Jaakuna guard's whip lingered in the air, ready to strike Yowai.

"Korudo. You should watch your own slave instead of taking over for someone's cur," Yuki said, stalking over to his son. They both glowered at each other. Korudo muttered a few choice words under his breath and lowered the whip, giving in to his father. Yowai sighed in relief.

"Besides," Yuki said, turning his gaze to the slave, "I think he's had enough work for the day." A smile followed his words. "Take him back to his cell."

The words chilled me and I shivered.

Yowai's guard took a firm grasp on him and dragged my friend to the slave establishment.

"Did I order for you to stop? Or do you want to join him?" Yuki turned to me.

I shook my head and resumed shoveling, my heart aching despite myself. Poor Yowai . . . it seemed none of the guards wanted to give him a second chance.

Even when we all returned to our cells for the night, Yowai didn't speak, or look at me. He sat curled in the corner, quivering, eyes distant. Trying to grab his attention didn't work so I settled for eating the dry, burnt knob of bread the stocky man gave to me. It didn't taste bad, but it left a peculiar aftertaste in my mouth once I swallowed the last piece.

The new moon glittered overhead behind the ceiling cracks, making the village look alive with shadowy silhouettes as I peered outside the entrance to the establishment. It made me think about the delightful story my mother told about the demons lurking in every village side, making sure everyone went to sleep. They watched over the village once all was quiet and kept a vigil, dispelling any threats from harming the people. However, if a demon caught a person who refused to sleep an incurable illness would fall on them every three years,

I shivered; those stories still had their frightful luster, despite me being a capable young adult. Yowai's whistle of his breathing indicated that he had fallen asleep. So in turn I decided that I too, should go to sleep as well.

Before my eyes could close however, a pulse of fear entered my senses. I rose to a seated position and glanced around, trying to find the source of my fear.

I saw it after a moment, fluttering in the breeze like a flag in the middle of the village: a *Gohei.* The white zigzag strips of paper fluttered, making my heart race. The one other time I saw one of these purification objects was when I had been younger. My mother took my brother and I to see a shrine in Nagasaki city. Three *Goheis* flew around in the strong wind from the Shinto shrine, making a strange buzzing sound. It fascinated me, but it also frightened me because I always thought a spirit would come and tell me I was cursed.

Kimu hobbled of out of a shelter, coming to a stop in front of the *Gohei*, looking around him. His eyes . . . I shook myself. Something just wasn't right about him.

As the morning sprung upon Nagasaki again people shuffled out their houses in delirium, as if under a spell. The *Gohei* had disappeared.

Yowai looked pale and his mouth curled downward. Even when I offered him a nod he didn't smile at me. His unusual attitude change made a crinkle form in my stomach. What could he have thought of that made him look as though he dreaded something?

As usual we slaves got to work upon retrieving our shovels. According to Yuki, we were close to the village— underground that is. After explaining this he roared out a laugh and snapped the whip to signal our start. Dirt pattered the ground behind us and extra slaves picked up the small soil piles, hoisting them into burlap sacks.

Kimu stared at us in scrutiny, as if searching for the evil he tried to accumulate last night. He locked gazes with mine, his lips moved in an inaudible whisper, and he slunk off through the group of slaves working near him.

I hadn't felt more fatigued in my life but in order to make the day progress faster, I had to dig. The darkness of the cavern augmented the further we went. This time I helped the others dig inside the cavern, the glistening jewels half buried in the walls watching us when Yuki or Korudo didn't.

I heard someone crumble to the ground and Yuki stalked over to give the person a lashing. I knew who it was without even a glance. Despite myself, a grimace rose on my face and stayed for each lashing I heard. I risked a look backward to see Yowai clawing the earth with his fingers, eyes wide, mouth open in a silent scream. Yuki picked him up and grasped him by the shirt.

"You make me feel disappointed," Yuki said and Yowai flinched, face white, his fingers twitching.

"He's done. Lock him in his cell. Tonight shall be interesting for him. A similar time his brother experienced." The Jaakuna leader smirked.

Yowai's face darkened in a flush of red. However, he said nothing as his guard clamped on the metal cuff and tugged him away from the digging site. A strange look now existed in his eyes, and I perceived it right away as an expression of giving up and letting go.

Men hauled the excess mud and dirt away, clearing the path. Mud slid down my face when I tried pushing my long hair from my vision, becoming damp with sweat.

At last, Yuki hollered to stop all movement and hopped inside the cavern. We all watched, faces stained with grime as he passed by, hoping he wouldn't find something he could use to punish us. The cavern, even though no light shone inside, glistened with so many jewels. They might hold the potential to blind us.

"Check this out . . . look at them all! One for everyone!" Yuki's voice sounded maniacal as he heaved up all the jewels he could hold after plucking a few choice pieces out the wall. Everyone, including slaves and guards, roared out a cheer, throwing shovels down and hands in the air. Thank the gods the deed was done. No one would have to dig anymore from now on. Korudo took me back to my cell amid the madness, a dark, but relieved look on his face. Yowai refused to look at me and his body quivered once Korudo left.

Once night fell my friend turned to me, a certain strength in his eyes.

"They've had enough," he said, "I've had enough . . ."

"What?" I cocked my head at him and he came closer to the cell boundary.

"My guard spoke to me. He said the Jaakuna had enough and that they hated weakness in men." Yowai flinched as a sharp clang sounded. "Sayuri . . . I know my time has come. They come now. The rats come to take me to my brother."

"Why? They can give you a second chance, right?" My eyes widened.

"They gave one chance too many, my guard said. He said enough's enough. I knew it all along . . . I knew it. I'll join my brother. My brother . . . My brother."

We sat in silence as his words sunk into my head. Then the watering in his eyes cleared and he looked at me with resolve now, limbs quelling their shivering.

"I want you to do one more thing for me," he said and I nodded.

"Anything, Yowai-sama."

"Just . . . hold my hand until the end. That's all I want."

I crawled over to the cell boundary and grasped his hand into mine as soon as I reached him. He closed his eyes and the first tear I ever saw him shed dripped down his face. He opened his eyes and looked at me. "My friend. My only."

I wanted to say something, anything to reassure him that the Jaakuna wouldn't come for him tonight or any night, but I heard the footsteps I knew too well.

"All right, cur. Ready to see your brother?" Korudo asked and a flame of rage entered me. Yowai tightened his grip on my hand for a second, then shook his head as he saw the look in my eyes.

"Why can't you give him another chance?" I said as the Jaakuna man I've come to despise came into my vision. Yowai just looked at me, his gaze never leaving my face.

"Another chance? You stupid girl, this slave was given enough chances to redeem himself. It's over now so don't even bother fending for your friend."

"That's just what Yowai is to me, Korudo. A friend." My voice shook now, which wasn't good at all. "Must you always kill people to prove a point?"

His eyes narrowed. "If you want to join him in death hand in hand, I suggest you keep talking."

"Sayuri-chan . . . don't risk your life. I can do this on my own now. Live, my friend. Survive," Yowai said, giving my hand a final squeeze as he stood, coming to his cell's door. Korudo let loose a guffaw.

I felt helpless as he took my friend by the wrist and walked out of the establishment. Every slave now watched, whether they had been sleeping or not. Anger welled in me and it continued long after I heard Yowai's screech in the distance. Every one of them turned and looked at me, sympathy in their desolate eyes.

Seeing that, plus knowing my friend had just died, overwhelmed me. My body jerked once as I lay on the dirty mat and my shuttering breaths were all I or anyone else could hear.

A soft rumble sounded deep underground, but I ignored it as a fresh wave of pain washed over my black heart. No one said a word the whole night as I laid on the mat, eyes staring up at the moon. Then came the scent, the all-too-familiar scent of sweet peas. I smelled them long after my eyes closed as the moon made its descent to the horizon line.

"Get up. No time for you to grieve over weak-hearted curs like your friend." Korudo's voice sounded outside my cell just seconds later. I refused to move as my eyes opened into the flickering light mixed with the genuine sunlight. It seemed, more often than not, that my nights flew past in a heartbeat.

"It's time for you to get to work." He unlocked my door. I stood and once he came close I burst out into a run, pushing him aside and fleeing out the slave establishment.

"Get her!" I heard someone yell as I made my way to the village gates, startling four Jaakuna men. Nothing else existed on my mind but to escape.

A rumble sounded and didn't fade. It became stronger and the sounds of panicked Jaakuna guards and village people sounded behind me. I turned to look, eyes wide, as a thunderous crack sounded from the earth. As if the world ran in slow motion, the ground slid together and caved into itself. Trees snapped, branches flew into the air, whipping all around and skittering to the floor.

Birds screeched and two crows flew from the tress they were in, circled once over the village, then departed. A groan sounded and my gaze whipped to spot a tree teetering on the unstable ground. A second later the tree collapsed to the ground in a flurry of snapped branches.

The rumbling became even more intense and I heard Korudo shout, "Run!" Screams rang in the air as the fissure in the middle of the village widened. I felt appalled, but also spellbound by the fissure, watching as it spread.

I took an initiate and raced away as best as I could on the shaky ground, trying to put as much distance between me and the village forever.

Sayuri
Early April 1947

Upon waking, the sunlight shone on my face. I stood off the forest floor, brushing away caked mud and sand. Trees colored white from petrification, branches bare, waved in the wind that came and went. Every so often the sound of a bird entered the air but most of the time it was silent. I found that I couldn't remember anything after escaping from the Jaakuna's village.

I looked back and, in the distance, could see a smoking village. A warm relief started up in me. Not because of the perished innocent slaves and villagers but because the Jaakuna wouldn't threaten me or anyone else anymore.

I thought of Akio and hoped he escaped amid the confusion. I should have went back and tried to help him escape. My hands still clenched at the thought of Korudo killing Yowai, my friend. I hoped he died a horrible death.

As I walked the scenery became greener and greener little by little the farther along I went. The forest must have not have been touched by the atomic bomb. Or it began to recover quicker than the other forests had. A road entered my vision and I looked both ways before crossing it, feeling the heat of the paving through my ratty shoes.

The sun shone down on my head in a clear periwinkle-colored sky and I breathed deep, still smelling ash and smog in the air from the bomb and the burning Jaakuna village.

After crossing the road I entered another part of the forest, seeing thick *Ume* trees bursting with fruit and bamboo stalks mixed together. Three *Umes* soon lay in my hands and I bit into each of them, the taste of real food spreading through me. I still didn't feel satisfied once the fruit hit my stomach and the cores fell to the ground. I proceeded to dig up bamboo shoots, gobbling them without a moment's hesitation. I didn't even care if the shoots weren't cooked in the traditional way. Usually bamboo shoots are cooked and steamed at least three times before they're deemed edible. The arid flavor of the shoots made me gag.

With a small burp, I and plucked two more *Umes* and continued on, not sure of a destination, but not caring in the least. In my mind, I felt comfortable in any environment without crazed armored men chasing after me for slavery.

In time, though, clouds raced to cover the sky, as if anxious to cover any source of light for the time being. Soon it rained. Humidity made my skin feel clammy and greasy to the touch. I wrinkled my nose, walking faster to try and escape it. No such luck; the trees let every raindrop past them, their thin mangled branches teetering under the weight of the water.

The sound of a river came from close by and, upon looking, I saw it. The river flowed parallel to my path, its gurgles and its slight rushing sound enticing me. I looked down at myself, feeling ashamed to see the grime of my slave-work staining my skin. This led me to the decision that I would bathe. And I did.

The water felt divine as I entered the river, scooping water and rubbing my skin, seeing the brown-black grime slipping off me, traveling downstream. Despite the rain, I didn't mind feeling cold. I felt clean and pure once again.

It stopped raining as I put on my clothes after washing them as well. The material clung to my skin, but at least they didn't look soiled. The clouds still lingered in the sky, ready to send their lashing of rain down on the earth again.

The sudden sounds of a dog barking in the distance entered my ears. I paused, my breath quickening and my body tensing. A wild dog could be dangerous if it craved fresh meat. All of this and more went through my head as the sounds of crackling branches and leaves came closer and closer. The dog knew I was near. I remembered my dagger being flung into the rubble back at my village and felt a wave of anger. If only I hadn't been so foolish.

A shape burst from behind the trees and bamboo, earning a flinch from me. An Akita Inu, a beautiful black and cream colored one, stared at me. It barked again as it padded to me, sniffing my wet leg with a black nose. The Akita's soft chestnut-brown eyes flickered and its trademark curled tail moved side to side as it looked up at me, cocking its head. To me it seemed as though the dog tried to piece together whether or not I served as a threat.

"What have ya got there, Rabu?" A man's voice sounded as branches snapped. I tensed again, not knowing whether to flee or stay put. It was too late to make a decision. An elder man came into view with a black patch over one eye and scars littering his arms and face.

"Ah, a fine young woman. What's the matter? Are you lost?" He turned to me after acknowledging the dog, his tone gruff.

"I'm homeless," I said as he came closer to get a better look at me, his one eye narrowed. The Akita trotted back over to the man, accepting a half-hearted pat from him.

"Rabu here bounded away quick as a whip when he heard your presence in this area. What're you doing out here all by yourself? You're sopping wet besides. Don't you realize this forest's Jaakuna lands?"

"They had enslaved me." I felt my fists clench, then thought better of it not to let too much emotion show and looked down at the mud below my shoes. "They murdered my friend because he was a coward. I escaped when a huge earthquake struck their village yesterday. They deserved the destruction that happened to them." I looked back up at the man. "They deserved it."

"So it was an earthquake," the man said, looking at me in thought. "It kept me up all night and day, it did, trying to figure it out; all the rumbling and shaking."

Rabu gave a short rapid bark, as if in agreement.

"Tell me straight, for you didn't answer my original question, what're you doing out here?" A hard glint showed in his eyes. I knew he didn't trust my words one bit.

"Trying to find a new home. The village I lived in before the Jaakuna enslaved me had been destroyed by the atomic bombing two years ago," I said and the elder man's eyes softened. Rabu growled, most likely sensing my fear, but he wasn't looking at me. Rather, it seemed he paid attention to the words I said.

"Nasty trick those Americans played on us . . . just to make us surrender from the war. You and I are in the same vein, I guess . . ." He heaved a sigh, soft and sad. "All these scars you see," the man gestured to the scars littering his arms and legs, "all of them were because of the bomb. Lucky for me Rabu here saved my life, fetching food for me while I recuperated. He and I . . . we haven't broken apart since that day."

The Inu barked again, wagging his fluffy curled tail, happy to hear his name.

"You know, there's something about you. Something— how should I say—something good," the old man said, scratching the area around his eye patch, scowling at the itch. "You seem innocent enough. I can tell also by the look in your eyes that you've experienced some sort of despair."

He was perceptive, just like Akio. Akio . . . I had to push the thought away about him. He would have came looking for me if he still lived.

"Did . . . the atomic bomb do that to your eye?" I asked, deciding to change the subject.

"Not so. I earned this wound from warfare back in the day. Had a nasty skirmish with my comrades and the result ended up with my eye being as it is now." He rubbed at it again, his face coloring as another itch came over him.

"Oh." I felt uncomfortable as he scratched at the eye patch, cursing under his breath all the while. The old man shook his head, as if trying to get rid of the subject.

"Call me Dansei, child. What of you?"

"My name's Sayuri, Dansei-sama." I bowed my head. Dansei's eyes widened.

"I had a niece with your name, but she was much younger than you. She perished in the atomic bomb blast." His tone sounded faraway and tinged with morosity. I frowned.

"Aye . . ." Dansei trailed off at my sympathetic expression, falling silent.

"Come with me Sayuri-chan," he said, then added after seeing me take a step backward, "Now don't worry, Rabu and I don't bite. No need for suspicion."

"Why do you trust me, Dansei?" I asked, still feeling wary of him. Rabu looked up at me, tongue lolling out of his mouth, tail thumping the ground.

"As I had said before, you don't look like the type of person who would seem dangerous. A young woman all alone in the woods? Doesn't give me a cause for alarm at all."

He looked friendly enough, I figured. Dansei waited for my answer, shifting his weight onto one leg, then the other. I envisioned him in the time of warfare, seeing him without an eye patch and with a group of men he trusted.

"Yes, sir," I nodded and followed behind Dansei, who had already began to hobble off into the trees. Rabu bounded ahead of us, eyes sparkling.

A large cabin in the woods appeared when I caught up to Dansei.

"You built this?" Incredulity took me over and my eyes scanned over cabin, seeing the dark brown resin tree trunks making up the house and the strange windows. A tiny orchard of different plants grew on the side of it, already full to bursting with fruit. Alongside the trees long stalks of green leafy bamboo rods waved in the wind, their leaves rustling in the gusts.

"Aye. Took me months of hard labor. Pulled it off with aplomb however."

"I have decided, Sayuri. Why don't you stay with me for a few days? Maybe get your strength up, eh? What do you say?" Dansei asked, something in his voice making me cock my head. I knew he must have seen the look in my eyes when I glanced over at his orchard.

"Well . . ." I still felt distrustful.

"I know you don't have a destination, considering the fact you told me you were looking for a home. Even more certain:

you're far too skinny. I know you haven't had a decent platter of food in ages."

His words unlocked something in me. I felt tired of running away from the past and living like a savage. Dansei was right about the food part. Two and a half years was a long enough span without a true meal for me.

My mother one time told me not to trust people who mentioned food in their pleas. She explained it as a technique people used to try and trip others up by lowering their guard. I looked at Dansei now and saw no trickery or deception in his gaze. What I saw was a man who wanted to do good. Rabu barked and weaved through my legs, looking up at me.

"Then I'll stay," I said with a bow. "Thank you for your hospitality, Dansei-sama."

A pleased smile cross Dansei's features for a moment before it vanished. I began to wonder if that was the first time he had ever smiled.

"Come along, Sayuri." He beckoned me with a finger, just as a crow called, indicating that sundown would soon approach and change the day into night. We walked together up the stairs and into the cabin, Rabu barking and trying to weave around us in his excitement. The sight made me snort. It felt good to feel at ease again.

"Have a seat." Dansei pointed to a table and I complied, kneeling on the floor cushions, hands folding into my lap.

"Good thing I made a large serving of food tonight." He placed a platter of dinner in front of me, handing me small chopsticks as he too knelt on the mat across me.

"I'm still shocked at how you made this cabin all by yourself and everything inside it," I said, marveling at the wooden kitchen made from the same tree bark as the house itself. A steaming plate of *Ume* stew and seasoned chicken awaited for me to eat it. Dansei sure knew how to cook; the food smelled delicious.

"It just gives me a place to make my own. Nothing neat about that." Dansei made a grunt after we both said the dinner prayer, picking up some chicken with his chopsticks, chewing his food. He stood and grabbed a spare cup off the counter, filling it with water and giving it to me. "Tell me Sayuri, how did the Jaakuna enslave you anyway?"

"Well," I said, giving him a nod of thanks and taking a small sip of water from the cup, "I was in my village, what remained of it after the bombing, then some Jaakuna men burst into my shelter. They claimed my village was now theirs and any other village they could take over. I tried to escape them but they captured me.

"They forced me to push rocks to the village so the Jaakuna could build more shelters. When the recent earthquake caused the village to cave in, I took the chance amid the confusion and panic to escape. Looking back . . . I think I had been the only survivor." I decided to leave out everything about Akio. I didn't want to make the story complicated and arouse emotions of pain in my heart. I had enough of that emotion for the time being.

"These're terrible times we live in now, dear. People will do anything to bring themselves back up to par with others." Dansei looked solemn after I spoke, his hand gripping his cup.

"I agree, Dansei," I said, taking a sip of the hot stew, "but why do they do it?"

The older man fell silent for a long while as he contemplated my question, then said, "They won't feel as though they're at one with themselves unless they display some sort of superiority to someone lower or higher than them. Times were different in the past, Sayuri. People, at one time, felt trusting and open with each other. Now everyone goes mad over our emperor and the people who will change the future of our country. If they focused more on humans as a race and not as the filling for a country . . ."

Once we finished dinner, Dansei showed me where I could sleep and gave me a tattered blanket along with other somewhat stained soft mats to lay on top of.

"I found the blanket in the remains of a village I visited not long ago. Must have been some poor child's blanket before the destruction happened. It'll provide for you while you stay here," he said. "Now don't worry, I washed all these sleeping mats and blankets well. I wouldn't want to have lice or any other ravenous parasite feeding off my body either."

I gave a nod at his words, feeling exhausted as my eyes threatened to close. In order to prevent myself from zoning out on him I forced myself to keep busy with getting comfortable under the blanket, wrapping it around my body and feet.

"Tomorrow we'll wake early so I suggest you sleep well tonight. No staying up late, all right?" he said after a moment, the gruff tone back in his voice.

I didn't bother to ask what he meant, for Dansei already started walking out of the room, taking the lantern of candlelight with him. The inside of the room was quaint and somewhat cramped in the gloom of darkness, but it sufficed for one person. If I breathed deep I could smell the nature and, if I concentrated long enough, I'd sense the spirits still lingering in the wood floors and walls. Thinking about that made me feel comforted in knowing some kind of presence stayed with me in the room.

As I dozed, becoming comfortable, a warm wet nose prodded my face once and a body plopped down beside me.

Despite the dog meeting me for the first time he sure seemed affectionate. The warmth of his body, combined with the augmenting warmth of the blanket, lulled me to sleep.

A warm meadow where small white lilies and rolling snow-capped mountains existed came to my mind's eye. The sun made me feel like dancing and shouting in glee. It was a wonderful dream and I never wanted it to end.

That's when I saw something that perplexed me: a small turtle emerged out of a hole and lumbered over to the forest. Not even my presence distracted it from its path. The turtle continued on and as soon as it entered the forest it seemed to disappear, as if it never was.

"Hey, Rabu. Decided to sleep with Sayuri-chan last night, old boy?" Dansei asked, his voice entering my dream, and I opened my eyes to see sunlight stream into the room. Rabu gave a happy bark at my side, licked my sleepy face, and hurried over to Dansei, expecting his master to pat him. When he didn't get one the dog put his paws on the old man's knees, whistling out a whine.

"No, get down, boy. I'm angry with you for not keeping routine," the older man admonished, although his voice had a playful tone in it. Rabu made another cajoling whine, circling the elder man's legs before coming over to me, accepting my pat.

"Bah! He knows I never stay angry with him for too long anyway." Dansei shook his head and beckoned me off the floor. "I hope you feel rested, Sayuri. I need help with cracking eggs for breakfast. You can't just do nothing while you stay here. Now come along."

I nodded, following him and Rabu as they left the room and entered the kitchen, pots and plates already set in their respectable areas, the area swept clear. It reminded me of my mother, who always kept a clean and methodical kitchen. This caused the default frown on my face to furl ever downward. A minute cooking fire blazed in a nearby fire pit and Dansei paused to look at it, narrowing his eyes. He shook his head and continued to lead me.

Outside the house, off to the side, a tiny coop stood on its own. Inside it ten brown and white molted chickens clucked as I neared closer to the small wooden house. They waddled with heavy steps, eyes trained on me.

"See them chickens? I traded some fruit for them and now I have a healthful breakfast every morning to last a lifetime. These chickens just eat what greenery sticks out the ground so I have no responsibility in feeding them. Grab four eggs, Sayuri, then we'll get started," Dansei said.

I did as told, giving the chickens a wary eye as I poked my hand inside their home to grab four warm eggs. I knew some could get protective and snap. One hen squawked as my hand neared her body and she puffed her feathers, backing away and colliding with another chicken who clucked in alarm and hustled to a clear area in the coop. I snorted at the silly display as Dansei and I headed back inside the cabin, ready to start breakfast.

"Why do you trust me to help you with breakfast?" I asked. Dansei looked at me, rubbing the back of his neck.

"You're just a young woman. I feel no threat coming from you."

His words infuriated me for a moment. I hated it when people called me young. All my life I've always wanted to grow stronger and feel older. Did that make me narrow-minded?

"Doesn't matter." I shook my head. "You can't act too trustful around strangers."

"You had all the chances yesterday to hurt or kill me somehow while I turned my back." A stern tone entered Dansei's voice now. "You didn't."

I went over to a bag that lay on the counter alongside the pots and pans as he ordered me to crack the eggs. Then he inhaled, giving me the indication he wanted to speak.

"Being alone in this world now isn't good anyway. You were in the destruction of the bombing, Sayuri, right?"

I turned to him, which gave him the incentive to continue, "Weren't you supposed to have been rescued a long time ago? Why do you still linger in Nagasaki without a home?"

My lips pressed to a thin line. "The rescuers were Americans."

His nod was my answer. While the silence lasted I got to work cracking the eggs, throwing the empty shells in the bag and picking up any on the floor.

"When you're done cracking those eggs place them in the pan there." Dansei ignited the cooking fire and made it blaze hotter and higher as he gestured to the pan. Soon fresh hard boiled eggs sizzled over the fire pit, the warm smells spurring my stomach to growl. I couldn't wait to eat them.

Once the eggs looked ready I placed them onto two plates, putting one in front of Dansei at the table, and the other in front of me. He handed me a pitcher of water, which I poured into our two wooden cups, before we knelt onto the cushions.

"Usually takes me forever to crack those eggs by myself. Arthritis gets to you faster than a fellow can blink," the old man said as he placed an egg in his mouth, his hands trembling as he tried to hold his chopsticks in a firm grip.

"Dansei-sama? How long did it take for you to build this cabin for yourself?" I asked after taking a slow sip of water.

He put his fork down and chewed as he contemplated my question. "About four months. Those stumps you may have seen about the forest where Rabu found you are the exact trees I used when I built this house," he said, scratching the skin around his patch, scowling as the itch persisted him. "Every once in a while I have to cut any rotting pieces of wood in the cabin due to insects getting at it and what have you."

"How long have you been living here by yourself?" A soft tone entered my voice, one that I hadn't heard before, and Dansei grimaced, pain flashing in his eyes. I knew it then as I had known it from the very beginning: Dansei didn't want to be alone. Rabu wasn't enough company. He wanted real human contact with other people.

"For almost twenty years." His reply sounded soft, as if he had said it in a whisper. My eyes widened. I've often heard stories about people who live alone with no human contact for years. They never ceased to shock me, and this was no different. For someone to live alone, they had to have no desire, and no hope to live around other people. Dansei was strong to live this long without help, I could tell, but sometimes strength comes at a price.

Hermits aren't uncommon in Nagasaki. My mother used to tell me the times when she saw a man walking about with no desire to enter villages or even speak to people. 'They just avoid your gaze, as if they're accused and guilty of a crime,' she told me and I'd often wonder how those people lived the way they did.

We finished breakfast afterward but Dansei didn't let me slack. Rather, he sent me out to the orchard to pick fruit and dig up bamboo shoots, ordering Rabu to watch me. The loyal dog barked, as if he felt pleased to do something. The playful Akita bounded around me as I plucked the ripe *Umes* and some *Ichijiyu* off their trees outside the cabin. I snuck the dog an *Ume* which he gobbled faster than I could blink.

"No more Rabu. You need room for lunch." I waggled my finger at him. The dog's wet nose bumped my ankle once as he sat down, watching me pluck more fruits. He really was intelligent, that much I could tell. Dansei must feel lucky to have had Rabu with him all these years in solitude. How different would he have been if the Akita never found him?

The air was alive with the sounds of insects and birds. Pollen drifted about in the slackening and rising soft wind. It made my nose tickle and I heard Rabu sneeze once or twice. The sunlight fluttered behind the tree branches and bamboo stalks, alighting on my face and the other areas the warm rays could touch.

I walked over to the bamboo stalks that loomed over my head and remembered when my mother told me a story about how one should never disturb the spirits resting in the bamboo. The story told about a small mischievous boy who was foolish, but brave. His mother warned him not to disturb the spirits in the Grove of Bamboo. The boy didn't heed his mother's advice and headed to the grove, yearning to see a spirit and keep it for his own. Bamboo stalks of all sizes appeared in his vision when he entered. A wood-chopping hatchet rested on the forest floor near a pile of white stones, which he took, a gleam in his eyes.

The foolish boy's temptation took him over as he chopped down a bamboo stalk, hearing the enraged scream of a spirit enter the air. Excitement entered him once the plant slid to the ground and withered into a brown color. He waited for the spirit to appear. Indeed it did appear, and in its rage of being disturbed it dissolved the boy's body and sent his spirit out in the wilds, to never return to its body again. Banished and alone, it's said that if you listen when the wind blows you can hear the boy howling as he weeps for disobeying his mother and the choice he made.

"How do you survive on just *Ume, Ichijiyu,* bamboo shoots, eggs, and chicken?" I asked Dansei while we ate dinner. Cooked bamboo shoots with some chicken and a side of chopped *Ume* for something sweet was our meal for the night.

"Got to make do with what you have, Sayuri-chan." He looked at me, not saying anything else to the subject. Rabu's wet nose bumped against my hand as I sneaked him some pieces of chicken, although I knew Dansei saw me.

"You can stay here as long as you like," he said when the silence stretched between us. I nodded and looked at his face, seeing a strange emotion in his eyes. He wanted me to stay . . . he felt too lonely to continue on his own. This alone convinced me to stay for another day or two.

Later on the next morning I picked more eggs, making sure to leave some behind so they could hatch into new chickens. The routine stayed the same everyday, but I never tired of it. It reminded me of the times when my mother would assign me to water the indoor and outdoor plants before weeding and watering them everyday. I liked doing chores, a rare trait among girls my age.

Rabu always followed me around, whether because Dansei ordered him to or just to see what I would do. A happy lopsided smile always lingered on his face in my presence, tongue half hanging out of his mouth, cocking his head. I would come over and give him a pat on the forehead. At my touch his tail began to wag as his eyes closed.

Dansei and I ground the *Ichijiyu* fruits into a paste for jam once I came back into the cabin. Rabu lingered at our feet, his gaze trained upwards in the event a piece of fruit would come sailing down into his open mouth.

"Dansei-sama?" I said after a moment of silence stretched between us.

He looked at me. "Yes, Sayuri?"

"What did your niece look like? The one who had the same name as me," I asked, then started to regret my asking when Dansei sighed, his chest moving up and down with the movement.

"My dear niece. Oh Sayuri-chan, how I wish you could have met her. She would have came here with me if she still lived, you know."

"Really? Didn't she have parents?"

"That she did. However my niece loved coming over to my house, back when I had one, and just help me with errands and chat. She loved to talk and I couldn't escape her without her striking up a conversation about something or other." Dansei chuckled. "I love her as much as I love my own daughter who now lives in Osaka, studying to be a nurse. My niece was every which way just like you, Sayuri. Except her hair looked like a flowing dark brown waterfall with black undertones. Her golden-colored eyes . . . they seemed to stare right into your soul. She knew how to make anyone laugh and she always wanted people to feel happy around her, no matter what."

I began to imagine this girl, the niece of Dansei who perished in the bomb explosion two years ago. It depressed me, for I wanted to meet her since he mentioned it. I wanted to see how that girl influenced his life and helped him with chores.

However Dansei continued, "When she was younger she always wanted me to brush her hair and put it up into a big big ponytail. She'd parade around the house afterward and blow kisses at imaginary fans, as if she was the most sought out girl in all of Japan. I loved her, as I've said, and when she died . . . my heart split into two. My brother was devastated, for he had lost his niece, his wife, and his house when the bombing happened. What more pain entered his heart for him to think his brother perished as well."

"But you're not dead, Dansei-sama." I wanted to smack myself for how stupid my statement sounded.

"That's the point, but how could I tell him in person in order to prove it? He doesn't live in Nagasaki anymore, child. Indonesia's where he makes his home, helping the children there and trying to forget the sad things that happened to him. No, I don't have a way of reaching him and when I think about it . . . it's better if it stays that way."

Silence grew between us again as we continued to beat and grind the figs. I felt bad for bringing up the subject and told him so.

"What're you sorry for? You wanted to know, so I told you. No shame in curiosity, Sayuri. When I look at you, I see my niece's dancing spirit and fire again. Don't hesitate to ask me anything. Besides, it felt good to let all of what I said off my chest. It's been lingering around for two years and I knew I'd have to tell someone at some point. Which brings me to thank you, dear." Dansei smiled, then he sobered and grounded the last fig.

"We'll have ourselves a feast tomorrow," he said, a mysterious glint in his eyes. "Come with me."

I felt confused but complied with a small bow and followed Dansei out the cabin.

"Rabu will watch over the house, so don't worry," he said after seeing the look on my face. "I do this all the time." He walked over to the side of the house and picked up a basket, walking among the *Ume and Ichijiyu* trees, plucking ripe fruits.

He rejoined my side once the basket looked full to bursting and we walked together again.

"So, where're you taking me?" I asked.

"There's a marketplace in a nearby village. I can use some money to buy more food by selling the fruits here."

It drizzled in light spurts, the drops plopping onto leaves and slipping off to wet the undergrowth. The sounds and scents of nature entered me until I felt I'd explode. Leaves crunched underfoot and I felt somewhat normal again. Walking beside a person again and just heading to a place for reasons other than survival put me at ease.

Guilt entered me as the thought of Akio bounced in my mind. He would've been with me right now. He's dead now . . . The thought of that made my chest feel heavy again.

Dansei and I continued to walk and then the sound of a car entered my ears. In the distance a village lay, a car leaving it and another entering it. I felt spellbound by the sight and could only stand and watch as the car passed and honked the horn. Dansei tapped my shoulder, indicating that I should walk and I shook myself out the daze I entered. We continued to walk and, upon entering the village, a few people gave nods to Dansei and arched brows at me.

"I feel for you, dear. I know you haven't been around normal people in a long time. So take your time adjusting," Dansei said and I nodded, feeling my lips part. I haven't seen this many people in a long time. The Jaakuna's village people didn't count; they weren't normal. These people lived and had lives. They walked, talked, and lived in a carefree world without slavery. Children squealed and scampered after running chickens, the birds squawking and trying their best to escape.

One woman gave me a sympathetic glance as Dansei and I passed her and I lowered my eyes. The westernized-looking clothes some of the people wore made me feel sick, but I envied them. I had no money and I must look like a ragamuffin to them. The sidewalk under my feet looked fresh and clean, as if people made it few days ago.

Dansei took me to a marketplace, where banners, overhangs, and people flashed pretty colors in the dismal weather. We walked over a bridge and I looked down at the small creek, hearing the water gurgling and rushing to an unknown destination. In all my distractedness I almost knocked into a man crossing the bridge in front of me as I rejoined beside Dansei.

Upon reaching the other side people waved at Dansei, sparing me curious glances. I assumed they knew him from his frequent visits here. Feeling even more out of place, I tried to look smaller and hunched my posture.

"This is my niece, Sayuri. She decided to come visit me this week," he said, covering up who I was. The marketplace people nodded, smiles returning to their faces. I tried to smile back but couldn't and settled for avoiding their gazes.

"Now Sayuri, you can wander wherever you like, so as long as you return to the marketplace once the afternoon sun sits on the horizon line. I'll need some time to sell these *Umes* and *Ichijiyus*. You might want to look around Kyroyoku." Dansei turned to me and I nodded, eager to walk around and busy myself with civilization.

Cherry blossom trees arched into my vision after rounding a corner and I found myself struck by how beautiful the sight looked. The way the flowers reached from their branches and how their pink color, darker in the middle and fading to light at the petal tips, shone in the light. I saw movement below the tree's branches and stiffened. There, sitting against the trunk a person sat. My eyes narrowed and the figure spotted me, lifting blue-green eyes to my vision. Before I could stop it, my hand moved to my mouth and a fiery blaze swept in me. No normal Japanese person has blue-green eyes. The person, who I identified as male, stood and came over to me, eyes unblinking, clothes rustling in the wind.

His lips moved and I stood stone still, not understanding him. My own lips parted and I backed away, knowing who he was. An American.

"Stay back," I hissed, even if I knew he wouldn't understand me. His eyes narrowed as if he tried to piece together what I said. The man stood tall, hands in his pockets, his golden-brown hair sticking in the air. His lips moved again and this time I could understand him.

"You okay?" the man asked in broken Japanese and my lips pressed to a line. How dare an American come here and sully our language! The anger in my eyes must have told him how I felt, for he backed up as well.

"Your people destroyed my life," I said.

He had to have understood something from what I said, for he looked at me straight in the eye. "I know."

At this point I felt so disgusted at his innocent tone that I looked for anything, anything at all, to serve as a distraction for me to get away from him. I looked up at the sky, wishing for it to change to the sultry oranges and purples of sunset. I regretted leaving Dansei alone in the marketplace . . . I knew I should have stayed alongside him.

"Your name?" He licked his lips again as his voice cracked and I wanted to laugh at his attempts to make conversation.

"Why would I tell you my name, *sir*?" Disgust filled me. The man looked hurt as I turned on my heel and stalked off to the marketplace. Sounds filled behind me; the man decided to chase after me.

"Please don't . . . leave," he said and something in his voice stopped me. I turned around in a huff.

"Don't follow me," I said and the American man shook his head.

"I mean no harm . . ." he said and I had to laugh at the irony.

"You meant harm when you and your American friends helped bomb my home."

"Almost two years ago."

Talking to him reminded me of Yowai, and the thought of my dead friend made me tense again, my eyes blinking. I understood what the man meant and felt a scowl furl my lips downward.

"It doesn't matter. Now leave me alone," I said and this time I hurried off, not stopping when I heard his shout. My head swam and my vision turned blurry as the marketplace surrounded me again. Traditional red lanterns swung from their hooks, golden tassels hanging in the air. It all looked like blurbs to my vision.

"Sayuri?" I heard and voice and felt relieved to see Dansei look at me in concern. "You look distressed."

I must have stopped by instinct in front of him in the busy marketplace.

"I just saw an American man," I said, a choked tone in my voice. I didn't want to show Dansei how affected I was but he seemed to piece it all together.

"They've come to Japanese villages since the bombing happened. They were army members once removed," he said and I sighed. That made it worse. I've grown to hate the American man and knowing one of them had attempted to talk to me made ripples in my stream.

"I just hope I never see another person like him for as long as I live." I scuffed my foot, my mood souring as I took my place beside Dansei. He received customers and sold most of his *Umes* and *Ichijiyu* by the time the sun looked ready to set. The pressure escalating in my chest puffed out as the tension left me. Relief followed after; at least the man hadn't tried to find me.

"You still look unsettled, Sayuri-chan. Did the man's presence disturb you that much?" Dansei asked as he packed the fruits he couldn't sell, pocketing his money. I nodded, feeling like a child and wanting comfort. I swallowed back those feelings and decided to look at the fancy tapestries fluttering in the wind, my lips pressed.

"I've collected more than enough money for the both of us," he said, but I wasn't paying attention to him. My mind focused on that American man and why he tried to speak to me of all people. How could my people allow him to just laze about the village without a care in the world?

"-get some more while we're here," Dansei said and I shook myself from my thoughts.

"I'm sorry, Dansei-sama, but get some more of what?" I felt ashamed to have drowned him out.

"Some bread. I have just a few more slices back at the cabin. Which reminds me . . . Sayuri? Would you do me a favor and buy some *saba*? I plan to use it tonight for dinner." He looked at me and I nodded as he placed the amount of yen I needed in my hand. All I hoped for while I went to the fish vendor was for the American man to have left the village by now. Remembering him revamped and reinvigorated my hatred for what happened to my family two years ago.

Upon reaching the vendor, my back tingled, but I didn't dare turn around and face what I dreaded to see. I didn't want him to feel the satisfaction for finding me again.

"Good choice, young lady." The man behind the vendor bowed his head as I bought fresh *saba* from him and hurried back to Dansei.

I heard the American man call out in Japanese, "Wait!"

His voice stopped me. It was a mistake on my part and I watched as the man came closer and closer.

"Why?" he asked and my lip curled in confusion.

"Why what?" I said. Now he stood a few feet away from me.

"Why run away from me?"

I couldn't respond, for Dansei appeared in that moment, rescuing me for continuing to talk with the man. The American man now looked uncomfortable and his eyes darkened with sadness. He wanted to talk to me, I realized. He wanted to try and make me his friend.

"Come Sayuri, we have to leave now," he said and took my arm with a soft grip. I looked at him, hoping he could see the gratitude in them. He did.

As Dansei took my arm and led me away from the man, giving him a wary eye, I held my head high and walked with purpose. I hoped to never see another American man for as long as I lived as we left Kyroyoku.

———————————————————————

Dansei and I got to work in the morning, making breakfast, spreading the jam on the bread and slicing *Umes*, kneeling at the table.

We ate the food after the prayers. I made appreciative noises while I ate; the jam worked out well with the bread, no matter if it tasted stale. I slipped Rabu some bread and jam and he pranced out the kitchen with his treat in his mouth, as if in triumph.

A crack sounded from the sky and Dansei stood. "Come quick, Sayuri-chan!"

"What is it?" I asked, feeling my eyes widen. "Trouble?"

"If we miss this moment, yes. Hurry, bring those empty pitchers!"

I did as he asked and hurried outside the cabin, seeing Dansei waiting, an impatient insistent look in his face. It startled me to see the intensity in his expression.

"Place the pitchers around the house." He pointed to several spots, taking one pitcher from me and placing it down by the stairs. I put the rest of them around the cabin's perimeter, feeling confused.

Dansei explained it all to me as we reentered the cabin. "That's how I acquire water. The same water you drank since you've stayed here. Rainwater doesn't taste bad and it helped kept me alive for this long."

It continued to rain later on in the night when I laid on my blankets, yawning. The pattering sounds lulled me to sleep, giving me good dreams of throwing Rabu a strange multicolored toy in the green meadow, the small white lilies waving in the warm breeze. Dansei appeared in my dream as well, a joyous expression on his face, while the Akita Inu and I played. His smile stretched from ear to ear as Sayuri, his niece, launched into his arms and gave the older man a kiss on the cheek twice.

Dansei woke me by putting a soft hand on my shoulder. My eyes flew open as he gestured for me to stand and follow him. The rain had stopped. We went outside to collect the large jugs, which looked full to the brim with water. I picked up one by its handle and carried it inside the cabin.

"Careful. Don't stumble or hurt yourself," Dansei said as he handed me two more jugs, seeing me lurch in my steps. His hand rested on my back as he followed behind me and I shot him a grateful glance for his help.

"Good work Sayuri. The gods above will favor you until the end," he said with a small smile as I place two jugs on the counter. His tone struck me. He sounded just like a proud and happy parent to me; he sounded like my father . . .

Akio
Early April 1947

"That selfish girl," Akio said aloud as he stumbled over a cracked barrel. His scowl deepened as he regained his balance, his arrogant eyes turning to everything in contempt. "How could she leave me behind like this?"

The Jaakuna were dead, Akio knew that for certain. He watched every single one of them perish and stand like ducks while the earthquake rumbled about them. He could have laughed at the memory, but all it brought him was naught. Trees lay toppled on the ground in the wrecked village, dark-brown roots reaching up to the sky like fingers. Clouds raced across the sky, attempting to block the sunlight. Akio narrowed his eyes, then shook his head in disgust, setting off from the village.

"Where would Sayuri go?" he wondered, holding back a sneeze. Three days have passed since the earthquake but Akio felt like he was back in the destruction of the atomic bomb again. His eyes had opened to find himself alone. With no ally or friend to call his own. He pinched the bridge of his nose, feeling dejected. It just occurred to him about how selfish people became when it came to their safety. He hoped Sayuri felt guilty for leaving him by himself. Akio knew now what he had to do: he had to find a place to live and call his own, and maybe forget everything that happened to him.

He continued to walk on, following a paved road, knowing his path would lead him to civilization of some sort. To him, the air smelled fresh and clean. He felt free for a while.

Akio walked, not stopping in his path for anything until he reached a village called Kyroyoku. He licked his lips and felt a smile breach his solemn features. In the distance a marketplace stood, banners flapping in the wind, its vibrant colors cajoling him to come closer. A transformation overtook Akio as he saw normal people for the first time since two years ago. It seemed to whisper of a life one had to live before judging. It held a certain beauty and a sense of protection from the taint of the outside world.

The market beckoned him closer with a finger of possibility and nourishment and Akio felt infected by it. He walked closer and closer and the smell of food and clean clothes entered his senses. At once a vendor popped into his vision, sporting delicious rice balls. Akio sauntered over, the marketplace consuming his thoughts and actions.

"Good day, sir!" the man behind the vendor said, voice rich with splendor and personality. "May I interest you in buying some of my hand-made rice balls? They're a delicacy in Kyroyoku."

"Yeah, I'll have one," Akio said and the vendor man beamed wider.

"A wonderful choice! That'll be eighteen yen."

"Eighteen yen," Akio repeated, then proceeded to reach into his pockets.

"Y'know, I can't give them out for free," the man said. Then Akio realized he didn't have any money and hadn't had any since the atomic bombing. At once the hopeful expression in his heart popped and deflated, destroyed. The beauty of the marketplace burned away and all he saw now were men and women desperate to earn money for a living. It made his scowl return.

"Sir?" the vendor man asked in innocence, seeing Akio's turn of expression.

"You're right. You can't." Akio looked the man straight into the eye. Then he turned on his heel and walked out of the market, footsteps clomping on the wooden bridge over a creek.

Akio's mother told him once that life was like an expensive kimono; you need money in order to buy your way into it. He shook his head and headed into the nearest building: a teahouse. He needed to earn money quick.

"Do you hire?" he asked, his voice resonating into the quiet atmosphere. Since it was early afternoon the place would have one or two people inside for tea. A women who just entered Akio's sight flinched and turned to him, long lashes batting her cheeks as she blinked. The sound of a bamboo fountain sounded, the faint clunking and endless trickling of water entering his ears.

"I'm sorry, sir?" the woman asked, looking at him.

"I asked, do you hire, ma'am?" Akio repeated, feeling impatient.

"Masaki!" she called, turning around to face the back room. "A person here wants to know if you hire!"

"What now?" a man asked from the back, boxes smashing and plates clattering together sounded in the air, before Masaki entered, a grouchy look upon his face. Akio had to refrain from making a face. The man's greasy hair reached to his elbows, each strand looking out of place on his scalp. With a mean, sneering mouth, Masaki gave Akio a once over, a faint tsk coming from his lips.

"You want me to hire you? Where do you come from, boy?" he asked, his rough voice set on edge.

"It doesn't matter where I come from, sir. Do you want to hire me or not?" Akio felt like walking out of the teahouse. The woman gasped at his forwardness and Masaki shook his head.

"Azuki, hush. The boy may seem bold but I must say, he's better than the lazy bunch of crooks I pay now. So you want to work, eh?" the man said after turning from Azuki.

"I said that before, didn't I?" Akio asked and Masaki scratched his head.

"Right you did." He looked clueless but the look faded. "If you feel brave still, then follow me." The man headed to the back of the teahouse, Akio following close behind him. The lights in the main room were dim and the tatami mats underfoot looked clean. Akio guessed Masaki cared more about what his teahouse looked like rather than what he looked like as a person.

"So what do I have to do?" Akio said after a moment of silence as they stopped walking.

"You get to clean the kitchen," Masaki said and shoved him through the swinging doors, cackling as he stumbled away from sight. "Use the rags and gloves inside and clean until everything sparkles."

Akio muttered a few choice words under his breath as he rubbed his arm, looking at his surroundings. The air had the wafting aroma of tea and saki. A ventilator fan whirred overhead, circulating the hot air in the room. The metallic counter tops looked rusty and caked with dried food. Akio shuddered.

"If it's the only way I can earn money . . ." he trailed off and picked up the nearby cleaning gloves, ready to get started. His nose crinkled as he took a cleaning rag in his hands, removing the hardened gunk from the counters. He knew nothing could help make the rust disappear so he left it. Masaki looked pleased nonetheless as he entered the kitchen after a few moments. Pleased to either see Akio working or pleased to see something getting done.

"What's your name, boy?" he asked and Akio placed the rag down, wiping the sheen of sweat off his forehead with his arm.

"Akio."

"You're the glorious man, eh?" Masaki chortled at his words. "The glorious man who cleans my kitchen for me." He gave another laugh at this. Akio grumbled to himself and returned back to cleaning the last corner on the counter.

"I've never seen a cleaner kitchen before in my life." Masaki preened his scalp with his index finger and thumb. "Tell you what, you can come here after open hours and clean my kitchen for ten yen an hour. How's that sound? The way you're cleaning this kitchen makes me think this isn't a big deal for you to do. Whatdaya say?"

Akio took the rag in his hands and turned it over and over, thoughts entering him of Sayuri and the plan they had for escaping together and living a new life. He thought of the way she snubbed him by leaving him in the Jaakuna village alone to fend for himself. Akio knew he could take care of himself. Why did he care so much that Sayuri left him?

"I'll take the job," Akio said and Masaki's mean little mouth stretched.

"That's the boy!" He roared into another laugh and left, leaving Akio to stare at the cleaning rag alone, the sound of the kitchen ventilator acting as ambiance.

Sayuri
Late June 1949

I sniffed as the aroma of Dansei's and my cooking entered my nose. Rabu sat at my side, expectant for a handout.

"No no, Rabu." I waggled a finger at him. "You have to wait until Dansei-sama says it's okay."

"Go ahead and feed him." Dansei had a laid back smile on his face as he turned to me. "I'm sure we've all waited long enough for the food by now."

The Akita Inu barked once and I slipped him a piece of a rice ball. As we knelt for dinner and prayers I felt a certain feeling enter me. Dansei must have guessed by my expression that my mind decided to wander, so he asked, "Sayuri, are you all right?"

"Just fine, Dansei. I'm thinking as I usually am." I looked at him and the elder man gave a firm nod, starting the prayers. While his lips moved, his voice lowered in respect, I felt the strange feeling enter me again. One reminding me of Akio. My thoughts returned back to the day the earthquake happened, which seemed so long ago. For the past two years I'd been so preoccupied with helping Dansei that I didn't think of Akio for a moment. It startled me how I had forgotten about him. The human mind adapts to change long after the death of a person happens.

"I can see that." A smile broke Dansei's features as he finished the prayer, responding to my previous sentence. "It looks like your thoughts have consumed you. I hope you paid attention while I spoke the prayers."

"I have," I said, nodding my head. "I always do."

"You know, Sayuri." He turned to me, his tone of voice changed. "You've stayed here for so long I'm beginning to think that you've been here with me since the beginning."

"That's a bad thing, right?" I asked, hearing the usual meekness in my voice.

"No," Dansei said, "you're just like my niece. Maybe even more so than her. You have a good heart for sticking around with me for as long as you've had."

His words gave me pause and I chewed my food. "It's the right thing to do."

"You're right there," he smiled.

After dinner, Dansei took out his shamisen and began to play it, the haunting sounds of the notes entering my ears. I watched how his fingers plucked at the cords, his gaze compiling a look of pure concentration. He had insisted I try my hand at playing, but I shook my head. I loved listening to him play, and knowing I had no experience with the instrument, I feared my inexperienced fingers would mar the magic I've heard every night. So I felt content to just listen to him, to close my eyes and let my mind drift away to a faraway land. This time though, my thoughts stayed glued on Akio. I wondered why I started thinking about him again.

I lay on my new blankets upon entering my room to go to sleep. The crisp moonlight from the quarter moon entered my window, alighting on my face. I thought back two years ago to the Jaakuna's old village, of the earthquake, and how the threat of the Jaakuna no longer affected my life.

For the next few days my mind went back to everything that happened before I met Dansei. Hands clasping and unclasping one night, I felt the sudden desire to make sure what I had experienced hadn't been some strange dream. Upon meeting the old man and staying with him, I felt like I was suspended in a dream world where things could do no harm. A place of protection for the innocent.

I stood and listened to Dansei's snores, feeling glad Rabu decided to sleep with him tonight. The loud snores would help me leave and return to the cabin without them noticing. I tiptoed down the hall and entered the kitchen, seeing the door just inches away from me, as well as my shoes. I raced outside the cabin, the moonlight offering me the way to my destination.

My blood raced at what I would find once I returned to the destroyed Jaakuna village. It made me shiver, but I longed to find out the truth of whether or not Akio had died or not. I felt sick of letting it become a mystery in my mind.

The paved road came back into my vision and I remembered when I first crossed it, my steps unsure, my heart in my mouth as I ran from the village. Now I ran across it with purpose, seeing the Jaakuna village not too far away, nestled among pine trees. In the two years I've been with Dansei, nothing changed except for the trees that continued to regrow their damaged branches. Now the area was in full bloom and, to me, it seemed the trees tried to hide the corruption that had infected the village.

The moon was free to shine upon me once I entered the village. Gravel, wood, and glass crackled underfoot as I walked. I blinked as the rank of flesh wafted into my nose. Nothing had changed, not even while the village lay empty. The smell of decay still lingered. Bodies lay, ones that I knew were Jaakuna men. With light steps, I picked myself around the corpses, heading to the slave establishment. The building looked half-sunken in on its foundation, but the front entryway still stood. Upon entering, the first thing I could see were all the steel bars of the cells. They still stood.

Avoiding chunks of rocks, I peered in every cell, seeing nothing inside them. I felt confused because every cell door stood ajar; no slave's bodies lay about inside them. Akio wasn't anywhere in the establishment either, and that's when it hit me upon reaching the last cell: he had escaped along with the other slaves. I knew the truth. In the two years I've spent with Dansei, I've always thought Akio died during the earthquake. Now my mind saw the light. Akio lived and maybe he scoured Nagasaki, looking for me.

At this, I straightened, knowing now what I had to do. If Akio was out there then I'd have to find him and set things straight again. I couldn't leave him hanging out there, alone by himself.

Once I found myself back in Dansei's log cabin I lay awake, unable to sleep, my blood rushing at the journey I would soon take. I knew Dansei would feel crushed when I'd tell him about my decision. In truth, even I felt reluctant to leave him without a person to keep him company. I'd miss the walks to Kyroyoku to help Dansei sell his fruits and bamboo shoots. We had even started cooking our food right in the marketplace and selling it to hungry people. Most of those villagers knew my face and name by now and they'd nod with smiles on their faces, should I appear in their vision. I'd miss all of it. There's a certain magic in earning trust and seeing the carefree smile pick you out to send its effulgence to.

With my heart drowning, I flipped onto my side, letting the moonshine hit my face, and slept. Upon hearing Dansei's voice in the morning, I stood and looked him straight in the eye.

"Have you figured something out, Sayuri?" he asked, his one eye bright and clear. His posture looked stooped, as if he had slept wrong in the night.

"I have." My voice sounded broken, and at once so did my confidence. We headed into the kitchen as Dansei prepared some fresh eggs for us.

"About what, dear?" His expression was open and curious.

I sighed. "I never told you about someone I met while in the destruction. His name's Akio and we were set on traveling together to find a home for ourselves."

"He's your boyfriend?" Dansei asked, a glitter in his eye.

"No. I hadn't even known he existed before the atomic bombing happened. We just happened to meet two years ago. We connected because we were both stuck in the same situation. The Jaakuna captured the both of us together and when the earthquake happened, I ran off without Akio. For a long time I've always thought that he was dead. Now I know he isn't."

A silence came between Dansei and me, then he spoke, "So you've decided to go look for him."

"Yes. I have this feeling that he's out there somewhere . . . looking for me. Even if it's been two years."

"I understand. No need to explain any further." Dansei looked dejected. Guilt rose in me but I ignored it. The sound of sizzling eggs filled the persistent silence.

"Dansei-sama . . ." I began but found I couldn't continue past the lodging of emotion in my throat. My eyes lowered.

"It's fine, Sayuri-chan. I know . . . I know," Dansei held up a hand as he said this, his one eye glittering. "Just stay for breakfast, please."

It amazed me how attached I felt to Dansei and Rabu, who padded into the kitchen while we ate breakfast. He understood the words we had said, for a whine whistled out from him. His curly tail drooped and his brown eyes became cloudy.

"It may seem selfish of me but I need to find Akio. I feel ashamed for leaving him alone." I reached and patted Rabu's soft head as he came over to me.

"I won't lie to you. Rabu and I have grown quite attached to you." Dansei seemed to be combating inner emotions from being let loose. He set down my plate and began to eat his eggs, his expression saddened.

"As have I but—" I stopped, not able to go on and complete my sentence, looking away from him.

"I know dear . . . You have to go, I understand, Sayuri. Thank you for sticking by this old man's side for all this time." He surprised me by coming over, giving me a full embrace. I embraced him as well, wanting to remember him. His breathing quickened as he drew away and the old man looked down at Rabu. Then he gazed at me. "You don't know how much you've helped me since we've met, dear. Here, take this."

My eyes widened as Dansei placed one hundred-fifty yen in my hand, his one eye gleaming with purpose.

"I can't accept this . . ." I trailed off as he waved my words away from him.

"Please take it. It's all I have left to repay you for all you've done for me."

I knew he wouldn't want me to refuse the money so I nodded and put it away, embracing him again. Dansei smelled like family to me.

I knelt and kissed the lovable Akita on the nose. Rabu whined again and licked my face, his ears flattening as I stood, my plate empty.

"Get going then, Sayuri-chan. Go find your friend, dear. Never forget me or Rabu . . . because we won't," Dansei said and I saw something glistening in his eye as he turned away from me just as his shoulders began to quiver. He composed himself and turned to give a smile, just to show me that he still could find some happiness in him despite feeling sad.

I turned around and walked out of the cabin I had called home for the time I had stayed there. Padding steps sounded behind me; Rabu whined. He jumped on my legs as I turned around. It made me think the Akita Inu wanted to find a way to bring me back to stay in the log cabin forever.

"Rabu, stay." Dansei's command sounded choked and forced. The sound of it spurred me to run, not wanting them to see the sadness I combated. The wind blew through my hair and I clenched my fist, trying to prevent emotion from overtaking me.

"Oh Dansei-sama. I'll never forget you either. May the gods above grant you good luck," I said in a murmur, looking back as I slowed my pace. Through the bamboo stalks and tree branches a place of safety and hope rested. A place where those of weak hearts can strengthen them. A place one does not forget: home. Past the tree trunks, I could see the dark wood cabin, but even fainter still I could hear the sounds of a mournful, doleful howl filling the air with longing and sorrow.

And in my dream that night . . . the old man, who I knew now had been Dansei, disappeared from the meadow. Now two people stood in front of me, their expressions the same.

Jaakuna
Late June 1949

"I'm very sorry, Commander Korudo. Your father . . . we found his body. H-he's dead, sir." The guard gulped, as if the words seemed hard to say. Korudo stood from his mockery of a bed, walking over to the man. The guard shifted a nervous step back as the Jaakuna leader's massive dark whip made its appearance in the candlelit gloom, sheathed at his side.

"Show me," Korudo said. With a hasty reply, the guard fled to tell the other messengers of Korudo's decision.

After the earthquake happened the Jaakuna, the little amount of men who survived, were left without a place to call their own. Korudo felt devastated; he had lost his mother and now his father. He knew he had no parental figure in this world anymore. Even if he had a silent resentment aimed towards Yuki, Korudo felt grateful to still have a parent in life when his mother killed herself.

He remembered the slave girl Yuki thrust into his care back and he remembered how she stuck with that coward Yowai. It infuriated him how she had trusted that thing enough to make him her friend. Korudo shook his head, dark feelings inside him. *I should have asked her for her name . . . But by the gods, despite looking emaciated, she had been the most beautiful thing I'd ever seen since my mother died.*

Korudo remembered searching the village for the girl, his father, and any remaining Jaakuna standing around with horror on their faces. He found the latter first by just opening his eyes after the earthquake ended. Their facial expressions made his lip curl: the sympathetic and worried phases of weakness. They helped him onto his feet, saying their sheer apologies.

They're idiots . . . they should feel grateful they weren't in the old village. They would've been dead just like the others. My father must have had some good sense in him to send them out on patrol instead of sending them to the cavern looking for jewels. Jewels . . .

the main thing Korudo always knew his father had a soft spot for during his life. That's the reason why, when the strange old man came into the village with the gemstone rumor, Yuki believed him without hesitation or second thoughts.

With no success in finding either the girl or his father, Korudo decided to take the job as high commander, disregarding what the Jaakuna wanted. Usually the clan held a ritual at night after the previous leader died or abdicated and a preferred leader would make himself known. Korudo didn't want to wait until the night fell. He never had patience and it showed now more than ever.

He knew he was a brutal commander. All the remaining Jaakuna were either frightened of him or had no hesitation in having orders thrown at them. Korudo knew the right way to rule over weaklings. *If people feel frightened to wrong you, they will listen. As is the way of human instinct; no one wants to be the person who acted brave in the eyes of danger, unless they were foolish and irrational.*

As a last resort, Korudo went to excavate the underground cavern and see if Yuki still lived. All he saw was a black whip. The long black whip that never left his father's sight or his grip. It was Korudo's now; he felt he should confiscate some object that represented his father's image. The whip fed on the fear and pain of the remaining Jaakuna and it gave the commander a rush of power every time he used it.

Korudo looked out the window to see the desolate village he ruled over: Kagayaki. Rumored to be the most prosperous village in Northern Nagasaki, it had been easy—too easy—to take it over and enslave most of the people. The Jaakuna man held contempt for what had jumped out to him upon entering the gates. The people looked unsuspecting and placid, the perfect combination for an ambush. Korudo grinned, remembering how they all leaped out their houses, hands over their heads, bodies crouched on the ground when the Jaakuna stormed the village. Those he deemed useful became slaves and the rest he cared not where they went.

The Jaakuna commander sat down at his desk, feeling the ornate cedarwood resin beneath his fingertips. Korudo had a flair for writing, a strange hobby he picked up after settling into Kagayaki. The things he wrote were just excerpts from famous war leaders, but today he wanted to try his hand at something different. In his mind, sentences formed, desperate to be conveyed through the use of a pen. He began:

The touch of a Rose seems too passionate, too silly.

I'd much rather the touch of a lily.

With soft edges and a pointed look,

It draws me to believe—

"Sir?" A voice ruptured his concentration and Korudo growled as he looked up, pen pressing into the paper.

"What?" He turned to glare at the messenger shifting in his position in the doorway. They just couldn't come at a better time, and now the moment Korudo dedicated to writing vanished. "Can't you see I'm busy?"

"I'm sorry sir." The messenger bowed twice. "You said you wanted to see your father's body."

"Why did it take you cretins so long to go find him?" Korudo slammed his pen down and stood. "It took you three days to even gather up the courage to leave Kagayaki and find your old leader. Then it took you even longer to find him."

"Sir, we had been busy with settling in Kagayaki—" "—Settling in nothing! Next I suppose you'll tell me you and the others couldn't find Yuki and you just brought me a look-alike just to "ease" my mind," Korudo interrupted the floundering guard and spared himself the agony of hearing a pity party. He had never known how foolish and stupid these men were until he took over the job of leading them. Korudo wondered how his father dealt with them for all those years. In a way he felt for his father and in another way he didn't. Yuki had been a poor father and an even poorer role model. Korudo still idolized him however, knowing that his father had ruled over the Jaakuna with mercilessness. He experienced a taste of his father's brutality once. Now Korudo was free, but sometimes he felt something still held him back.

"As Korudo commands." The guard bowed low again and left. The Jaakuna commander growled and stormed after him, a dark look brewing on his face. All the other messengers and guards backed away upon seeing their leader clomp out into the open. Contempt rested in him for a moment for his men. Korudo glanced down to see his father's corpse and all emotion faded from him.

A serene peace existed in Yuki's face. One that hadn't existed before in Korudo's family. Not even his mother's face harbored the same expression when he saw her on the tatami floor, blood congealing into the mats. The old Jaakuna commander's eyes were closed, dried blood residing in the corner of his lip. His body looked as pale as a banshee's skin. Korudo sighed and knelt onto the ground, his hand moving to his father's arm.

"Father . . . you were a glorious man. Now may your revered soul rest in the sanctuary of the gods above us," he said, the tone in his voice half-hearted and forced. Korudo had never known how to help a dead person's spirit move on to the next life. He would just stare at the bodies and keep his mouth shut. The other men murmured in respect and gave their condolences, not noticing that Korudo didn't sound sincere.

He turned to look at his men. "Two years it took for you men to gather up the courage to go find him." Silence bloomed at his words. "From now on I'd expect each and every one of you to redeem yourselves, unless you want to join the slaves." A loud crack of a whip on bare skin sounded in the distance as the sentence hung in the air. Then came the thin high wail of a slave. All the Jaakuna men blanched.

"So what'll we do?" one man asked, daring to break the silence.

"An insignificant question." Korudo looked at him. Kagayaki wasn't enough for Korudo—he wanted more. He wanted . . . what he couldn't have. "We'll go and pillage more villages. It wouldn't hurt to make our reputation known, right?"

The other men remained silent. Korudo wondered if he ruled as his father would have if he still lived. He knew he had no leadership quality to call his own. In a way Korudo was still a child, the same child his father took and enslaved a long time ago. *That will change*, Korudo thought. *It will.*

"Tomorrow, men, we'll head out to regain what my father ignited in us. Gather up supplies today. You have ten minutes. Now go."

"As Korudo commands, so shall we obey," the men chorused, then they departed. Korudo looked down at his father's body one last time. His lip curled and he left it outside, going back into his room to plan. He knew one of his guards would bury Yuki somewhere.

Leading these foolhardy men is easy enough. All you have to do is say a command and if you instilled enough common sense and fear in them from the beginning, they'll do whatever you say, Korudo thought as he sat at his desk once more and picked up his pen, before dropping it with a curse. An ink splatter stained his hand and he muttered, peering amongst his maps and documents for another. A map of Nagasaki lay in front of him and it too had a black ink stain on it. Korudo narrowed his eyes as he noticed the spot the ink stained and there, a village was chosen. *Planning takes no effort. All it takes is a brain and an able hand.*

—*It draws me to believe that my heart the lily has took.*

"Korudo sir, the packing of supplies is finished. We're ready to move out tomorrow . . . Commander?" Korudo heard a guard ask from behind him. He turned to him and made sure his gaze looked pointed.

"Good, good, now leave me alone and tell the other imbeciles that," he said. The guard shifted a foot in hesitation, then left Korudo's sight. It annoyed him how the guards always acted meek around him, as if they didn't have a mean bone in their body. They even hesitated to snap at slaves and make them feel weak. A few of the Jaakuna guards were exceptional; the ones Korudo grew up with in the old village. They were the men he valued. Not these cowards who had been around since Yuki led the Jaakuna.

The moon's beam glittered on his arm like a band as Korudo blew out the lantern light in his room. Outside, the sounds of uneasy chatter started up from the village people. It amused him to know the Kagayakians felt so petrified of him. They felt it was safe to come out at night. Once the sun came up again, the villagers retreated into their homes, closing their blinds and locking their doors. Korudo never worried about a revolt from them; they were too scared to even look a Jaakuna man in the eye.

He closed his eyes and let the lull of people's conversations take him away to sleep, trying to imagine himself back to a time when he didn't have to rule or lead anyone.

Korudo opened his eyes upon hearing the sounds of birds singing as morning came again. A snarl sounded in his throat. *How could those birds sing while we're down here struggling to survive?*

His mouth ready to form the usual scowl, he stood from the bed and stalked over to a chair, putting on the pieces of his armor. That's when the words of the slave girl reverberated in his head: *I don't know who or what the Jaakuna are, but I can tell you guys don't realize that armored men only exist in stories now.* These words gave him pause and he looked down at his armor. His brow creased in thought and for a moment he saw the attire on him as foreign material. Korudo shook his head and continued strapping on his boots and breastplate. *Who cares if the Jaakuna don't have the generic Westernized look? It makes it easier for people to recognize us.*

As he walked outside he could see solemn and grim faces on his men as they made their way to him. A large supply bag lay on the floor, bulging and full to bursting. A cruel smile stretched onto Korudo's face at this sight.

"All right men. Here's where it stands. There's a village about four miles from here, a quaint one called Chinmoku. Our objective? We'll travel there and take over everything. Leave no house unchecked and make sure not one villager raises a finger in protest. Got it? We need to assert command now while the country still lives in recovery," Korudo said to the Jaakuna assembled before him. A ragged cheer started up at his words. His grin augmented as a vision of Chinmoku becoming his own entered his mind. While his thoughts wandered, Korudo hefted supply bag over to three guards, who grunted, helping each other in supporting its weight.

"Carry this with care. We'll call it our "survival decider" should we get lost," Korudo said to the three red-faced men. "Jaakuna assemble yourselves. March!"

At his words, all sixteen of the men assembled into rows of four, as they had been taught. An answering roar started up as the Jaakuna began to move, for glory and power.

Sayuri
Middle July 1949

A month passed, a long tough month. I had to ration the money Dansei gave me as I traveled. I tried looking in Kyroyoku, for Akio. Asking around for someone named Akio wouldn't work for me. I preferred to find someone without help. Frustration soon became my main emotion to grapple with and I doubted my chances of ever finding him. Then I'd remind myself to keep pushing on because he might just be in the next village over, looking for me.

I continued on my path, not knowing which direction I traveled in, but not caring all the same. I went through village after village, buying some food and water to supply me on long routes where no civilization existed. I crossed roads, avoided cars, walked over bridges, and finally received the notion that I should buy a map. However, I was unsure of when I'd see the next village. I could very well be lost and not realize it.

Now I lay at night, counting my yen and seeing the same stagnant faces of past emperors staring at me. When I stayed with Dansei I felt human. I wasn't used to living like a fugitive once again. It made my stomach twist to find myself back at square one again—all alone—and without an ally.

The next morning, as I walked, an unfamiliar sound entered the air. It soothed me. As the trees parted I could see a glittering expanse of water stretch across my vision. At once I knew this was the ocean. I remembered my mother telling me about it one time—how the water stretches for miles and miles, remaining the same. However, she also told me about the variety of life that lived below the surface of water.

I walked onto the sand, feeling the hot grains from inside my shoes. The water kissed the shore and doubled back, as if afraid. It surged back again, crashing higher little by little after each cycle. Curious, I reached with my finger and touched the foamy water before it could recede. The water felt light and I stuck my finger in my mouth, puckering my face upon tasting salt. I wondered if Akio knew about the ocean. The wind came and rustled my long draping hair.

As I looked about I saw a small house upon a promontory above the ocean. The water lashed at the rock face, determined to break it down and level it. A house meant people, and people meant a greater direction. I set off for the house, taking my small satchel of food with me.

The grassy fronds stuck up from the ground in all different directions and they brushed against my legs at my passing. The wind blew in stronger tones the higher I went. I stopped cold as a song hung in the air, faint, but full of cadence.

"In the dawn of light, may it whisper, whisper in your heart. Dewdrops fall, caress your soul. Shimmering unseen, stars of heaven. Sleeping peaceful, soft as dove's down. She rises . . . she rises."

That lullaby—my mother used to sing it me in the morning when I was younger. It startled me to hear this again and I began to wonder if the salt water I licked off my finger made me delirious. I continued on my way and soon the porch of the house was under my feet. The singing continued, unhindered, stronger now.

"Hello?" I called out, rapping on the door with my hand. The singing stopped, then a young woman came to the door and peered out it, her face open.

"Yes? Do you need something?" she asked and an older woman also joined her in the doorway, eyes glinting. What did I need? I couldn't figure out why I decided to knock on the door of the house in the first place. I couldn't just stand there and stare at them, so I decided to free up my vocal cords and speak.

"I, um, think I'm lost." My face flamed at this. I surmised I must sound immature to them. Then I remembered the reason. "I need a map."

"A woman in need of a map. Wait here and I'll get you a spare one." The older woman shuffled out of sight, the younger woman watching her then turning back to me.

"How did you find out that we lived here?" she asked, her tone suspicious and accusatory. It chastised me. Her voiced sounded borderline angry.

"I . . . I heard singing and wanted to know where it came from."

The woman sighed and said in a mutter, "I knew I should have told her not to sing while the windows lay open to let in the breeze."

"Why?" I asked, but the look I received in return made me want to back off and leave the woman alone. The older woman reappeared and handed me the map, a smile on her lips.

"Here you go, honey. I even marked on the map where you are right now," she said, and the younger woman turned to her, enraged.

"O bachan! How could you do such a thing like this?! Suppose this woman decides to show this map to others— then what'll we do?! They'll definitely find us!"

"Hush, On'na-sama. The lady in front of us wouldn't tell anyone anything."

"About what, may I ask?" I asked. Their expressions looked intense and, as they swung to look at me, I wondered if I should just leave. As usual though, I had to feel curious about everything.

"Don't tell her!" On'na said, her eyes wide with panic now. O bachan turned to her, silencing her next words with a single look.

"Sweetheart, what do you know about destruction?" she asked, looking at me now, and I wondered if it was a trick question. Of course I'd know what destruction was—every single detail about it.

"I survived the atomic bomb two years ago, O bachan-san. I know destruction's dark reaches and how it ruins people without remorse."

"Ah." The word came out as a sigh from the older woman. "You've suffered much. You'll understand our plight."

On'na shot her a pleading look, but it was waved away.

"We've suffered as well. The Jaakuna took over our village, Kagayaki, and turned it into a nightmare. We ran away at the slightest chance we had."

"The Jaakuna?" I felt like laughing at O bachan's words. "The Jaakuna are dead. They were killed by an earthquake in their village."

"No, dear. They're indeed alive. On'na and I escaped them a week after they appeared and wrecked havoc."

"How could they still live? I watched them die when when the earthquake happened." My head shook. I couldn't believe her words. I just couldn't. The pain they inflicted upon me and Yowai came back to me. I wanted to get away from the conversation and pretend everything was still the same.

"So you too have learned of their brutal ways." On'na's voice sounded tight and reluctant, as if she still didn't trust me.

"As I've said before, my precious granddaughter, this lady here wouldn't tell anyone of our secret. I can see it in her eyes," O bachan said, a triumphant smile on her face.

"How did they survive?" I asked, feeling bemused. On'na turned to me, her expression loosening, giving way to defeat.

"The gods salvaged them," she said, then took out a cigarette and a lighter.

"Indeed not, On'na. The gods wouldn't allow such creatures of evil to run about Nagasaki," O bachan said while On'na lit the cigarette and inhaled it.

"No, something else saved them."

"They're looking for you?" I asked, and On'na nodded her head, a puff of smoke lingering around her before dissipating.

"They wouldn't let people get away. We knew we had a short amount of time to blend in and "disappear". This house was abandoned upon our discovery of it. Not too far away, the village of Han'ei rests so it seemed as though fate called to us to stay. I make frequent trips to Han'ei to gather nourishment and supplies."

"We couldn't live like recluses while our meager food supply diminished," O bachan added, a smile on her face.

"We're careful though, if suspicious characters come into the area. I fear the Jaakuna will one day come destroy Han'ei as they've done to the other villages and find us here," On'na said.

Han'ei . . . it seemed like the kind of place where nothing bad happened. A place where one would feel safe. For the Jaakuna to want to even touch a village with that sort of magic—it made me clench my hands.

"You forget Han'ei has a powerful ally in itself, On'na. Kotei-sama wouldn't stand to let the Jaakuna overrun his village," O bachan said, and I felt something come over me. Perhaps this Kotei could help me in my search for Akio. Sure it seemed strange to ask a man to help me, but I needed an ally. A valuable one.

"Kotei . . . who is he?" I asked.

"Ah, he's one of the most revered people in all of Nagasaki." Here O bachan's eyes glittered. "He doesn't take violence and despair in light regards and he's a charming person. All the village people love him because he's a just man. We owe him a great debt for making Han'ei a peaceful place. He fought in World War two, you know. He may have lost the fighting but his determination marks him high in our standards."

"So he was a war general . . ." My sentence trailed off as my mind began to work. If I could go see Kotei, then perhaps I could live in peace after I found Akio. I wouldn't have to worry about looking for a home.

"One of the best," On'na said, her eyes showing affection. Her turnabout of attitude surprised me, but I kept it to myself.

"Thank you for the map," I said, feeling out of place in their conversation. I bowed once to each of them and added, "And thank you for telling me about the Jaakuna."

"It's no trouble, dear. I can see you're willing to leave. It's nice to receive visitors every once and a while. I'd suggest you head to Han'ei yourself. Perhaps you'll find your dreams there." O bachan sent me a smile. I began to back up and turn around as On'na blew another puff of smoke, its gray fingers curling in the air before it disappeared.

"Don't tell anyone what we've told you. Ever." Her voice sounded tight and controlled again and I nodded.

"I won't. I promise." I looked at both women and the tension drained from them at my words.

"Good," On'na said, then she entered the house with O bachan, closing the front door behind her.

Han'ei was indeed a place of peace and prosperity. I could tell the moment I stepped into it for the first time. Cherry blossom trees blossomed their flowers and children laughed, chasing each other with twigs and other objects. Parents watched from their doorsteps, looking healthy and full of vibrant life. Each house in the village looked alive with life and love, something I haven't seen in a long time. If I didn't have to find Akio then I'd feel convinced enough to stay here.

I breathed the air in and whistled it out with a sigh. It seemed so peaceful here. I had to check the map to make sure I was in the right place. This village seemed like a wonderful dream to me.

A horn sounded, and I looked in surprise as people raced out their houses, expectant looks on their faces. I felt confused until I heard voices say, "He comes! Show him respect!"

I began to wonder who it was, then my breath was snatched as I saw a man of dignified power and authority exit from a house. I came over, wanting to get a closer look at him.

"Isn't he dashing?" a woman asked someone beside me and I looked at them for a moment.

"Kotei's always attractive. That's a man every woman should marry," the person said in return. No wonder Kotei held such a large authority in Han'ei. The people loved and respected him. O bachan was right.

Upon my first glimpse of him, Kotei sounded just like the man O bachan described: a man full of dignity and love for his people.

"People of Han'ei!" Kotei said and everyone fell silent. "While villages around us quiver at the sight of evil we alone stand tall. I want you to always cherish that we've survived this long without being threatened. Chinmoku, Hebi, and Taka, have been destroyed by the Jaakuna. As if they never were."

Kotei's voice held a surprising effect on his people, for they hung their heads, as if taking the blame for the villages' destruction.

"However," he said with strength and everyone lifted their heads, "their memory and their struggles will live on in our hearts. I know I've failed in helping Chinmoku but it's an incentive to grow stronger. Our ally, Kagayaki, still stands and they are well. If the Jaakuna even think to touch that village . . . I will show no mercy."

People cheered at this and I wondered why the O bachan said that Kagayaki had been taken over by the Jaakuna. Did she lie to me?

"Everyone, you're dismissed and free to return to your duties," Kotei said and everyone bowed as they left. I knew this was my chance to speak with him on the subject while it still lingered. Before my wits could escape me, I hurried over to him.

"Kotei, sir!" I stopped short in front of him, making sure to bow. "If I may have a moment with you."

"Anything to please the lady." A smile grew on his face. He seemed joyed to have someone speak to him. A tingle went through me. The notion that he assumed I was one of his villagers made me feel as though I belonged.

"Well?" Kotei said as the silence lingered between us.

"I . . . the Jaakuna have ruined my life as well, Kotei-sama," I said and Han'ei's general's eyes softened.

"So young . . . you are too young to have evil touch your life. What's your name?"

"Sayuri."

"Sayuri." He nodded. "Tell me, what have the Jaakuna did to you."

I told him about the Jaakuna enslaving me and how they killed people they deemed useless. Kotei's expression darkened. He continued to listen to me as I also told him about my exploits to find Akio and how they led me to Han'ei.

"Hmm . . . you seem to have gone through a lot to get to here, and to find a friend as well. You're brave, Sayuri, to have come this far to northern Nagasaki. Though why do you tell me your struggles?"

I felt reluctant to tell him my reasons for speaking to him. I shrugged it off. "I need a friend—someone to travel with while I search for Akio. The Jaakuna may be anywhere now and . . . I don't want to be caught off guard."

"An ally." Kotei looked solemn. "At least you're thinking ahead, Sayuri. That's commendable. I would like to help you but I can't leave Han'ei alone without protection. You understand, right?"

I nodded despite feeling dejected. Of course my problem wouldn't matter to Kotei when it came to the protecting the village.

He continued, "However, if you need anything at all don't hesitate to come to me. I'll help you in any way I can. I wish not to see people in peril from a common enemy."

"Thank you . . . Kotei." I bowed, feeling grateful to have spoken to him.

"It's no trouble, madam." A smile returned to Kotei's face. I knew this meant I was dismissed and I walked off, feeling the Han'ei general's eyes on my back.

A sudden question rose in me and I turned to face Kotei again. "The Jaakuna were supposed to be dead, Kotei. An earthquake destroyed their village and they perished."

Kotei was silent for a moment, then his eyes looked straight into mine. "The Jaakuna never truly die. They're inside all of us."

Jaakuna
Middle July 1949

Korudo watched as his men ravaged the village Dokutsu, and a smile stretched his lips. Since they've settled in Kagayaki, things became much easier for the Jaakuna commander. The people of Dokutsu were weak and helpless to the attack, just as all the rest of the village people had in Hebi, Chinmoku, and Taka. All of those villages were now destroyed. Dokutsu was his next obstacle; a village built into a rock wall. If the situation for his "visit" had been different, Korudo would have imagined for a moment or two about how the Dokutsu people accomplished in creating the village.

Korudo felt so sure of his victory that he paraded amongst the houses, watching his men race in and out of them, gathering antiques, money, clothes, and other valuable items. Children cried and women with shaky voices hushed them.

He flinched as he saw a girl watching him from the shadows of the flames and houses. He had to convince himself that she wasn't the slave girl he wanted to recapture. He turned and raised his sword at her, but the girl already vanished.

"Damn!" Korudo said, then he turned to see a sight that widened his eyes. There, behind the flames, men stood, firing guns straight at him and his men.

"Reinforcements? Hm . . . so these village people have some brains after all. Jaakuna! Assemble and attack our armed enemies!"

A roar sounded as his nine chosen men barged from the houses, eager to prove themselves to their new leader. Korudo smirked and headed off back to the camp. He knew all of them would die anyway.

"Sir? A command to throw the grenades?" came a meek voice and Korudo turned to face the man, named Katsu, in charge of throwing grenades. He was a man of weak stature, in short he was comparable to a hermit. Korudo found the man slumped to a wall two years ago and in need of a drink. 'I have no money or any drink. Please spare me' he had said. Korudo asked him what his talent was, if any, and Katsu told him he created bombs for fun. Korudo knew how useful it would be for his plans if he had a man who created weapons of destruction.

"Yes, unleash the god's wrath on Dokutsu and everyone inside," he said and the man flinched.

"But . . . but what about your men, Korudo sir? Aren't they still inside the village?"

"I know what I'm doing. The Dokutsu hired reinforcements for themselves. They have guns—I know full well about long-range weapons and how they pose a greater advantage over hand weapons." Korudo continued to walk to his tent. "Throw the grenades now."

"U-understood!" the man said, wiping his brow. He took a grenade in his hand, pulled the pin with his teeth, and threw it, his lip quivering.

Akio
Late July 1949

Akio walked, his eyes scanning the scenery. Working for Masaki had given him a taste of the working world, and it also gave him some pocket money to keep for himself. Now he was over the job. He wanted to find the place that clicked inside him. The village he'd spend his life in until he grew old and sinewy. A sigh whistled from his lips at this. It wasn't easy to remove himself from the demands of the teahouse owner. Akio had even been in love with Azuki after a few months of playful banter and they hung out together. Her shy sweet demeanor touched him, since he never dated a girl in his life.

Akio was over Azuki now as well. For when he went out with her she reminded him of Sayuri.

Sayuri . . . two years had passed since he saw her last. Akio wondered where she went and if she felt guilt for abandoning him. Even stranger still: he missed her sharp look and distant personality. He wasn't in love with Sayuri, Akio knew, but he didn't think about her with hatred anymore.

Another sigh ripped from him. Kyroyoku seemed like an ideal place to live, with the marketplace and the peaceful atmosphere. It hadn't been enough. Akio needed more.

As he traveled, Akio's eyes darkened as he saw abandoned and annihilated villages here and there and an occasional car passing by on the road. It sickened him to have an idea on who destroyed the villages. He felt his lips press together. He knew they still lived.

Later on another village entered his vision, still standing and full of life. It gave Akio pause to see such a sight. It drew him to come closer, then he stopped as he felt a presence appear behind him.

"You too have sensed the village's aura." The voice sounded chilly and borderline bored. Akio swung around and saw the man responsible for everything. Korudo. His brother.

"I'm surprised you survived the earthquake, but I'm even more surprised that some of the Jaakuna survived as well." Akio said with impassiveness. Korudo's mouth twitched at the statement but nothing more.

"A fact I wonder about every day," the Jaakuna leader said. "The village we look at now is my next target. It's too cheery. Too . . . carefree. None of those feelings should exist. Not after what the Americans did to us. You understand, right?"

"The Americans," Akio repeated, not looking at his brother.

"If people act happy and all life-is-back-to-normal, then they must be spies for America."

"Don't be ridiculous," Akio said, turning to face Korudo. "Your paranoia seems to have increased since you joined the Jaakuna."

"So? I've never known how to lead people before in my life. I want what Yuki would have wanted for his Jaakuna."

"They're your Jaakuna now."

"Yes, Akio. Yes they are."

The two brothers fell silent, Akio wondering if he should move on and leave his warped brother to himself.

"How did you survive the earthquake anyway, brother? You were in the slave establishment when it happened." Korudo's tone sounded casual. Maybe too casual.

"Yeah, I was. Does it matter? It's just us two surviving members of our family now."

"So it is. Now Akio, what brings you to these parts? Not looking for me, are you?"

"No. I'm looking for a place to stay," Akio said before he could hold himself back. He knew this would give his brother the incentive to try and take the chance to persuade him to do something, which he always did.

"A place to stay . . . Well, why don't you join the Jaakuna alongside me? I'll even give you free room and board," Korudo suggested, making Akio grimace.

"Don't act generous, Korudo. It isn't like you at all, the cold, calculating member of the family. The thought of you growing soft scares me."

"Pah!" the Jaakuna commander snorted. "Me becoming soft is the same as you falling in love. It's impossible."

Akio felt the barb of his brother's words and had to steel back a defensive reply. He did date Azuki, but that didn't count to him. Once again Sayuri resurfaced in his mind but he shoved the thought away and glowered at his brother instead.

"I meant every word about joining the Jaakuna, Akio. I'm in need of some new members at the moment. Seems my last village visit caused me to lose nine of my guards. How pitiful." Korudo made a sneer, sounding contemptuous of his own words. "You and me, Akio. It's what father would have wanted."

"Even after he enslaved me?" Akio shot back, raw anger now in his voice. "After he whipped me?"

"That was just a phase, I'm sure you know this by now. He wanted to test your loyalty. He did the same to me." Korudo's own eyes flared. "He locked me in a cell for ten years before he realized I was grown up enough to be considered trustworthy. You had it off easy, Akio. Know that."

"I'm likely to never forget it."

"Enough of that now. Why can't you answer my question in a straightforward manner?"

"Begging me to join your group of killers, Korudo?"

"Must you always label things in such a prudish way? We don't kill for sport. My Jaakuna kill in order to prove."

"Prove what?" Akio began to turn away, ready to walk.

"Prove what happens to weakness. That's why Nagasaki was bombed by the Americans in the first place. We're nothing but a bunch of cowards dressing in Western clothes."

No, Nagasaki wasn't bombed for that reason, Akio wanted to say, but he knew he couldn't argue with Korudo once he started with his paranoia.

"Doubt me however you like. Go ahead. When America decides to come here again and wipe us off the planet for good, don't come crying to me." Korudo let loose a forced laugh. "Now will you stop acting adamant and just join beside me for the gods' sake? You have no one now. Might as well stick around with people you know, right?"

Akio huffed, looking up at the overcast clouds. Sayuri entered his mind. Again he tried to oust her, but it did no good. For some reason a mental image of her stuck to him like a burr. Not a painful burr either. Akio had to admit she was cute, if he looked past her distrustful expression and quick movements.

"Well?" Korudo prodded when the moment of silence lingered.

"You're hiding something, aren't you. You only beg for me to stand by your side if you need something."

"Why, begging has nothing to do with this. I don't grovel. Ever." Korudo's eyes leered.

"What are you planning, to make your brother turn into one of your men?"

"It seems my younger brother's mistaken." Korudo shook his head, as if in pity. "You don't trust the one family member you have?"

"Not since he became a Jaakuna member."

"Akio, you're trying my patience. Either answer my question, or get out of my face." Korudo's teeth gritted.

Akio crossed his arms. "Fine. I'll join your little group. However," he added upon seeing the Jaakuna leader's eyes brighten, "if I have to get involved with any killings, then it's your loss when you realized I've hightailed it out of your village."

"Coward." Akio's brother made a mean smile.

"I don't like to flaunt killer weapons around like you do, Korudo. Feel glad I even decided to take one of your suggestions." Akio looked at his older brother, the strange armor he wore, the cold calculating look in his eyes. He surmised that he knew less and less of his brother with each passing day.

"For once you've done the right thing. Now come with me. We have much to discuss." Korudo stalked off, his heavy black armor glinting in the sudden sunlight. Akio looked at his surroundings, seeing peaceful Han'ei, before he followed behind his brother.

"So . . . Akio." A strange tone was in Korudo's voice now.

"What?"

"Who was the girl we captured alongside you two years ago?"

"She was just a girl I met in her destroyed village." Akio felt the urge to defend Sayuri. However, his older brother didn't sound callous or contemptuous. He sounded interested.

"Indeed. Why for?"

"You ask a lot of questions, Korudo. I felt curious and wanted to find out if any survivors still lived after the bomb hit. It felt strange . . . seeing a live person again after two years when I met the girl."

"Hm . . ." Korudo looked deep in thought. "Did she tell you her name?"

"She had."

"Most interesting." Korudo didn't pry further. Akio felt glad for that.

"Why ask?" He raised an eyebrow at his brother.

"Curious," Korudo said in reply. "By the way, father's dead."

"I've known he died. He would have never survived the earthquake, especially if he was underground at the time." Akio felt nonchalant.

"I felt nothing for his death. It gave me the chance to rule." Korudo looked at his younger brother for a split second, then returned his sight to the road ahead of him. "All my life I've wanted to prove I'm greater than a coward."

"I know, Korudo. You've always been ambitious."

"Ambitious?" Korudo barked out a laugh. "Your words amuse me, brother, they do. Ambitious? That's a word you'd say to a scholar or a five year old. Not to a grown man with dreams to spread his influence."

Akio sighed and shook his head as his brother continued to laugh, feeling sick of speaking to him for the moment. *If he wants to act stubborn, then that's his problem. I want no part in it.*

Sayuri
Early August 1949

Mosquitoes buzzed in my ears as I walked, the village of Han'ei behind me. I felt pleased to have spoken to Kotei, despite not getting any clues of where to find Akio. Before I departed, the Han'ei general sought me out and told me if I needed help for any reason, I could write or come to him anytime. At least I had someone I could fall back on in case I needed support.

The allure of Han'ei convinced me to stay for two weeks. It seemed like the perfect place to live and I had to convince myself that I wasn't in a dream, but in reality. Birds chirped, children sang, and the air danced with a mystic quality. It drew me in and kept me there, showing me how life was supposed to be.

During my stay I happened to pass by a mirror, seeing a woman who looked damaged, her mouth a stagnant line. Her soft brown-gray eyes bore into mine, her skin pale, her hair long and flowing. Her long lanky frame and the way her clothes seemed to hang on her made me grimace. Then I saw that the woman was me and I flinched. What happened to the girl who survived the atomic bomb and looked into puddles to see what she looked like? Now I saw a hardened person who wanted to belong somewhere, anywhere. It broke my heart.

Now I walked on, my purpose to find Akio once and for all and end this chase I've started. Upon looking at the map I could see three villages past Han'ei, all three were possibilities of where Akio could have went. My feet thudded the ground in soft tones as I moved, the sun shining on my head.

My hand covered my mouth upon reaching the first village and the smell of ashes stained the air. The houses sagged, as if they held up a heavy invisible force. No birds sang and no people populated the area. I came closer and saw a blazing fire, its angry orange fingers reaching for anything in its path.

My neck hair rose as I saw eyes watching me from the eaves of the rubble and collapsed houses. Three people watched me, their expressions wary, their bodies tense. It brought me back to when I had been in the same situation as them. Distrustful and careful of every moment.

As I neared closer and closer, the people shrank back and I perceived one of them to have long hair. I wanted to call out and ask what happened to the village but I didn't want to startle them. I realized they were speaking amongst themselves.

"Scare her off, please Maiko. That person's one of them, I know it."

The woman spoke, "Hush Isamu. The woman isn't here to harm us." She swung a look to me, to make sure I didn't have a weapon of any sort.

"But Maiko . . ."

"Hush!"

"Maiko, how are you so sure of yourself?" the man next to her asked.

"Katashi, when do you ever doubt me? If this woman was out here to hurt us, she would have done so by now and would've been on her way." Maiko's eyes flashed.

This encouraged me to come closer and Isamu and Katashi withdrew from my view. Maiko rolled her eyes.

"Excuse me for asking, but what happened here?" I asked, looking at her.

"Our village was destroyed, can't you see that?" a voice said from the shadows. I assumed it came from Isamu. His voice had a scornful air to it.

"How?"

Maiko shuffled out from under the eaves of the collapsed house. I had to hold back a flinch. She wasn't young as I thought when I came closer. Her hair was drizzled with grays and whites, wrinkles creasing her eyes and the corners of her mouth. Her eyes themselves threw me off, for they looked bright and full of youthful energy.

"A group of unscrupulous armored men came and destroyed everything. I believe they called themselves the Janku . . . Jakka . . . something around those lines. Katashi, what did those men call themselves by when they destroyed our village yesterday?" Maiko asked.

"The Jaakuna, Maiko," Katashi said.

I stiffened once the dreaded name entered my ears. "What?"

"You've heard of them?" Maiko turned back to me, interest in her bright eyes.

"I have," I said with a nod of my head. "They enslaved me two years ago."

"As I said, they're unscrupulous." She shook her head, gray hair swaying. "I watched as the rafters for my house collapsed onto my couch. It was an explosion. An explosion. As if the atomic bombing happened all over again."

Katashi made his appearance and stood next to Maiko, clasping his hands behind him. "Maiko, suppose the Jaakuna come back again to kill any survivors? What then?"

"We head to another village. Goodness knows we aren't the only people around here," Maiko said.

"What direction did the Jaakuna go after leaving here?" I asked.

"They headed farther north, ma'am," Katashi said and I felt my lips press together.

"North," I echoed him and Maiko nodded.

"Yes. I hope I never see the likes of them for as long as I live. Though, I did see something strange about them. Wasn't there a man who looked out of place, Katashi?"

"There was," Isamu said as he joined beside Katashi, throwing me a wary look. "He had a scowl on his face and everything. To me he looked like a man the Jaakuna hand-picked off the street and forced to come along with them."

"Yes, that's it. The man looked out of place and not thrilled to watch destruction happen."

"Maybe he's a slave—I've heard it from my cousin in Kyroyoku that the Jaakuna enslave people to do their dirty work."

Isamu's words unlocked a flood in me and I felt my lips part halfway as the thought of Yowai entered my mind. My slave friend—the one who didn't have enough chances to prove himself. Now another man might face the same judgment. My fists clenched.

"Thank you for telling me this," I said. My voice quivered as I tried to get it under my control. Maiko's eyes widened as she caught wind of what I would do.

"You can't possibly have the desire to chase after those armored men, do you? The man will be dead by nightfall."

"I had a friend once while the Jaakuna enslaved me." My voice broke. It sounded soft. "They killed him one night. Killed him without remorse."

My words made Isamu, Katashi, and Maiko blink and they looked at me with undisguised pity.

"I must go to save the man now," I continued, "so what happened to me in the past doesn't happen again to another."

Maiko made a respectful noise under her breath and Isamu's indifferent expression wavered. Without another word, I began to walk, my sights pinned to the North, my objective clear.

"Good luck, ma'am!" I heard a voice and turned to see Katashi looked at me, his hand raised in farewell. I inclined my head and continued on, feeling the familiar heaviness settle on my shoulders.

It seemed strange how my journey could end with me heading back in captivity again. On top of that, I still needed to find Akio. Perhaps the Jaakuna village would hold all the answers for me.

As I walked, my dirty and ripped shoes scuffing up dirt and dust, I thought about why I had even decided to go find Akio anyway. Was it all just to make ends meet? I couldn't find a reason. My mother one time told me to follow my instincts as well as my heart, because one day they'd prove valuable.

Guilt took me over as I remembered the words Akio told me back in the Jaakuna's old village. How we'd try to escape, together. I wondered if he'd even find it in him to forgive me somehow. I just needed to see him again and make sure I hadn't hurt him.

Another village sprang into my view and once again, just like the last village, it was destroyed. On impulse, I decided to check the village for survivors. What made the Jaakuna so ruthless and power-hungry? What did they get from destroying villages?

A black shape darted across my vision as I entered and my heart leaped to my throat. A crunch sounded and I whipped around to see the black figure dive under the rubble, kicking wood and glass pieces around.

"Hey," I said and came closer to where the shape fled to, hearing a small squeak. The black figure burst from the rubble with a yelp and I recognized it as a girl. She stopped and rubbed her arms as she shot a glare at a small rat that tumbled into the open.

"Oh how I hate rats." The girl shivered. Then she noticed me and put a hand over her mouth to conceal a gasp. "Don't scare me, lady! I thought you were one of those freaky looking people."

"Freaky looking people?"

"Yeah. Some guys in armor came along and destroyed this village. I watched it with my own eyes!" The girl looked at me, her short black hair turned brown by the sunlight.

"The Jaakuna . . . I knew it," I said to myself, then in a louder voice, "Did you live here?"

"Nope. I lived in Dokutsu before it was burned down like this village."

"Dokutsu?" I remembered someone telling me about a village set in a rock wall named Dokutsu. How could the Jaakuna have destroyed that?

"Most of the other villages call us Dokutsus "Rock-heads" but I don't care." The girl looked at me as I took a step closer. "Why do your clothes look so big on you?"

"I haven't had a real life in four years since the atomic bombing. I've wandered the land since then," I said and, at once, the girl's eyes darkened.

"My brother died in the explosion. Did you really travel all over to look for a home?"

"It's not just that." I gave a sigh. "I'm also looking for someone. A friend I need to make amends with."

The girl nodded once. It bemused me as to why she didn't act wary or defensive in her conversation. It reminded me of Korudo and Akio, who both were eager to tell their life stories upon my asking.

"What's your name?" I asked.

"I'm Seishin."

"I'm Sayuri, Seishin-chan."

"Why do you look angry?"

"I'm heading to Kagayaki, to confront the Jaakuna. I want to stop this endless destruction. For too long those men have tormented me. Maybe my friend will be in Kagayaki as well. I just have to hope."

"Well, I want to come with you."

I blinked once, startled. "What? Why?"

"I just can't live like a hermit, can I? I've been stuck in this village for the past few days. I've had enough of darkness." The girl looked at me as if my questioning deserved ridicule. It made me think back to when I was back in my village after the bombing, still choked by the depression. Perhaps people need to break free from what holds them back every once and so often. Maybe that's why I wanted to find Akio. He had a different kind of life in him. One I always wanted.

"Didn't you get tired of being sad all the time, Sayuri-sama?"

Her question startled me and I said in reply, "Yes."

"So, there's another reason why I should go alongside you. I mean, what else will I do? Just sit here and rot?"

"Even if I had no place else to go and I passed through here, would you still have asked to come along with me, Seishin?"

"Yeah. I don't feel comfortable on my own. I've never had any siblings so I was an only child. Since my parents left me alone to survive when Dokutsu burned I've been alone for a long time. Too long." She shuddered.

"Don't you think it's weird how you're eager to join beside me?"

"Nope. It's life, Sayuri-sama, and I want to live. I know I will if I stick around someone."

Akio flashed into my mind once more and I failed in pushing him out, shaking my head.

"Fine then. Let's get going," I said and Seishin came over to my side. We began to walk, feet stepping in a synchronized fashion.

"So who were those crazy men? You acted like you knew them."

"I do know them. They're called the Jaakuna, Seishin. They enslaved me and killed the one person I could trust."

"What about the friend you're trying to find?"

"It's different," I said, not knowing how to explain. "I just . . . have to find him."

Seishin nodded and looked off into the distance, her hair flowing behind her. I couldn't help but compare my past self to her. She looked like she was fourteen years old. When I was fourteen my village still stood. None of this destruction ever happened.

"Why did the Jaakuna destroy my village?" Her voice lowered and became soft.

"They want full control over Nagasaki."

"So they're taking advantage of us while we recover from the war," Seishin said and I nodded.

"Exactly."

Later on, when night fell, Seishin and I took turns keeping watch. The moon rolled across the sky each time my eyes opened for a slight moment. When I woke to do my third and final watch Seishin didn't fall back asleep. She lay on the leaves and bracken of the wood's floor.

"Seishin? You all right?" I asked after a moment. The girl turned over and faced me.

"It just feels weird—how everything happened. One minute I was in Dokutsu with my family and next . . ." Her sentence trailed off and I nodded.

"I know what you mean. I felt the same way. Being alive—to just live—counts, doesn't it?"

"Not while your parents and friends are dead."

Her words made my lips furl lower. Seishin and I were alike in more ways than one. More ways than we knew.

"How old were you when the bomb hit?"

"I was seventeen."

"Seventeen?" Seishin rose to a sitting position, mouth agape at me. "You're lying!"

"I'm not."

"Sayuri-sama, you're a grown woman. How old are you now?"

"Twenty-one."

"Gods," Seishin whispered. "I wouldn't have guessed it just by looking at you."

It startled me how much I had changed. The girl had been in my presence for a few hours and she already noticed.

"Seishin, what do you think of me?" I asked.

157

She gave me a once over with narrowed eyes. "I think you're a bit guarded."

"Guarded?"

"As if you have a big secret you don't want to let go of for anything."

At this I began to wonder what it was that Seishin saw in me. The only secret I had didn't even count as a secret: it was the truth.

"What about me?" she asked and I blinked.

"I think you're an open and trusting person." *Maybe even too trusting.*

"My mother used to say that until . . . well, you know. She always told me I'd leave with a stranger if I liked him or her well enough."

"Well, she was right about that," I snorted.

"Am I easy to read?"

"I guess so. I'm just noticing these things while we talk."

"So, who's your friend anyway? The one you're trying to find."

"Akio's his name. We were separated when the Jaakuna captured us. When an earthquake hit their village I made my escape, leaving him behind."

"Why would you do that to him?" Seishin's voice sounded angry, almost reprimanding.

"I was in so much pain . . . I couldn't linger anymore and risk being caught if any of them survived."

"Pain? Did they hurt you?"

"Besides whipping me during labor? No, I was in pain because . . . I don't want to talk about it. I just didn't want to stay any longer."

"You still left Akio there all alone."

"I know." I felt my face twist into an expression of pain. "That's the reason why I'm going to find him."

"If I had a friend alongside me I wouldn't leave his or her side for a second, Sayuri-sama."

"You'd feel willing to give up your life just to stick around him?" My words sounded too harsh to my ears. Too defensive.

"It's what I would do. It's what friends do."

"Then that's the difference between you and me."

Seishin looked at me, then she turned over, her back facing me. I made a mute sigh and looked at the stars above, seeing them twinkle from the holes in the cloud cover. The girl's breathing slowed and I knew she had fallen asleep. Her words made me feel guilt, anger, annoyance, and something else. Longing. A longing for completion.

Had I sounded selfish? I wondered to myself. Did I sound like a bad guy? Is it wrong to try and save yourself first before anyone else brings you down?

I stared at Seishin's back before returning my gaze to the surroundings, my heart heavy. When the first splotchy colors of dawn entered my vision, I woke Seishin and continued on our journey. Neither of us spoke and neither of us looked at each other.

Once the sun sailed over the horizon line I saw a village up ahead. One that still stood. My heart began to thrum a fast beat in my chest. The Jaakuna village was just up ahead.

"Is that it?" Seishin asked for the first time since we started walking.

"Yes, there's the Jaakuna village: Kagayaki." I looked at the village and saw its size. Kagayaki was the largest village I had seen since Kyroyoku, its houses rising up into the sky. Birds soared overhead: crows. We surged forward, my intent to complete my mission, and Seishin's intent to follow me. I thought about the man the Jaakuna scooped up off the streets and forced to march alongside the armored men.

Upon entering Kagayaki the first thing I could see was that the village was empty. Not a soul walked around or talked. Every house's windows were shut and blinds were pulled to cover them. The trees were the few things full of life, their branches swaying in the wind.

"What happened here?" Seishin's question echoed among the silent houses.

"The Jaakuna took over and left everything behind like exoskeletons," I said.

"I don't think your friend would be here, Sayuri-sama."

I heard sound just then and flinched, looking around. The noise sounded again and Seishin and I turned to each other.

"I'll go find out what the sound is. Stay here where it's safe."

"You're kidding, right? I'm going with you," Seishin said. "You think I came here just to stay on the sidelines?"

"Well don't yell at me when you get caught. This is my mission alone," I pointed out and the girl crossed her arms.

I moved down the road, feeling my blood enter my veins. In this moment I knew something would change forever. I still kept going.

Then, I identified the sound as a whip lash and hurried faster, the houses blurring past me, my surroundings turning into a small village square. In the middle a Jaakuna man stood off to the side, while another had a whip raised, standing over a cowering person.

The Jaakuna man standing off to the side turned and flinched upon seeing me. I saw the look in his eyes through his silly black-armored helmet. We both stared at each other, then the man took off his helmet. Now it was my turn to flinch. The Jaakuna man was Akio.

"Akio?" My voice came out hoarse. "What have you done?"

Even though two years had passed I still recognized him by the scar running through his eyebrow. His brown eyes still shone with life, however they seemed harder now.

He continued to stare at me, not saying a word, putting his helmet back on just as a force slammed into the back of my skull, turning my vision as black as the Jaakuna's armor.

My vision returned and I found myself in a cell. For a moment I wondered if I was back in the Jaakuna's old village with Yowai's cell next to mine. I turned to see Seishin in a cell adjacent to mine. Her hands were roped together. Mine weren't.

"I told you," I said, no trace of gloat in my voice. "I did say you'd get caught."

She still stared ahead, her eyes blazing. "You saw your friend, didn't you."

"Yes, he's one of them now."

"You deserve it." The girl's voice grew hard. "He'd be with you now if you hadn't left him alone like you did."

"This again? You think I don't know that?" I asked. "You think I don't have any regrets?"

"I saw the look in his eye when they took you here. He was hurt, Sayuri."

Her words gave me pause. I didn't see any hurt and pain in his eyes when I saw him,

"When did the Jaakuna catch you?"

"A few minutes after you. I stuck around and got myself into this mess."

I said nothing and lay there, breathing. No Jaakuna came to bother us and nothing happened. Three days passed. I sat on the small bed in my cell room, feeling blank. A bed . . . it was new to me since, in the Jaakuna's old village, I used to have to lay on the ground. The Jaakuna didn't provide a blanket, but since the weather was hot anyway I felt glad.

Seishin and I hadn't spoken since the first day, a certain tension between us. However, today the girl turned towards me, her eyes staring into mine.

"So you're just gonna give up? You got this far so why don't you try escaping?"

Seishin's words entered my mind, but I pushed them out, shaking my head.

"An earthquake won't happen this time to provide as a distraction." I looked at her.

"So you *are* going to give up, I knew it! You took one look at your friend and you froze like a rabbit in the headlights. You traveled all over to find this guy and now that he's joined the bad guys you just decide to throw everything away? You're laying there like you'd rather be dead now instead of living. I'd be trying to escape with whatever I had."

Her words bit into me. "Seishin, we're both different people."

"Yeah, you said that to me already. Does that mean you're eager to relive the mistakes you made in the past?"

I froze. Relive the past? That's what I wanted. A time where I had my family and a life. It's normal to think back to better times. I've lived the life of a refugee for so long I couldn't imagine not having a normal life ever again.

"Say something, please. I hate being ignored," Seishin said. I gave a sigh.

"Maybe you're right," I said, but no sound of triumph came from the girl. "Maybe I did freeze up because I couldn't accept how things changed."

Seishin never got to speak, for a clang sounded and a Jaakuna man entered my sight.

"Well well, look who's back in a cell again!" It was Korudo. "Couldn't survive for long after your little escapade from us?"

I glared at him, hating him even more than I had.

"You even brought along another slave for us to use. How sweet of you. You won't be used for slave labor though, oh no. Instead, we Jaakuna could use a new cook." His voice flattened as a mean smile curled his lips. "And I'll be the one who watches over you. Just like in the old days."

"Drop dead, Korudo." I tried a weak attempt at intimidation but he laughed at my tone.

"You've turned into a pretty little thing since the last time I saw you. Perhaps that's why my brother never went on dates while he could. Maybe he's too busy feeling smitten with you. I saw the look in his eyes when you came near him."

I felt Seishin's gaze settle on me, but I refused to look at her. Korudo leered at me as I stood and came over closer to the bed. Then, I spit on his face. His eyes bulged for a moment and a scornful snort bubbled out my lips. Korudo's face twisted and he smacked my face, the impact enough to turn my head. I didn't feel anything but the blood rushing to my cheek.

"I see you still have your spunk. That won't change anything for you now." Korudo glared at me before clomping away from my sight, wiping his face of spit.

I looked at the ceiling, which was covered. No cracks showed the sky behind them. I felt detached from the world.

I must have dozed off, for the sound of my cell opening jolted me to my feet.

"Ma'am? I-I'm very sorry to disturb you. But I have to take you to the kitchen. You have to work." It was a Jaakuna man, however he didn't seem like it. His voice sounded too jittery. All the Jaakuna men I knew sounded blunt and cold when they spoke. Could this be the man Maiko said looked out of place?

"I have no choice I guess," I said, swinging to look at Seishin. However her back faced me, her breathing deep.

"Come," the man said and I sighed, following behind him.

We didn't speak as he led me out into the open, taking me to a long building with a golden thatched roof. Kagayaki itself looked clean and modern looking, red and white lanterns swaying in the breeze. No paved roads existed in the village, but dozens of rickshaws lay abandoned near alleyways. The trees about the village bordered the houses, their branches thin and their leaves thick.

Inside the long building Korudo waited, a grin on his face. The setting of the room looked like an *Izakaya* with the dark resin walls and clean tatami mats. A few other Jaakuna men bustled about, sporting aprons and chef hats.

"You've done well, Kawa. You're dismissed," Korudo said and Kawa nodded, giving me a look before he left.

"Now come with me, lady." The Jaakuna commander's voice dripped with contempt as he took my wrist into his own. I remembered something from long ago, about Yowai telling me to show them I could work. At once my vision heightened, my heart began to pound, and my lips parted. His memory lived on in my heart, and now his words could save me a second time. Seishin's words interlaced with Yowai's and I knew she was right. How could I give up now?

We walked through two smaller hallways before a large kitchen opened to my view. Korudo shoved me in the room and locked the door behind me, standing with his arms crossed.

"Now let's see how well you cook. I want you to make us Jaakuna miso glazed cod. For the slaves I want you to make them *Dashi* soup."

"Wouldn't a real cook order me around on what food I should cook?" I asked, giving him a look.

"We don't have a cook and since I'm in charge of all my Jaakuna and every slave, I have every right to order you," Korudo said. "Now get to work and stop questioning what I do!"

I rolled my eyes and went over to the sink, running the water and filling up a pot halfway. My mother's words entered my mind as I searched the new-looking electric refrigerator for what I needed. *'Take a small teaspoon of herb and scatter it about the fish. Don't let the gods see any waste. Every ingredient must be used to its full potential.'*

Soon enough I had the sablefish cooking, a wonderful aroma entering the kitchen. Out of the corner of my eye I saw Korudo try to hold himself back from breathing in deep. I took that as success.

"Very good," he said once I poured the *Dashi* soup into small bowls. "You cook better than my mother had."

"Now what?" I asked, feeling weary.

"Now, you have to go out there with the miso glazed cod and serve it to my seven men waiting at the table. I bet they've waited long enough."

I held back a huff and picked up the individual plates, walking out the kitchen doors, Korudo in close tow. I focused on the smell of the food, which galvanized my stomach. The Jaakuna just gave me stale bread and a small cup of water for nourishment.

"Your dinner has arrived, men!" Korudo announced as we reached the initial room. The seven Jaakuna kneeling at the table picked up their chopsticks, ready to eat. They looked at me in expectation, a few licking their lips.

"Compliment your new chef well." Korudo's voice flattened, sounding contemptuous again. I stood off to the side while the men ate, grimacing each time they spilled some food on themselves. I waited for Korudo to take me back to my cell, but he didn't budge. He just watched his men eat with a sick fascination. My appetite left me.

Akio walked into the door at that moment and I tensed, turning my gaze away from him. He didn't look at me and instead he went to the empty seat at the table.

"Haw haw!" one of the Jaakuna men laughed. "Looks like our cook ran short of food! Guess you'll go hungry tonight, Akio." Now they all laughed. Akio sat in his seat, glaring at the other men.

"I bet the chef didn't even know he existed. Maybe this'll teach Akio to act more sociable and prompt." More laughter sounded at this.

"Maybe our cook hates tardy people."

"Either way Akio, you're missing out on this!"

"I'll go make another plate for him." The words tumbled out my mouth before I could stop him. This made the men and Akio turn to me, surprised expressions on their faces.

"Lookit that! We have a generous chef here tonight. Let her cook more often, commander. I like her!" The first Jaakuna man who spoke looked at his leader.

I turned to Korudo and he shook his head. "The cook will be dismissed for the night. Akio, you will just have to go hungry. Or you can try to cook something for yourself."

The Jaakuna roared at this, nudging Akio and rubbing jokes in his face.

"Come." Korudo took my arm. "We'll leave these men to their fun."

I followed behind as we left the building and entered another where the jails were. Seishin's cell lay empty. I guessed she had been taken out for labor. Once Korudo locked me in I lay on the bed and thought to myself. A slave groaned deeper in the establishment and another shushed him. It made me grimace.

I woke from a doze as Seishin's cell door clanged open and a Jaakuna guard thrust the girl on the tiled floor.

"Don't think to talk back to me again, you hear me?" he said and Seishin curled her lip. The guard sniffed, locking the cell door and leaving our sight.

"You all right, Seishin?" I asked and she nodded, rubbing her arm.

"Stupid Jaakuna guy . . ." she said under her breath in a vehement tone, stomping to her bed and throwing herself on it. "Did they do the same thing to you?"

"Korudo did worse to me when he took on the role as my guardskeeper."

"What did you do today?"

"I cooked for the Jaakuna men and . . ." I choked on the next words, unable to get them out.

Seishin knew what I hadn't said and she nodded. "So what are you gonna do?"

"About what?"

"About escaping. I mean, the whole point you came here wasn't so you could get captured again, right? You're still going to give up, Sayuri?"

"We're going to try and escape. I can't afford getting stuck in the past again."

The girl looked at me and a smile rose onto her face. "That's the spirit!" Then it faded. "How will we escape, though?"

"We're going to show them that we can be trustful, so their guard drops. It may take a few days to make it work, but I know we'll succeed."

Akio
August 1949

Akio sat on the bed in the room Korudo gave him to live in and he scowled at the armor he had to wear. It was hot, clunky, and it reeked of body odor. He felt glad when night fell, so he could take off the armor and feel like a regular person.

"How does Korudo stand this?" he asked aloud as he looked at his reflection. Akio saw a man with enough coldness in him to melt glaciers. A man who lost something dear to him. It startled him to know how much he changed over the years. No longer was he able to produce a smile.

Since Akio joined beside his brother, Korudo felt he could do anything. A mad glint had entered his eyes and it refused to budge.

A knock sounded at Akio's door and he said, "Come in, Korudo."

The Jaakuna leader strode into room, closing the door behind him. His armor shone in the dull moonlight and his posture was one an accomplished man attains. Akio heard a small rumor amongst the other men that said Korudo slept in his armor at nights, dreaming of victories. It caused a shudder to go through Akio.

"My brother!" Korudo said, coming ever closer. "Have I disrupted you in any way?"

"No. Go make yourself at home. Why have you come to me?"

"I'm here because there's something bothering me."

"Bothering you?"

"Yes, about what our new chef."

"Go on."

"Why would she offer to make you a serving of food? Do you know her?"

"I've never seen her before in my life."

"Oh really?" Korudo's tone was one of interest. "Then tell me, if you don't know her then why did she pause upon seeing you a few days ago?"

"I don't know." Akio shook his head, hoping Korudo would drop the subject. He wanted to hide that he knew Sayuri was the new cook. Even if he held a grudge against her, he still wanted to protect her from him and from Korudo.

"It would make sense why she looked so eager to make you dinner if you knew each other. I feel you're hiding something from me, brother. That's something I don't like one bit. Siblings aren't supposed to hide secrets from each other, right?" The mad look entered the Jaakuna leader's eyes. "Right?"

"How are we siblings if we never did things together? We've been separated since we were ten years old. If you had stayed behind instead of going with father to the Jaakuna then we would've been together."

"We're together now, brother! Nothing changed. Only that our father's dead and I rule the Jaakuna." His eyes gleamed. "The power is all mine, Akio, don't you see? My men are powerless to my orders. Drop the guard you have for me and tell me what you hide. You and I are family, remember?"

Akio didn't respond as he looked at himself in the mirror. Again his cold and brutal looking reflection made me pause. *Is that me? Is that what I look like to others?*

"I see a man of great purpose, Akio. You just have to awaken him." Korudo looked at Akio's reflection, a grin on his face. "Acting like a petty boy won't help you."

"How did you know it was me when we crossed paths by Han'ei anyway?"

"I know my brother like I know my own self. I knew he'd coming looking for me someday, for power out of reach. Once Nagasaki is mine, you can have some power as well!"

"You're getting the insane look in your eye again, brother."

"Now listen to me, Akio. Tell me how you know the woman and we can both be free."

"Korudo, I'm not in the mood for you to bother me now. I don't know the woman but I feel somewhat touched she wanted to provide for me. I'm not hiding anything from you and that's all I have to say. Now go away."

"Fine, but this doesn't end here. I'll find out the truth, and then you'll see." The Jaakuna leader edged to the door. "You'll feel sorry for hiding things from me."

The door slammed and Akio lay on his bed with a soft groan, rubbing his temples.

"Why must he act so childish?" he asked the air as he closed his eyes, wanting to sleep away the night.

Akio woke early and stared at the black armor, which lay on the chair, gleaming in a dark radiance. It disgusted him, yet he knew he had to put it on his body. 'For protection', Korudo told him.'In case one of the slaves wanted to get bold and attack.'

The slaves don't even look like the type who'd attack anyway. They cower in the very sight of any Jaakuna man. Except for Sayuri. She stands up to danger. Akio gave a snort at this thought. He heard Korudo stomping about, groaning on about how a slave spit in his face. The thought was laughable at best, but pathetic. Akio knew who spit at his brother once a guard filled him in with the details. 'What're ya laughing about, Akio?' the guard had asked. 'Nothing,' Akio had said. 'It's just funny how Korudo let a slave spit on him. That's a first, right?' Much ragging was done to Korudo that day.

Akio stood and put the armor on, doing his best to look fearsome. He felt awful, knowing that trying to act like someone different wouldn't make him better than before. He knew though if he let any weakness show he'd never hear the end of it from Korudo or the other men.

He wondered himself why Sayuri would want to show kindness to him regardless of the tension between then. *She left me. She's selfish and not worth it.* Somehow, though, he didn't believe those inner words. Sayuri was brave to come to this nightmare just to get captured again. *But for what reason did she come here?*

Once he finished buckling the armor boots, Akio made his way out into the sweltering heat of August. A bead of moisture already got to rolling down his neck and back. Korudo waited for him as he always did by the long building, looking comfortable in his own armor. He'd just get away with saying he wore it like a second skin.

"Top of the morning to you, my dear brother," Korudo said as he made his way to Akio. "I have much work for you to do today. First, your job for tonight is to lead our cook to the kitchen. I'll make sure to watch her in case she does anything erratic."

"Like spitting in my face this time instead of yours?" Akio couldn't help but humor his brother. Korudo's expression darkened.

"Especially that."

"Come on, lighten up, Korudo. It's just spit. She hasn't done anything to ruin you now, has she?"

"She dared sully my image! Now all my men ridicule me because of it!"

Akio had to admit his brother was right in a sense. All the other Jaakuna men, even the ones who feared him, looked at him with contempt now.

"Now, tomorrow I will lead my men to the village of Jundo. I need a worthy individual to watch over things while I'm gone."

"Me, right?"

"Yes, Akio. I'll choose you for the job. Make sure to stand on your guard at all times."

"Fine," Akio nodded and Korudo grinned.

"Father would feel proud of you, Akio, if he still lived."

"He would," Akio echoed in an impassive tone. This pleased his brother, for his grin widened and he strode off to the slave building.

When dinner hour approached Korudo sought him out and led him to the slave establishment to let Sayuri out her cell. When Akio looked into her eyes and saw her flinch he had to force a cold expression on his face. *How she had changed* . . . Akio blinked. Sayuri transformed from a girl with no sole purpose to a woman who bore the weight of confidence. Her long flowing hair reached her bony elbows, framing a mature thin face and a soft mouth. He couldn't help but feel taken with her.

"Akio, what's the matter with you? Take her out and lead her to the kitchen." Korudo leered at him. Akio shook his head free of his emotions and unlocked Sayuri's cell. She stood, her movements flowing and strong, her eyes bright. He knew she wanted to speak with him, but with Korudo around, that wouldn't be possible.

Instead he said in a curt voice, "Come."

Sayuri obeyed, her eyes dimming then. Korudo's teeth reveled themselves behind his lips as he smiled in contempt.

"Make sure you cook us a good meal tonight. We'll need it. Since my men have taken a liking to you, I'd suggest you watch your step not to enrage them with an unsatisfactory meal."

She said nothing in reply and Akio walked in front, making sure she followed behind him. She did. He felt her eyes on his back but he ignored it, not wanting Korudo to see how much she affected him.

"Oh and Akio? I want you to lead our cook back to her cell after dinner hour ends so I'd advise you don't stray too far."

Upon entering the long building again Korudo dismissed him, leaving Akio with no choice but to leave, his thoughts roiling. Sayuri had a slight defeated expression on her face as he turned around once to look at her. Then he squared his shoulders and left the building.

Part of him dreaded seeing her again when Korudo called him back into the long building an hour later to eat dinner.

Part of him rejoiced. He had to admit that Sayuri was a good cook and, as he stole looks at the other men, he could see he wasn't alone in his opinion.

"Akio, you may take our cook back to her cell now," Korudo said once the last Jaakuna man finished his plate. Akio held back a sigh and nodded, beckoning for Sayuri to follow him. She did so and, when the Jaakuna commander was no longer in their sight, Sayuri looked at him. Akio kept his gaze everywhere but at her. A painful silence existed between them, one he found hard to bear. He remembered how they trusted each other. How they planned to escape together. *Times are different . . . she's a total stranger to me now.*

Once they entered the slave building, Akio took her arm to make sure she wouldn't escape, even when he knew she wouldn't and unlocked her cell door. He thrust her inside and locked the door.

"Akio . . ." Sayuri trailed off, her voice low and full of hurt. He looked at her, saw the look in her eyes, turned his back, and left the building. His chest hurt and he tried to conceal it. Unbeknownst, Korudo watched Akio, his gaze thoughtful, a cruel smile on his face.

Sayuri
August 1949

"Sayuri, are you okay?" Seishin asked, and I nodded.

"Just fine," I said and went to lay down on my bed. Next time Akio leads me back to my cell I would try to speak with him again.

The next day news reached my ears about Korudo's victory in the village of Jundo. It sickened me to know that the villages the Jaakuna destroyed didn't even work up the courage to fight them.

"Jundo's destroyed!" I heard a Jaakuna man declare outside the slave building. "You listening, slaves? That's what your leader does right!"

A week passed. I hadn't seen Akio since he led me back to my cell. I did my duty, then Korudo escorted me back to the slave building. He looked crueler, if the thought was possible. His eyes glittered with the prospect of future victories. I swore I saw a mad look in his face as he locked me in for the night.

"Sayuri! Guess what!?" Seishin sounded like a ball of energy once her guard left the building one night.

"What happened, Seishin-chan?"

"I have this amazing news! We can escape now if we do it right!" The girl bounced in her place as she came closer to the cell boundary.

"Slow down! Now tell me what you mean."

"My guard told me today while I worked about this thing coming up called the Slave Inspection day." Upon seeing my confused look, she continued, "It's where the Jaakuna gather all the slaves together into the village square and inspect them for illnesses or weapons. My guard told me they have one every year to keep the slaves in check."

"Why would your guard tell you all of this without thinking you might use the information against him?"

"Because he's stupid and plus Sayuri-sama, you were right! It did take some time but now the guards trust me! My guard even lets me take breaks every once and so often."

Hope fluttered in my heart for the first time in years. Finally we both may get out of this place and find a new life for real!

Seishin reached into her pocket and held something in her hand.

"What's this?" I asked as she reached one small hand through the cell and put the substance in my hand. It was gravel. "Why do I need this?"

"I have some too! I had this plan figured out in my head all day while I worked. What we'll do with the gravel is this: we'll throw it into the eyes of our guards once they unshackle us for the inspection. Then we'll escape while there's chaos!"

The plan seemed worthy. I had to give Seishin credit for her quick thinking.

"Are you sure this plan will work? Suppose they keep us shackled so we don't try to escape?" I asked. Seishin's expression didn't dim at my words.

"It's like you said in the beginning: we had to show the Jaakuna that they can trust us. Now they do! Trust me, Sayuri, I know this'll work!"

I looked at the gray rock bits and pieces in my hand, imagining them in the eyes of Korudo as Seishin and I made our escape. The shocked expression that came upon his face as the attack happened.

"All right, let's give it a shot," I said and Seishin made a soft exclamation of triumph.

"My guard told me the inspection will happen soon, so I guess we have to wait until he tells me a date."

"Fine. Once we escape though, where would we go?"

"I didn't think that far, Sayuri!" Seishin made an accusatory look. "I don't know. When we escape, then we'll figure out where to go."

At least we had some sort of plan to escape the Jaakuna. I placed the rock bits and gravel in my pocket, giving it a small pat.

One day passed, then four. I did my duty to feed the Jaakuna and do my job right. Each night, expectation rose in me and Seishin. We knew the Slave Inspection day would soon come and we waited for it.

Once the Jaakuna men finished their meal one night I turned to Korudo, waiting for him to take me back to my cell. This time he turned to Akio and said, "Why don't you lead our cook to her cell this time, Akio? I feel quite lazy tonight."

Ice entered my veins as Akio rose from his knelt position, heading over to me. Korudo gave a nod and a smug look came into his face. As if he knew something we didn't.

"Come on," Akio said and I nodded, following him out the building, leaving Korudo behind.

Before I could snatch the words back, I spoke, "Akio, I have to talk to you. You can't keep ignoring me."

He didn't say a word and heavy feelings entered me. Once we reached the slave building he took me to the side, out of sight, and looked at me, his eyes flaming.

"Well? Say it, Sayuri." Akio looked angry, even uncomfortable if I looked close enough. Then the facade faded and a hardened man was all I could see.

"How could you switch sides, Akio?" I asked, a soft tone in my voice. "What made you do it?"

"You duped me." The words were said in a growl. "All you cared about was for yourself. I felt sickened by that, Sayuri. You left me to fend for myself in a place I know little about."

I felt the first blaze of anger rise in me. "I thought you died, Akio! Anyone would have thought the same if they looked at the village's remains!"

"Dead, huh?" His tone was now one of contempt. "Yeah, I thought you were dead too until I saw no trace of your body. Then I remembered how you escaped from Korudo when the earthquake hit." He laughed, the sound chilling me. "But you don't care, do you. I should've known you were heartless."

His words struck me and I felt chagrined—reprimanded. I felt ready to cry. Seishin's words bounced in my head as well.

"Why would that make you turn to the Jaakuna of all people?" I looked at him. "Don't you see how evil they are?"

"Are you any better, Sayuri? Plus I needed someone I could trust. I wanted to stick with someone I knew. When I saw my brother again it was either join beside him or wander Nagasaki without a destination."

"Your brother?" I arched a brow at him. He sighed then, all the anger leaving him.

"I have to tell you something, Sayuri, and don't take this as a way of me forgiving you. First, Korudo is my brother."

"No." I covered my mouth, concealing a gasp. "That can't be . . ."

"It is. My mother and father never perished in the atomic bomb blast. My father did run out the house when it happened, that much is true. However, he left me to go to his Jaakuna, not to get help. Ten years before, my father took Korudo to the Jaakuna village after our mother died. I didn't go because I had been at my grandparents' house and they protected me from my father's wrath. He came with Korudo and demanded that I was to go with him. My grandfather refused to let me go. He knew how my father changed and he didn't want me to be influenced by that.

"After a great deal of time my father left, giving up and dragging Korudo away with him. My brother cried as he reached for me, terror in his eyes. But I could do nothing . . . I lived with my grandparents for a few weeks until they told me my village must be safe to live in by now. I agreed, wanting my independence from my restrictive life, and left the house that became my refuge.

"When I came back to my village to find it vacant of people I decided I wanted to stay. Call it strange, but that's what I did. I took on odd jobs to pay the bills for my house whenever I could. When the Americans dropped the bomb though, I knew I couldn't stay any longer. So I left my annihilated village to find a place where I could live and one day see my father and Korudo again."

"Then you met me . . ." I trailed off, my gaze falling from his. It all made sense now.

"Yes, I met you and decided, since we were both in the same situation, that I could trust you. In the beginning you looked as though you needed something. Something to complete you, just like me. How wrong I was in the end."

"Akio." I couldn't say anymore. Korudo's and Akio's story coincided in my head, fitting together like a puzzle piece. Akio didn't tell me the truth after all when I first met him. I realized he was too scared I'd reject him if he did. So he had conjured up a lie in order to make me believe him and lose my doubts. Why would he care whether or not I'd believe him? Back in the destruction I would have believed anything he said.

"Sayuri, when I first met you, I took you as a person who'd make the right choice every time. I . . ." It was his turn to trail off now.

I looked at the man Akio had become, wearing the Jaakuna get-up, his expression wavering now from rage to pain. I remembered the mature and perceptive teenager he had been when we planned to find a place to live.

"I'll tell you the reason why I escaped the old Jaakuna village without you."

"You'll tell the truth now?" The soft tone in Akio's voice hardened again.

"Yes. Saying "I'm sorry" doesn't cut it for me because it's said too much and not enough."

"Go on, Sayuri," he said, his gaze not straying from mine.

"I made a friend in the old Jaakuna village while I lived as a slave. His name was Yowai. He helped me think of an idea to escape, one I'd use to help you escape as well if it succeeded for me. I wanted to tell you about the plan but we never got the chance to talk to each other. Yowai bolstered my hopes and kept me company while I lived in agony and loneliness. I trusted him and he trusted me.

"The night before the earthquake . . . Korudo killed Yowai. Your brother took my friend away from me and, in pain, I ran the next day when I had the opportunity, not wanting to stay any longer. Nothing mattered to me than to escape and grieve for Yowai by myself. I was in so much pain, Akio." I looked at him, a desperate tone in my voice. "You must understand now, right?"

Akio fell silent for a moment, his lips forming a grimace, then, "Was I even considered as a friend to you, Sayuri?"

"Yes, and you still are, Akio. Even if we haven't seen each other since now. Times are different between us. Now you're something else to me."

"I'm not worth anything to you." He shook his head. I could tell he wanted to believe me. "All you're saying is lies."

"I speak the truth. I searched Nagasaki for you for two months when I found you weren't dead. I knew I needed to make amends with you for leaving you alone. I did feel guilty, and I felt angry with myself for abandoning you, although you won't believe me. When I heard that the Jaakuna captured a man who looked out of place I felt enraged, not wanting another person to die like Yowai had. I needed to go save him. At first I didn't know who the man was, but now I know. That man is you, Akio."

He didn't speak, his jaw clenched.

"Please believe me. You're all I have now . . . and I may have been shallow by leaving you alone; that's true. But now I know there's nothing left in my life if I don't make amends with you."

"You traveled through Nagasaki just to find me, Sayuri? After what you did? Did you even think I'd forgive you?" An incredulous tone existed in Akio's voice now.

"Yes, I did and I still do." With this said I headed by myself into the slave building and stood by my cell, waiting for Akio to come. He did and after locking me in, he looked at me. I waited for him to speak, but he left, his steps strong and sure.

Seishin came soon afterward, her guard thrusting her into her cell and locking it.

"My guard told me that the Slave Inspection day will be here in four more days! Do you still have your gravel?" she asked once the guard was out of earshot.

"Yes, I do," I said, surprised my voice didn't tremble once after speaking to Akio. "How about you?"

"I have even more now." Then, after a moment. "Sayuri-sama? What's wrong? You look sad."

"Sad?" I looked at her. "No, I don't feel sad. I'm just thinking about things."

"Think about our escape instead!" she urged. "I can't wait to laugh in their faces, mentally of course, when the plan works."

The thought satisfied me and, not wanting to linger on Akio, I focused on that instead. I created different scenarios in my head, anything to keep my mind off Akio's words.

The night before the Slave Inspection day arrived. My gut wrenched as I thought about escaping. My body began to feel heavy and that's when I knew what I must do. As my hand moved to brush a strand of hair from my mouth I felt a warm chain around my neck. It was the locket I picked up long ago and kept. I opened it to find the words '*Wakai raibu ka shinu*' jump out to me again. I closed it and lay awake, staring at the ceiling, the gravel weighing in my pocket.

The morning of the fated day of our escape felt humid and the heat rose from the hot pavement. I could feel it even through the cool slave building. Upon waking I could hear Seishin muttering about how her hair would look frizzy. I had to snort. There were better things to worry about now than appearances.

She heard me and turned, a smile on her face. "You ready?"

I gave a wordless nod just as Korudo, Seishin's guard, and eight other guards came into the building.

"All right! All you slaves will be inspected today for any kinds of weaponry or sicknesses. So get up and come with us," Korudo said. Seishin looked at me as the Jaakuna leader took me out my cell and clamped a chain to my wrist, but I stared ahead, my mouth dry.

We walked through Kagayaki, the sun sending the full brunt of its heat on our bodies and heads. A small river trickled under us as we walked over a small wooden bridge. The trees sagged under the heat, some of their leaves turned yellow from dehydration.

Dozens of people waited in the square, some in medical attire who I assumed were nurses, others just regular Jaakuna men. They stared at us, waiting for Korudo to arrive in the middle.

"Here's what'll happen. Three slaves will be let off their chains at a time to be inspected. If you're asked any questions you must answer them." Korudo swung a hard gaze on us all.

Out of the corner of my eye I could see Seishin tremble with anticipation, her unshackled hand resting near her pocket. Three slaves were chosen after we formed rows, their steps shaky, their eyes wide. The nurses came over and inspected their ears, eyes, noses, mouths, and skin with medical tools. Once they were deemed healthy and free of any weaponry, the slaves trudged back to their guards, who shackled them again.

It was a long time before Korudo called for Seishin, me, and another slave to go to the nurses to be checked. This was it. This was the moment Seishin and I had waited for. Korudo unshackled me and pushed me forward just as another guard unshackled Seishin. I turned around and watched as she took one step, reached into her pocket, and flung the gravel bits into her guard's eyes without a moment's hesitation.

It was a perfect throw. Seishin's guard emitted a loud curse and rubbed at his eyes, trying to pick the gravel off his face.

"What happened?" Korudo asked and just then the other unshackled slave wailed, expecting the blame to settle on him. This caused the other slaves to moan, fear in their eyes, and the other Jaakuna guards hurried over to the scene. Everything soon became chaos. Seishin was right, the plan worked.

When I looked to find her I saw that she had escaped without being noticed. She was free. I stood while the guard yelped and groaned, his fingers clawing at his eyes to remove the gravel.

"Will you cut that out!?" Korudo smacked the guard's face. "You're causing a scene!" He looked around, at the mess of crying slaves, noticed Seishin missing. Anger flared in his face and he shouted, "A slave escaped! Go find her!"

I watched as three Jaakuna, including Seishin's guards, took up arms and raced in different directions to find her. I knew they wouldn't find her so easy.

"You wouldn't happen to know about where the slave went, do you?" Korudo asked me, his jaw tight, and I shook my head.

"The audacity of it all!" A dark look crossed his face. "She dared take advantage of us."

I saw Akio looking at me, but I didn't look at him. Korudo growled to himself as he shackled me and said, "We'll call off the Slave Inspection for tomorrow. I want more men to search for that girl. If any of you find her, kill her!"

"Yes sir!" all the Jaakuna said. I felt dread line my stomach and I hoped Seishin was far from Kagayaki by now.

"I'll be watching you from now on, just to make sure you don't get any ideas to retaliate either," Korudo said as he took me back to my cell.

I worried about Seishin all day, and each time a search party would come back to Kagayaki without reports I'd feel tremendous relief. Then Korudo would send another group of men out to find her and my relief would plummet.

Time passed and soon I found myself cooking the Jaakuna a meal that night, my thoughts wandering.

"Watch it!" Korudo said as he heard a sizzling sound from the pan. I held back a curse and raced to shut the flame off, feeling frazzled. I'd been too busy worrying about my friend's whereabouts instead of my duty. I didn't want the trust I had instilled in Korudo to fade away over a petty mistake.

"Focus on our food, not on yourself."

I turned to face him, hating him even more for reprimanding me, and for how he corrupted Akio. Resisting the urge to make a face at him, I turned around and administered to the food.

As I added the soy sauce I heard an exclamation of breath from Korudo. "No! Don't add that to the food!" He slapped my hand away and took the bottle of sauce from me.

"Why not?" I asked.

"One of my men has allergic reactions to soy sauce."

"Why didn't you tell me?" I looked at him, feeling annoyed. He didn't answer and he pointed to the food. "Watch and make sure our dinner doesn't get burnt tonight."

"It won't."

"Good. Now cook."

"Without the soy sauce I can't cook this recipe. It won't have any taste."

"Make something else, then. You have plenty of time. So do it!"

I huffed and looked at the half cooked food. "What about this?"

"I'll feed this grub to the slaves. They'll feel pleased to have something different than bread for once. Just do as I say."

Rolling my eyes, I scanned my mind for another recipe I once helped my mother prepare. While I worked on making another batch of dinner Korudo stood beside me and asked about every ingredient I needed to add. It just made me more frustrated.

It didn't stop there. Korudo went on to annoy me for a couple more nights afterward, ordering me around on what foods to make.

"Make the miso glazed cod again. My men like that dish," he said once. I went on to explain that I made the dish a few days before. He growled.

"Do as I say and stop arguing with me. Got it?"

I became sick of his orders and ignored what he'd tell me to make. In the end, this usually ended with me getting whipped after dinner. I took it all without the slightest yelp.

One night as I placed the food down on the table on of the Jaakuna men took a bite and began to choke, his face turning red.

"What happened?" Korudo asked, giving him a dark look.

"I think our chef added at bit too much pepper tonight," another Jaakuna man said with a chuckle. "Look at it, the pepper just covers the food."

"I guess I misjudged how much pepper to add," I said, not knowing how I could have added too much of the ingredient. The recipe called for two pinches of black pepper.

As I took a closer look at the dish I saw the ingredient clinging all over the beef, making a black covered powder.

"You sure slipped tonight, chef. I'm not eating this, not with all that pepper on it," another man said.

"I'll just wipe it off for you," I said and prepared to take the dishes back to the kitchen.

"Oh no you don't. You'll prepare a new dish for them." Korudo came over to me.

"Why? So we have to wait here another hour before we get served? Why can't we just scrape off the pepper?" the man who had his first bite said after a long swallow of water.

"Our chef needs to prepare a fresh meal for you. It's unlucky to eat a tampered meal. Go on, back into the kitchen you go."

I held back a sigh and headed back into the kitchen with the dishes, Korudo following behind while his men called out their protests.

After that horrible day I figured Korudo would lay off, but he didn't. The next night he continued to banter with me on the food. However this time I made sure to add the precise amount of ingredients to the dinner.

Things went fine until the next night Korudo asked for me to make the dinner Black Pepper Beef. The same recipe that made one of his Jaakuna man choke.

I knew better than to argue and this time I made sure I added the right amount of pepper. I cooked the beef enough to make it succulent and juicy and looked over the meal. It smelled delicious to me and I wished I could have a bite of the food I made.

"Go wash your hands," Korudo said. "I'll look over the food."

I sent him a glare at the order but I heeded it nonetheless. Over the weeks I've noticed ho childish Korudo acted if things never went his way. I wondered if he acted that way because of a poor role model. Maybe Yuki never had a chance to teach Korudo how to be mature.

As I went to grab a towel to dry my wet hands, out of the corner of my eye I saw Korudo lean over the dishes, shaking his head.

"What are you doing?" I asked, coming over to him, feeling suspicious.

"You added too much pepper again." He stepped away from the food and I flinched, seeing the black pepper coating the meat again.

"How?" I said. "I made sure to add the right amount this time."

"Why ask me? You prepared the food, so fix it."

I mulled over how all the extra pepper ended up on the meat as I scraped it off with a napkin. It looked fine before I went to wash my hands. Then I saw the opened container of pepper by the dishes and remembered putting it away after I finished using it.

I handed the dishes to the Jaakuna men in the dining room and waited for one of them to comment about it. None of them did and Korudo looked at me.

"Don't add pepper to this meal from now on, all right? You seem to keep making mistakes when you do."

"Can't you lay off my back for a couple of days for once?" I asked, feeling sick of him.

"You forget that I have the right to order you around while you're my slave."

"Hey commander, don't argue at the dinner table. It's bad luck," a Jaakuna man said.

"The chef and I aren't eating, dummy," Korudo said. "Eat your food and stay quiet."

Once the last of the Jaakuna finished their plates and left I went to fix the tablecloth and the kneeling cushions. I watched Akio, the last person to finish eating, as he looked at me before leaving.

"Must you always act self-righteous around me?" Korudo asked as he thrust the gathered dinner plates into my hands. "Maybe that's why the girl left you behind here. She found out who you really are."

I refused to speak, knowing he was trying to antagonize me. Why did Korudo want to get on my nerves? What came over him?

As I lay in my cell that night I looked at the flickering light, watching as it shut off several times before it came back on. It reminded me of a brave warrior getting back up each time he was knocked down, despite his injuries.

My eyes closed and the dark surroundings melted away, turning into the meadow with the white lilies. Korudo stood, his gaze stoic and faraway. I wanted to go over to him and yell at him, and maybe throw a kick or two. I knew it wouldn't change anything about him. He wouldn't react to my presence.

It took me a moment once my vision changed again to a ceiling with a flickering light to realize I had awakened. With a small sigh, I turned and looked through the bars, seeing a Jaakuna man pass by, his boots clinking and clumping on the floor.

"Sayuri."

At once I jerked in my position and glanced at the person who spoke my name. It wasn't Akio. It was Korudo and his smile widened as he saw my face. This moment must have been something he had waited for the whole time he knew me. He wanted to shake me and try to break me down to size. I couldn't show weakness or vulnerability anymore. My mouth set and my body returned to its looseness. How did he know my name?

"Yes, I know your name now. A fellow Jaakuna guard told me for a small price." He looked at me. I sucked in a response and stared right back, feeling disgusted.

Instead I said in a blank tone, "I have no name. I'm the property of the Jaakuna, forced to cook for them for no pay."

Now his smile tightened. "You may think you're witty, but we're keeping you alive, Sayuri. Where would you be now if we didn't provide for you? In a shanty-town? More than half the villages are either mine or destroyed. I intend to claim the rest with any means I can, even if I have to wipe the villages off the planet."

"You're crazy!"

"In fact I feel very much insane with joy."

"Just leave me alone until I have to do my duty, please?" I said with a groan.

"Your duty changes now. Instead of cooking for us, you'll provide for our sick. Our nurses will teach you the various methods of healing and purifying."

"Why change what I have to do?"

Korudo ignored my question. His eyes blazed instead. "Again I ask, why must you always question my orders? Just follow what I say!"

"Fine." I rolled my eyes.

"Now come here Sayuri and I'll escort you to your new workplace."

I had no choice but to get off the bed and go over to him. His sardonic mouth stretched ever upward as he opened my cell and took hold of my wrist. We left the slave building to have the heat blister us. It felt much cooler back in my cell. I wanted to retreat back there and stay in the shade, away from the sun.

We kept going, the hot gravel and concrete crunching underfoot. A large building with many banners hanging from the roof appeared in my swimming vision.

"This will be your new place to work, Sayuri. Make sure you never forget it."

I couldn't forget it if I tried. The building was a sad gray color with a brown thatched roof. Even the banners and their many varieties of color didn't brighten the building. Brown traditional hanging beads acted as a door and two red lanterns hung from the overhang.

Korudo tugged me inside the building and I could hear the swish of the beads as they trying to regain their stillness again.

"Ah, commander." An older woman stood from her knelt position on the tatami mats. "What brings you here?" A small pot lay by her feet, the smell of incense pouring out it.

"I have a proposition for you, Iyasu."

At these words Iyasu lit up, her eyes sparkling.

"A proposition you say?"

"Yes, I have with me here a woman who I'm enlisting into your service. She, however, does not have the adequate skills to cook. My men were very much displeased by her skills. I decided why don't I see if she do a better job in a different work setting."

What? I whirled to face Korudo. How dare he lie about my cooking? The man had to force himself back from breathing in the aroma of my food!

The old woman shook her head in pity. "I see. We'll take her. My nurses have been taking off work because of the heat. Your proposal must have come from the gods, commander. I do need more hands to help. Your men can't seem to get themselves out of trouble."

Korudo made a forced laugh. "That they do, Iyasu. I can't keep a quick eye on them. Also, if you take on Sayuri here, I'll increase your pay as well."

"Then it's a done deal, Korudo sir." Iyasu bowed low. "The nurses and I are in debt with you."

"Never mind that. Just think of it as a favor." He turned to me. "Now Sayuri, I want you to do a good job this time. No messing up or you'll face your punishment. Got it?"

I swallowed my pride and gave a nod, not wanting to argue. I wanted him gone from my sight. He grinned and walked through the beads back outside.

"Come, Sayuri was it? Time to meet your new advisers." Iyasu beckoned and I followed behind, the smell of herbs and tonics becoming stronger the nearer we came to a brown folding door with iridescent cranes on it.

As the older woman pushed the doors aside my vision opened to a large room with four medical tables and six cabinets filled with jars. The dark beige wallpaper had black swirls lining the corners and edges. Three women stood straight, their eyes focused on Iyasu. On each medical table lay a patient and near each medical table was a small stool and desk. More banners, toned down in color, hung from the cabinets.

"Iyasu, ma'am, what held you up from the traditional prayer?" one woman asked, her long black hair tied back in a ponytail.

"We had a visit from Korudo. He brought us a woman to enlist into our practice as a new apprentice."

"Golly! It's been so long since we've had fresh prey," another woman said, her strange eyes glittering. To me she looked like a weasel, her forehead shiny, her eyes black as night, and her nails long and yellowed.

"Remember Hageshi. You were once a newcomer here as well." The first woman turned to her. Hageshi folded her arms.

"Can't I say that it's not everyday we get a new nurse in training?"

"You can, but just don't act like a predator all the time."

"I don't!"

"Ladies!" A stern tone now entered Iyasu's voice. "If you want to bicker like children then I'll just treat you like children."

"No, Iyasu ma'am, we'll stop now. We understand we have to hold a persona of maturity in order to keep our business running. Money won't come to us if we don't," Hageshi said.

"Excellent. Now greet our newest member, Sayuri."

"Haikei," both women chorused. I looked at the third woman who hadn't spoken.

"Introduce yourselves," Iyasu said.

"My name is Hageshi," Hageshi said.

"My name is Rin," Rin said.

The third woman did not make a sound.

"What about her?" I asked, hoping I sounded meek.

"She doesn't have a name. In Kagayaki's nursing clinic, you have to earn your name." Rin turned to me. "That's how I received my name.

Her words made me think. In order to earn your name you had to be a successful nurse?

"And I can't believe how she's been here longer than me and she still doesn't have a name." Hageshi pointed to the other woman. The nameless woman didn't say a word in defense. I decided to call her Hisoka in my mind. She fit the name well, as I could see. She looked reserved and innocent.

She still didn't speak as Rin took me to the medicine cabinets to show me all the jars.

"You have to understand that working as a nurse is risky business." A serious lilt entered her voice. "If you don't, the probability of making a person sicker or close to death is certain. When you're an apprentice nurse, you don't want that to happen."

I gave a nod and watched as she took out some jars to show me their contents. By the time we went through all six cabinets my head spun and I felt like telling Rin that I wanted to end it for the day. She still didn't stop and this time she took me to a small drawer where ten gleaming medical tools jumped to my eye.

"These here are what we nurses depend on to keep our business alive," Rin said. "If we use them right we'll save another life and receive more money."

I decided that Rin and the other nurses were greedy, wanting nothing but money for all their troubles. I always thought nurses took on their job to help people for nothing at all. However, meeting Hageshi, Iyasu, and Rin changed my belief.

"Now Sayuri, from now on you're nameless until you've earned your true name here." Rin's tone turned strange. "Once that happens you'll be accepted here as a full-fledged nurse. The Jaakuna need fresh aspiring nurses to keep them alive."

I nodded when all I wanted to do was laugh. The Jaakuna were just using the nurses as they used the slaves and villages—for their own benefit. It made me think of Akio one day becoming like them and my disgust and determination flared.

"When you're done daydreaming go tell Iyasu-sama what you've learned today."

"May I ask where she is?"

"Down the hall to your left. If she's in the middle of prayer, so help you if you disturb her."

I followed Rin's instructions, ducking under another banner as I went through an open doorway. The smell of incense grew stronger and it made my nose tingle. Somehow it reminded me of when Kimu put up the *Goehi* in the middle of the old Jaakuna village. Three other folding doors opened to rooms where I figured the nurses slept. Another doorway lay open, the incense flowing from it in a smoky waft.

Upon nearing the room I heard a soft hum and peered in to see Iyasu sitting in the *seisa-style*, her forehead touching the tatami mats. Rin's words ran through my mind and I contemplated turning around and going back to the main room. Until I heard Iyasu speak.

"You may come in, Sayuri. I hear you out there."

I trudged over, not faking the meekness I displayed. The old woman stood in one fluid motion and stared at me, robes fluttering. "Well?"

"Rin-san sent me here to tell you what I've learned."

"Oh Rin—always so paranoid about her mentoring. She always wanted to set an example for others. Pray tell, what did you learn today?" Iyasu's eyes twinkled.

"Well, Rin showed me all the herbs and explained their uses in healing people."

"Ah, a basic herb walkthrough then."

"If I may ask, why is Rin paranoid?"

"Now that's a question I have no true answer for," the older woman laughed, "but I'll try my best."

I waited for her to speak.

"This goes back to when Rin first turned up at my door, looking miserable and out of a job. I tried turning her away but the woman persisted in persuading me to accept her. 'No' was never a word to her, it seemed.

"In the end I grew tired of Rin standing behind the beads, peering in at me with large innocent eyes. So I took her in and explained that she would have to listen to every command and adhere to it in order to stay. She was diligent and hardworking, often repeating my words to the other apprentices. Rin called herself Sasuke, which she claimed 'was an unoriginal name'.

"In time, as she became an accomplished nurse, she told me her name was Rin. 'Because I've become a new person now,' she had said. I assumed she wants to keep her record clean so anyone lower than her can vision her as a role model. Now she keeps to the rule that everyone must earn their name in this business in order to have recognition."

I wondered where the greed came from, then. It seemed Rin wanted a job just to earn money. Knowing it wouldn't be wise to speak about it, I dropped the question and gave a nod.

"I'd suggest not hampering the standards Rin set for herself. Her temper is one to contend with, Sayuri."

Again, I nodded and waited for my dismissal. Iyasu came over to me. "I know you're just starting out today, but let me warn you that being a full-fledged nurse takes time. It'll be a long road for you, Sayuri. So I'd expect you not to shirk whatever duties you have to do. Understand?"

Upon returning to the room, I saw Hageshi there instead of Rin, blinking once. Almost as if she wasn't expecting me to appear in the room.

"You're our new apprentice, right? Get to work cleaning and sterilizing the tools!" she said and I had to hold back a flinch. Her strange eyes narrowed and a predatory expression entered her face. "What're you waiting for?! Do it!"

Iyasu's words ran in my head. I remembered where the tools were and walked over to the desk, taking them into my hands.

"Sanitize them well, apprentice. Slather them with the sterilizer near the sink and wash them. If you prove to be a better cleaner than Nameless maybe we'll be able to count on you for something while you're here."

I figured 'Nameless' was the woman I decided to call Hisoka. I wondered why the other nurses called her by that nickname. As I came over to the sink and ran the warm water I heard someone come over to me, and a pressure built up behind my head. Taking the bottle of solution in hand I poured it onto each medical tool, expecting it to be Rin behind me.

"You're new."

Her voice stunned me and I turned to face Hisoka, my hand paused under the hot water. Those were the first words she ever said to me. For some reason they impacted me. She stared at me, her mouth a line and her eyes blank. Only when a burning pain made jerk did I return back to my task, gritting my teeth at my throbbing red hand.

"I am. I just came here," I said, as if that would make all the difference. Hisoka stayed silent, watching me clean the medical tools, her eyes seeing everything and nothing. Her presence unnerved me then and I willed the last tool to get cleaner quicker.

She spoke again, "Your name. What is it?"

I contemplated telling Hisoka my true name until I remembered Rin's words.

"I don't have a name yet." I turned to her. "I have to earn it."

The woman nodded. "Same as me. I've been here for five years and I still don't have a name for myself."

That's when I wanted to tell her about the name I made for her. As I opened my mouth to tell her I saw Rin enter the room and I turned back to my task.

"Cleaning the tools today, apprentice?" An interested tone entered Rin's voice.

"Hageshi-san ordered me to clean them." I capped the sterilizer and gathered the tools together.

"Let me see how you did." Rin came over and as her gaze slid to mine, she seemed to take in the sight of Hisoka beside me. Her expression darkened.

"What're you doing here, Nameless? Trying to make our new apprentice fail?"

Hisoka flinched. "No . . . I . . ."

I noticed she seemed normal around me. However, around the other women, she crumbled like a blasted wall.

"I don't want you staying around our apprentice, Nameless. You understand me?"

Hisoka inclined her head after a long moment. "I understand . . ." She shuffled out the room, posture slumped.

"Don't speak to Nameless the next time she stands near you. Got it apprentice?" Rin's voice sounded too harsh to be normal. Did Hisoka do something to her?

"Yes Rin-san."

"From now on you call us senior nurses ma'am, got it?"

"Yes ma'am."

She looked pleased. "Good. Now come with me. Your day's far from over, apprentice."

By the time I collapsed into the bed in my cell I felt ready to peter off to sleep. My head spun from all the herb and tool names and from walking the layout of the nurse's building during chores. I hadn't seen Hisoka the rest of the day and I felt somewhat worried. Why? I didn't even know.

As I closed my eyes I heard a pattering sound outside my cell. I looked to see the flickering light above had shut off for good. The pattering continued, sounding like the eager paws of a brown rat. Rats never bothered me.

However, when I looked outside my cell, I saw a dark shape behind the bars, tapping them in insistence. My blood froze as the figure continued to drum his or her fingers on the bars. I tried laying awake to fool him or her that I hadn't heard, but it didn't work.

"Sayuri-sama, I know you're awake." The voice sounded familiar.

"Seishin?" My voice rose in shock as I leaped from the bed, hurrying over to her. "Why are you here?"

"Why are *you* still here!?" she asked. "I thought you'd escape with me!"

"I remembered something and couldn't escape without it," I whispered. "Why did you come back, Seishin? Do you want to get killed?"

"No. I came back because I can't leave a friend behind. You know that."

Her words stopped me and I remembered her saying about how she'd stick with a friend until the end. She thought of me as a friend . . . My eyes misted over at this and I forced the tears away, ready to speak. However Seishin continued, "I felt really angry when I found out you didn't escape with me. It took me a while to find out why you stayed here instead of escaping. Then I didn't feel angry anymore, y'know?"

"Thank you, Seishin-chan," I said, my voice a warbling mess.

"So what'll you do now?"

"I'm going to let the Jaakuna trust me some more. When that happens then I could think of something to use. I know I missed out on my chance but—you know why I didn't take it. You shouldn't linger around here, waiting for me to escape. It could take years."

"I doubt it. I think you could come up with something if I stuck around to help. Why don't we meet up every day?"

"What if you get captured again?" This was my main concern.

"You think I'll be that stupid to come here in full daylight? I used to read some strange books a few years ago. Books on these things called "stealth tactics". One of the pages said something about the night being your best friend for sneaking missions."

"That's true," I said. "Now look, we have to set a time for when we meet. When do you think would be best?"

"Don't worry about me. I'm a chronic night owl, but what about you?"

"I'd say this time is good. No one's awake now to hear us. If I could just tell what time it is now anyway." I had to grumble after saying this.

"You don't have to, Sayuri. I'll just tap on your cell's bars to wake you. And I won't forget so don't worry." I heard a smile in the girl's voice.

"You're taking a big risk by doing this. Thank you, Seishin."

"Look, I hate these Jaakuna guys as much as you do. I'd try anything to stop them from taking over other villages."

"I feel the same way."

We chatted for a few more moments on some ideas for my next escape plan, but the both of us came up empty each time. We parted after a bit, promising to meet again tomorrow night and speak to each other.

As I lay on my bed again, hope spread its tired limpid fingers through me and I felt as though anything could happen now for the better.

The next morning Korudo woke me, serving as my escort to the nurse building. I said nothing to him, ignoring him as he spoke.

"Welcome." Rin was the first person I saw once we entered through the beads. Her face looked drawn today, her fingers moving without stopping. "Thank you for escorting our new apprentice here, Korudo sir." She bowed.

"My pleasure." Korudo's lips peeled back into a toothy grin. He sent me a look as he walked out, boots clinking.

"Now, follow me. We have a very important schedule for you today."

My important schedule involved me standing by the bed of a man with colic and handing Hageshi and Rin the supplies they need.

"I need some more hyssop, apprentice!" Hageshi said and I hastened in handing her a small cup of the herb. Rin stuck her pinkie finger into the cup to make sure the water was the right temperature. Her tongue stuck sideways out her mouth as she held the groaning and wriggling man still.

Hageshi poured the boiled hyssop into the man's mouth, pinching his lips together to make him swallow. I watched everything, wanting to prove to the women that they could count on me. A tingle happened in the back of my head and as I turned I saw Hisoka, her gaze settled on me.

"Hand me the chamomile from the cabinet, please," Rin said.

"Make sure you know which one's chamomile," Hageshi warned. I felt a pit drop in my stomach as I tried to remember what the herb looked like. Upon opening the cabinet I remembered Rin's words the day before about the jars. To me though, they all looked the same.

As I scanned the jars, hoping I'd spot something to clue me in, I heard a whisper, "The jar with the crinkled green leaves."

There, on the middle shelf, I saw the crinkled leaves and took the jar in my hands. I looked to see Hisoka give me a nod before she vanished.

"Hurry up, apprentice!" Rin cried. "This man can't wait forever!"

"Coming ma'am!" I hurried over, handing her the jar.

"It seems she's useful after all." Hageshi sounded surprised.

"She'll earn her name if she keeps it up." Rin took out a handful of chamomile leaves and put them in the man's mouth.

"Now chew," she said and the man wheezed as his jaw worked, his eyes red and tearing. I stood back as the man choked and green bits of the herb shot from his mouth.

"Let's try that again." This time Hageshi placed a handful of the herb in the man's mouth. "You want to get better, don't you? Now chew this time and swallow. I don't care if you choke."

The words sounded harsh but they worked. The man moaned after he swallowed and his head drooped, his eyes closing.

"There, see what happens when you cooperate?" Rin rubbed the man's forehead.

"Did you see everything we did?" Hageshi turned to me. I told her I had.

"Good. Perhaps we'll gain more service now if people hear we have an able new apprentice. Iyasu-sama won't have to worry about the rent anymore if that happens." Rin's eyes gleamed. "Then we can have some leftover money for us two, Hageshi!"

"Why don't the people ever leave their houses, ma'am? I never see anyone around except for the people here," I asked.

"They're cowards." Hageshi grinned. "Only when they're sick do they leave their "private oasis" for treatment."

"Since our commander took over Kagayaki, people became afraid of even the sun." Rin capped the jar, going to the cabinet to put away the chamomile. "I'd go crazy if I stayed inside my house everyday, never seeing life outside my window."

"Now, apprentice, go take the other man's temperature over there. You see him, the man with the all-over-the-place hair?" Hageshi handed me a thermometer. I went over to the man, who watched me with a furrowed forehead.

After sticking the thermometer under his tongue I waited, resisting the urge to tap my foot. This moment reminded of the one time I had gotten sick when I was younger. I had woken to feel my mother place a cool rag on my head. Upon seeing my look she said, 'You have a fever, Sayuri-chan. You're not going to school.'

Somehow, looking at this man reminded me of when I had the fever. I took the thermometer out and held it to the light, seeing the mercury touching the ninety-nine mark.

"How's his fever?" Rin asked. "Lemme see." She grabbed the thermometer out my hand. "Hmm . . . ninety-nine. At least it's better than yesterday."

She stole a look behind her and I looked as well to see Hisoka standing in the doorway. She held a tray of new tools.

"Took you long enough." Hageshi stalked over to her and took the tray. "Nameless, you've been here for five years and you still can't learn how to do things in an efficient way? Shame on you."

I wanted to open my mouth and tell her to stop bullying Hisoka, but Iyasu came in and looked at both women. "I hear an argument. Is there a problem here?"

"No, Iyasu-sama. We're just finishing up with the men who needed treatment. Nameless was tardy with the tools again," Rin said. The older women gave a bob of her head, then beckoned me forward.

"Sayuri, I need to speak to you."

"Iyasu, the apprentice doesn't have a name until she earns it. Don't you know the tradition by now?" Rin whined.

"No, I don't know the tradition *you* made up for yourself. I can call Sayuri by her full name all I want or any other name for that matter while I run this clinic."

Rin seemed to slump. "Fine. I apologize, Iyasu-sama."

"Good. Now go to the Main Room. A woman is up front. You wouldn't want to keep her waiting, do you?"

"No, ma'am." Rin nodded and headed out the Medical Room. The Main Room, the initial room upon entering the building, seemed like a lobby of sorts. A place where people waited for assistance. The Medical Room, the place all the patients entered when Rin called them, was the place I frequented in the most when Hageshi didn't assign me to do chores.

"Now Sayuri, if you please." Iyasu began to walk off, leaving me with no choice but to follow.

"Following orders from Rin and Hageshi without hesitation Sayuri?" This was the older woman's first question as we walked through the hallway. The tatami mats' color, a strange orange hue, appeared to pop out at me. The walls, an olive green, darkened in their color the further down the hall we walked.

"Yes ma'am." I nodded my head.

"Korudo-sama wouldn't like to hear that the new apprentice he chose for us decided to cause any trouble early on, right? Rin and Hageshi are your senior nurses so I expect you to look to them if you have any inquiries."

"Yes."

We exited out an opened folding door into a small courtyard surrounded by bamboo stalks and smooth Japanese maple trees. A small wooden bench was propped under a canopy of bamboo leaves and Iyasu invited me to sit.

"Why do Rin and Hageshi bully Hiso—I mean Nameless for?" I said, glad I caught myself. The older woman gave a sigh.

"Perhaps to feel more powerful. Since Rin was our latest newcomer, she wanted to prove her greatness. You do know that Nameless has worked in my clinic for over five years, right?"

"Yes. Why didn't she earn a name yet?"

"Let me tell you something, Sayuri." Iyasu leaned close to me, chapped lips close to my face, her breath sour. "Nameless has a slow complex problem. You understand? Her mind works differently than ours. That's why Rin refuses to tell her she's ready for a name. It's because of contempt. Judging by that, I think Nameless shall stay nameless for the rest of her life here."

I felt such pity for Hisoka from Iyasu's words. "What was her name before she was called 'Nameless'?"

"She never said."

"Why not?"

"I don't know everything now, Sayuri." Iyasu shook her head. "Perhaps Nameless will learn from your example, if you don't mess up your reputation."

I heard an underlying warning in her voice. "I won't, Iyasu-sama."

"Good. Now why don't you head back to Rin and tell her I said that you can help assist with patients this time. I think you're the kind of person who likes being hands on rather than just watching from the sidelines."

"What if I make a mistake?" I resisted the urge to tug at my hair.

"Then may the gods punish you until your death. See to it that you don't make any mistakes if you wish to make Korudo and me happy. Now go back to Rin.

"Yes, ma'am," I said and stood from the bench.

"How old are you anyway, Sayuri?" she asked.

"Twenty-one."

"I see." Iyasu fell silent, looking distant. I decided to leave and head back inside the clinic. Hisoka appeared from a room on my right and I stopped as she came over to me in the hallway.

"You got in trouble?" she asked and I could see what Iyasu meant about Hisoka having a 'slow complex'. She seemed to hesitate with every word she spoke, as if she would regret every one of them.

"No. Iyasu-sama had to speak to me about my next chore. She wants me to assist Rin and Hageshi from now on."

"Stay away from Rin and Hageshi." Her voice sounded clipped.

"Why?" I asked, feeling a chill down my back.

"They'll ruin you however they can."

"I'm still new. They have no reason to do so. Besides, Korudo wouldn't feel pleased if Hageshi-san and Rin-san decided to bully me."

"Just listen to me! No one ever does that!"

I started to edge away from her and I felt grateful when Hageshi appeared, looking at Hisoka with reproach. "Nameless, what did Rin tell you about talking to our new apprentice?"

"I just . . ." Hisoka's previous expression faded and her voice returned to her usual jitter. "I wanted to meet her."

"Well you can't." Hageshi took my arm. "We don't need another person like you here. Let's go, apprentice."

She tugged me along and I spared Hisoka one last look as we passed her by, seeing the blankness return to her face. It irked me why she always acted frightened of Hageshi and Rin. I intended to find out the truth if I ever saw Hisoka on her own again.

"Don't tell Nameless anything anymore, you hear me? She'll ruin you, apprentice."

That's strange. Hisoka said something similar about how Rin and Hageshi would ruin me. Whose words could I believe?

"Now what's your next chore? Did Iyasu-sama say?"

"Yes ma'am. She told me I have to help assist instead of hand out supplies."

"Did she?" Hageshi looked at me, her eyes narrowing. "Interesting."

We didn't speak another word until we entered the Medical Room. Rin attended to a woman, who looked fatigued, her expression frustrated.

"Ah, perfect timing, apprentice. I want you to interview this woman and relay to me what's wrong. You can do that, can't you?" She turned to me. I gave a nod and the woman on the exam table made a withering sigh.

"Why are you here today?" I asked. The woman sighed again.

"I've sprained my foot the other day. Can't you nurses just hurry up and attend to me? Isn't that your job?"

Rin scrunched her nose at the woman's attitude. "I now know two things about you, ma'am. One, you're impatient, and two, you're ignorant. You understand how condensed a nurse's job is, right?"

"Oh stop with this nonsense!" Hageshi stalked over to the woman. "She wants to get healed, then let's get her healed. Keep our apprentice out of this."

"Iyasu-sama said . . ." I started to say, but Hageshi glared at me.

"Forget what she said. Right now we have a grumpy patient who needs tending. She needs an Epsom salt poultice. Make yourself useful and get me the jar of lavender and the container of Epsom salt. Rin you get the rest sorted out."

I went to the cabinet to get the herbs she needed while Rin filled a pot with water and huffed.

"Come here, apprentice. Bring the ingredients to me," she said and I heeded her order, watching as she prepared a mixture in the pot. After grinding the lavender down with a mortar and pestle she threw the herb along with the Epsom salt into the pot. Within seconds a strange, however soothing, smell overtook the room.

"Go grab four fabric gauze strips for me," Rin said. "Make sure you get two large and two small ones."

Soon Rin spread the mixture on the long fabric and beckoned me over to her again.

"Now, I want you to place this piece onto the woman's leg where she tells you to, got it? Don't mess it up or it won't be just our patient who's on the edge."

Walking over to the woman and seeing her stare made me hope in fervency that I wouldn't mess up anything.

"Where did you sprain your leg?" I asked, "so I can put this poultice on you."

"Right there," the woman said, gesturing to her ankle. "Make it snappy now!"

I took her foot in my hand and wrapped the long piece around her ankle, making sure to place the side with the mixture on her sprained area. Hageshi watched, nodding every once and so often while Rin and I worked. Once the poultice wrapped around the woman's leg, tied and sturdy, I stood and took a deep breath.

"Lay down and relax now," Hageshi said and the woman nodded. It looked somewhat funny to see the woman hesitate in moving her leg in order to get comfortable.

"Here, apprentice. Wash out the poultice pot will you?" Hageshi asked and I had to hold back a sigh. Would I ever escape from people ordering me around all the time? As I ran the cold water and cleaned the inside of the pot I heard Iyasu's light footsteps enter the room.

"We have another patient, Rin. See to him, all right?"

"Yes ma'am," Rin said, walking off to the Main room.

Later in the night I heard the soft tapping sound and knew Seishin had arrived. I stood from the bed and came to my cell's door, seeing her standing with a small smile.

"Hey," she said.

"Hey Seishin-chan."

"Still alive I see."

I snorted. "Yep."

We began to chat once more about the goings on and I mentioned it to her that Korudo made me an apprentice nurse.

"That's great!" Seishin smiled again. "If you impress those nurses, then you'll get more support."

"I know. I did notice something about Korudo over these few days."

"What did you see?"

"He looks a bit—I can't describe it—but he looks angry."

"Why?"

"I don't know. I don't think I did anything to him. However, he does know my name now."

"You told him your name?!" Seishin gasped.

"No, I didn't! He came over to my cell door to let me out and called me by my real name. I don't know how Korudo found out, but it chills me. No one else in the village knows my name but . . ." ". . . your friend Akio, right?" Seishin finished my sentence. Confusion entered me. Why would Akio want to tell Korudo my name? What would it serve?

"Have you spoken to Akio since I escaped?" Seishin asked, scratching an itch.

"I haven't seen him since and it worries me." I shook my head. "I do hope he's okay."

"I know he's fine. You shouldn't worry at all."

We fell silent for a moment. Then I looked at her. "Seishin, like I said, I may not escape for a long time. I don't think you should stick around for long."

"This topic again? Look, I'm not abandoning you because you're stuck in a cell and I'm not. I said I wouldn't leave a friend behind, right? So I'm not going to leave you alone to face these jerks."

"I just feel bad for getting you into this mess."

"You know, if I wasn't captured on the same day as you when we first walked into this place, nothing would change. At nights I come find you and we'd talk about escaping. Just pretend I wasn't ever captured and we've done these meetings at night since the beginning."

I didn't respond, feeling thoughts take over my attention. Thoughts about Akio entered my mind. Then, Seishin spoke.

"Hey, Sayuri-sama? When's the last time you smiled?"

Her question struck me as odd. The last time I smiled? I probably smiled before the atomic bombing happened and I told her so.

"Why do you ask?" I asked afterward.

"I don't know. I just feel you'd look better with a smile on your face."

Her words stuck around in my mind long after I closed my eyes again for sleep once she left.

Seishin
Mid-August 1949

Seishin's long hair whipped in the warm night wind as she snuck out Kagayaki after leaving Sayuri. Her thoughts boiled as she headed to the small abandoned shack she took up residence in since she escaped.

These stupid Jaakuna men can't find me. They've searched for me for three days already. Seishin had to snort. *I've never met such stupid people in my life. Not even my brother could compare if he still lived.*

She looked up at the sky and sighed, feeling grateful to have escaped. She would have gone mad if she stayed cooped in that cell any longer. Seishin entered her little shack and wondered how Sayuri tolerated confinement for so long. Until she remembered that the Jaakuna captured the woman once before.

"Why does she have to suffer?" Seishin asked aloud, rubbing sweat off her nose with one hand. She settled on the small mat and tried to think of a way to help Sayuri, anyway to help her. An idea surfaced in her mind, a risky one, but still an idea. A small smile rose on her face as her plan ran a rapid pace in her head, spreading its hope throughout her.

Tomorrow . . . that's what I'll do. For Sayuri. She thought as her eyes closed and she slept.

Upon waking the next morning, she imagined Sayuri heading to her new nursing job. Seishin headed out the shack into the sunshine, her stomach rumbling and her mind set. She ducked behind a tree as the sound of Jaakuna boots clinked past, then stopped, the foul men muttering to each other.

"At this rate we'll never find the girl! She could have traveled all the way up to Hiroshima by now!"

"Hush! If she's still in the area our voices might scare her away. You have no common sense."

"What does it matter? I bet that woman the girl came with into our village plotted this escape."

"Then why didn't the woman escape? She stood like a statue while Korudo humiliated Kawa."

"Maybe she got scared. Women . . . always cowards in the face of risk."

Seishin felt the first burnings of anger in her. *How dare they talk about Sayuri like that!?*

"Though I wonder why she stopped dead in her tracks when she saw Akio. Remember that?"

"Yeah. Maybe he's in on the girl's escape as well. Korudo might as well get involved in this instead of standing around on the side and worrying about that woman all the time."

"Look, if we find this girl, Korudo will pay us big! Big I tell you! Let's get going while the morning still stands. Perhaps we'll catch the girl while she sleeps."

The boots clinked off and Seishin breathed a sigh of relief. "Stupid men," she said in an undertone. She felt such contempt for the Jaakuna and Korudo. As Seishin headed back to Kagayaki she stuck to the shadows, following the mantra of "Shadows give the spy a larger advantage". *And my mother always wondered why I read stealth books. They sure help me stay out of trouble.*

Once the surroundings turned into the houses of Kagayaki, Seishin stuck to the alleyways, her heart pounding. Once more she walked through enemy territory and once more the threat of a Jaakuna member finding her skyrocketed. She had to enact her plan and she had to do it fast.

Seishin entered the heart of Kagayaki after crossing over the bridge, looking around for a certain guard. One who didn't appear to fit the bill for a Jaakuna member. She hoped she'd see him—the one link for helping Sayuri.

She heard a sound and spirited to the shadows, watching with widened eyes of the new threat. Her mouth curled upward as she recognized the Jaakuna man stalking past her, his helmet off, the sheen of sweat on his forehead. He headed into a nearby house, shutting the door.

That's him. The man I need to see, Seishin thought. *I'll wait until tonight though, so there's no risk for another person catching me.*

Memorizing the house's location, Seishin left Kagayaki, feeling pleased and accomplished. Her one hope? That soon the Jaakuna would fade away and become a part of history. Just as the atomic bombing and the destroying of Dokutsu did. She hated destruction and she hated evil. In her mind she hoped the world would one day turn to peace and love.

Seishin bided her time and, once the beginnings of night fell, she set off back to Kagayaki. Once more her heart rate increased, her eyes widened, her gaze flung everywhere. On occasion she had to wipe her palms on her clothes. She hated having sweaty hands.

Even at night Seishin made sure to make her steps light, quick, and smooth. She couldn't trip or hesitate. The bridge's boards creaked underfoot as she moved and her heart rose to her throat. No one came out from the houses. No one and nothing made a sound.

It confused her as to why no one left their homes. Seishin knew people still lived in Kagayaki despite the Jaakuna taking it over, but she wondered why they stayed holed away from sight. She couldn't come up with a good reason and asking one of the village people wouldn't help in the least.

As she headed to the house anticipation and adrenaline entered her. For the first time she doubted what she planned to do. The door stood in front of her and she raised her hand to knock.

The sound resonated through the silent village and, just before Seishin decided to make a break for it, the door opened.

"What do you want, Korudo?" the man asked. His eyes widened in surprise as he saw that he wasn't speaking to the Jaakuna commander, but to someone else.

"You're Akio, aren't you?" Seishin asked, looking up into Akio's handsome face.

"You're the girl who escaped."

"That's right. I'm here to talk to you about Sayuri."

Akio's forehead bunched. "Why?"

"It's important. Will you let me inside so I can explain?"

Sayuri's friend hesitated, as if mulling over the thought of refusing Seishin and closing the door on her. However he sighed and beckoned for her to follow him.

"You're taking a risk coming here to talk to me."

"You think I don't know that?"

"No, but you should still take it into consideration."

"Whatever." Seishin crossed her arms as Akio closed the door behind them. "If you tell Korudo or anyone else that I was here then you're in trouble."

"What would you do about it?" His brow arched. "It's not as though I break secrets anyway. Why would I tell someone a girl visited me last night? I'm not involved in the search parties Korudo sends out to find you anyway."

"Good, because I need your help."

"Concerning Sayuri?"

"Yes. Since you're the guy she trusts I think I should try to convince you to help her escape."

"Now that's a big risk."

"Listen to me, Akio. I know Sayuri-sama left you and I know you have sour feelings over it. Don't you think you should try to *forgive* her?"

"I suppose she told you about how she decided to come back looking for me after two years." Akio's voice sounded tight.

"Yes she did, but she's sorry, Akio. I mean, I know you have a grudge right now against her but . . ." ". . . A grudge?" Akio interrupted. "What makes you think that?"

"You don't even try to talk to her. I bet you just mope around and keep hating her because you can. I met Sayuri when she passed through the village Yujo. I was on my own without anyone to talk to and she took me along with her. Well, really I just forced her to take me along, but you understand, right? She's all I have now and you're all she has. She's doing this for you, Akio."

Akio fell silent, his jaw working, his expressions fighting between annoyance and pain.

"Please tell me you'll talk to her." Seishin hated pleading, but she couldn't think of anything else to say.

"I can't assure you of that," Akio said and Seishin put her hands on her hips.

"So that's it? You're just going to abandon her now? Who's in the cell from night to morning without freedom? Who's the person who traveled half of Nagasaki looking for you? You probably told Korudo Sayuri's name just so you can hurt her even more than you do."

"What?" Akio looked incredulous.

"Why else would Korudo know Sayuri's name? I know you told him!"

"Look, Korudo asked me about Sayuri and he wanted to know her name. I slipped up and told him. That's it. I have no intention of hurting her." Akio put up his hands. If Seishin didn't know any better she'd think the expression in Akio's face now was one of guilt.

"Why do you care that Korudo now knows Sayuri's name? What would he do to her? Ruin her for life?"

"He could do anything; that's the point, Akio. I thought maybe you were one of the good guys, but now I see I was wrong for once." Seishin backed to the door. "You know what? I'm done talking to you. You aren't worth it. If you don't want to help Sayuri, then I'll do it by myself."

"Fine," Akio said and Seishin gritted her teeth, heading out the door. *How did Sayuri tolerate this guy? I'd ditch him too if he spoke like that to me everyday. He fits in with those Jaakuna guys without a doubt.*

Seishin still saw red from speaking to Akio as she headed back out Kagayaki to her shack. However, she decided not to tell Sayuri later on about visiting Akio. *She doesn't have to know about how indifferent Akio is.*

Sayuri
Mid August 1949

Time sped. My roles as a nurse's assistant became more involved. Soon I became the one who called in patients and asked about what they needed. I knew Iyasu was involved in this and I remembered her words about how I'd do better with hands on activities. In a way I had to feel grateful. I hated being cast into the corner, just watching.

A few times I saw Hisoka, but I never got the chance to speak with her or even give her an acknowledging nod. I began to have the sinking feeling that she despised me because of my rising popularity. She refused to look me in the eye and if I walked past her in the hall she seemed to crumble. Just like she did when she saw Hageshi and Rin.

"Oh, Sayuri has adjusted well to the nursing environment, commander," Iyasu said to Korudo one morning as he escorted me into the Main Room.

"That so?" He swung a surprised look to me. "She hasn't made any mistakes yet, has she?"

His tone of voice made me tense. It sounded too annoyed. Too angry. However his expression contradicted my observation.

"Nope and she's a hard worker, Korudo, sir. We're lucky to have her here. Thank you, commander." Iyasu bowed, taking his hand into hers.

"I wish to see all my people succeed," he said, his voice distant as he looked at me again. There it was again, that annoyed look. I blinked, trying to appear passive and unsuspecting. Why did he look so irked?

"We share the same ideal, commander. Why, before you took over our village, we were the lowliest village in Nagasaki. I hope our apprentice here does herself good. Perhaps I can rely on someone to take care of other people.

My other nurses became no shows because of the heat, you know this." Iyasu smiled, beckoning me over to her.

"Yes, the heat sure makes people stay away from work." Korudo nodded, heading out through the beads. As Iyasu turned her back to walk to the Medical Room Korudo turned around and I saw the full flames of rage in his eyes. Then he left.

"Come Sayuri. We have much to do today. Since I've made you active in your apprenticeship, I'd expect you do to do well enough today to set an example."

"For Nameless?"

"Yes."

We headed down the corridor and entered the Medical Room. My sight opened to Hisoka handing a few towels from Hageshi.

"No no and NO!" Hageshi slammed the towels onto the floor. "I still see dirt spots on these! Either you do the job right or you don't do it at all."

"Those spots . . . they're old stains." Hisoka managed through her warbling voice.

"What was that?" Hageshi inched closer to her, voice dangerous.

"No-nothing." Hisoka fled the room, leaving the towels on the floor.

"Come back here and pick these up, Nameless! You won't get away with that!" Hageshi watched Hisoka, her neck tight.

"Hageshi, I believe you should pick those up. You threw them on the floor," Iyasu said.

"Yes, I did, but it's her responsibility to do her chores right!" The words were said in a hiss.

"I understand, but for now would you please pick them up and dispose of them?"

Hageshi huffed, but did as told.

Iyasu leaned in and said into my ear, "Don't become like everyone else, Sayuri. I want variety."

"What did you say about me, Iyasu-sama?" Hageshi looked between me and the older woman.

"I just told Sayuri about how I like variety in my nurses. I hate people who act the same," Iyasu said and Hageshi narrowed her eyes, but knew better than to argue.

"Right. Now apprentice, come here. I want you to make a count of the herbs in the cabinet. Make sure we have jars for every one."

"Yes, ma'am." I heeded her order, feeling Iyasu's eyes on my back the whole time. In times like these I'd wish for a patient to come in and complain about their aches and pains. To me, counting the herbs was a bore. I did know the importance of this chose, though, and I made sure to count all the jars.

I paused as I saw one empty jar labeled: Fennel, and took it into my hands.

"We're out of Fennel," I said and Hageshi made a sound of acknowledgment.

"I'll make sure to let Rin know." Was her response.

Once my herb counting job finished Hageshi thrust the towels at me. "Here, at least I can depend on you to do your job right. See if you can clean these better than Hisoka can."

I headed down the hallway to the Laundry Room and saw another nurse, who I've never seen before, walk in a dainty way to the Medical Room. Perhaps she was one of the nurses Iyasu complained about when she mentioned the women who didn't come to work.

"So you're the new apprentice, aren't you sweetie?" the woman asked me.

I gave a nod and she laughed.

"Well, let's hope you can prove to us that newbies can do jobs right." She tittered again and sauntered on her way. Rolling my eyes, I headed to the Laundry Room to see Hisoka there, grumbling and leaning over the sink. Her jaw tightened as she glared at the cleaning product near her. Then, her body stiffened and she turned to see me behind her. With a hasty nod she left the room before I could stop her. It made me wonder if she avoided me for a reason besides jealousy.

I didn't find out more about this until I saw Hisoka in the Laundry Room again a few days later. It rained in sheets outside, the weather a relief from the constant sweltering heat that lingered for the past few weeks. Hageshi had ordered a full wash of all the fabrics and towels, declaring that the rain had cast off the grime of misfortune. 'In doing so,' she stated, 'it introduced the cleanliness of summer.'

While I worked in the Laundry Room, cleaning towels, I heard a shuffle and saw Hisoka enter, looking preoccupied in her thoughts. I rinsed the towels, rolling my fingers over troublesome spots to get rid of the stains. Hisoka glanced at the door often as she tried to clean a towel herself. On occasion I saw her steal a glance at what I did, as if trying to copy me.

After I caught her looking at my work, I said, "Hisoka, why don't you ever fight Hageshi-san or Rin-san back?"

At my words Hisoka flinched, her eyes growing wide. "Hisoka? You . . . you named me? Why?"

"Everyone has to have a name in this world or else they're nothing."

She looked shocked still, then a small smile lit her face. "I guess I fit the name then, right?"

"You do fit the name," I said. We continued to wash the towels on the washboards in silence, hearing the sound of rain patter the window. The rustle of the trees in the wind sounded and I longed to open the window and just listen. My mother cherished nature and believed, when it rained, it was good luck to open your window.

"Don't tell Rin or Hageshi about me naming you, Hisoka," I warned and she bobbed her head in a nod.

"I won't. Thank you."

As we handled the sopping towels and squeezed the excess water we shared a knowing look. Her words about staying away from Rin and Hageshi confused me. However, each day I believed in Hisoka more and more.

"Why should I stay away from Rin and Hageshi, Hisoka?" I asked one night before Korudo was to come escort me back to my cell. Hisoka had crossed my path in the hallway and came over to me with an open face. She glanced about in a quick fashion before beckoning me to follow, a finger on her lips.

"It was a long time ago. Sometimes I forget what happened but it always comes back. Always." Hisoka shivered as she guided me into a spare pantry. The jars of unopened and fresh herbs stood to attention behind the glass cabinets.

"Tell me."

"You know the reason why I act like this?" she asked, her voice sounding normal, almost anguished. I had to blink at the raw emotion.

"I act like a coward around them because I want them to ignore me. They've put me down for so long and I wished that one day they'd stop. They never did. For five years I've tried to impress them, but now I see that's not possible. Both women have made my life miserable, slapping me and yelling at me. In time a person will react to abuse, and react I did. Have you seen the dark red stain on Rin's hand?"

I began to think, conjuring up Rin's image in my head and seeing her walk, her hand raised to call the next patient into the room.

"Oh, the dark stain that stretched from her knuckles to her wrist?"

"Yes, that's the very one."

"But, how did you get involved with that?"

"Hold up, I'm not finished explaining. Rin's stain was caused by an overdose of Gingko Biloba extract. Do you know it? It's the herb in the jar with the blue cap."

I nodded, understanding.

"Too much of that herb causes skin discoloration, which is why we nurses recommended giving it to patients in small doses. Well, Rin's stain appeared just days after I enacted my plan. Rin eats a bowl of Ramen noodles and rice every afternoon for lunch. The night before I thought of my plan she corned me into the wall and flogged me because I had failed to mix two mixtures together.

"In a blind revenge I planned to discolor Rin's skin by a small amount every night, just to make her worry. She's stingy about her appearance. All I had to do was grind up many Gingko leaves and sprinkle the juice into her noodles. In the beginning things were fine, Rin saw a few unpleasant blotches on her skin, nothing more. She worried over them without fail, annoying Iyasu, Hageshi, and the other nurses about it.

"Then I grew bold. I created more Gingko than was required and Rin's whole hand became as red as a blood clot."

"No!" My mouth dropped.

"I made a fatal blunder at that. I used all the Gingko, meaning that soon someone would find out it who used it all. After much hysteria from Rin, Hageshi looked on impulse to the herb cabinet and saw the jar for Gingko was empty. Once her gaze slid to mine, it was all over for me. They knew without even saying anything. Rin and Hageshi held in their rage throughout the day but at night they burst into my room. Oh the abuse they did to me. Once they left I cowered in a ball and cried. There, not a foot away from me, lay a chunk of my hair.

"They didn't stop there. Every night afterward Rin came into my room to abuse me and I tried to fight it. Until another plan entered my mind. Perhaps if I acted slow and hesitant, maybe Hageshi and Rin would find no triumph in abusing me. For two years I acted the way I have, slurring my words, tripping over my feet, and becoming quiet. Over time my plan worked, but now I have a new derogation. Have any of the nurses told you I have a slow complex yet?"

"Iyasu-sama has," I admitted, feeling guilty to let this out to Hisoka.

"I bet that was the true reason why she took you out to the courtyard. To talk about me, right?"

"Well, no. She told me about you but she also told me she'd put me on the active status."

"Watch out for Rin and Hageshi now, okay? Since you're now a higher rank than me, they'll look for any opportunity to push you down again. Trust me, I know." A light shone in Hisoka's eyes, as if she had just become someone new. The blankness in her eyes spirited away and an intelligent look replaced it.

I gave a nod, not knowing what else to say. After a while she nodded back and gave me a brilliant smile.

"Apprentice! Where are you? Korudo-sama has arrived to take you back to your cell!" Iyasu said. Hisoka dimmed at her words, her body crumbling inward again.

"I have to keep this act of cowardliness going. It's all I have left. What's your real name by the way?"

"Sayuri."

"My real name was Shinjitsu."

Over the course of four days my skill in being an apprentice nurse increased and Iyasu took note of this with a pleased smile. Hisoka got her wish; she was cast aside as Hageshi and Rin depended on me to do chores and work. Each night Hisoka and I met and chatted, exchanging stories. I told her about my mission and her eyes darkened.

"I went through that love thing once. It destroyed me, Sayuri." Hisoka took my hand. "You're still young to have an infatuation."

"I'm not . . . !" My sentence trailed off and faded as a thought came to me. *Is that the reason why I feel intent on saving Akio?*

"What happened to you when you fell I love?" I asked instead. Hisoka sighed and took a seat on the spare stool in the pantry.

"When I fell in love with a man named Kurosaki it seemed like it came right out of a story. The blushing, the giggles, the kisses, everything. I reveled in it all, my heart expanded. We traveled all through the land, through Kyoto, Tokyo, and even Osaka. Until we came to Nagasaki." Here the nurse's eyes lowered. "He left me for a geisha he met on the night we stayed in Kyoto. He told me he couldn't bare the separation anymore. I let him go and the feelings that accompanied our break left me without breath. It seemed to get harder each day for me without Kurosaki there to bolster me. However, one day," she stood onto her feet, "I learned to breathe and feel again. This woman you speak to, Sayuri, has been the same woman since my revitalization, perhaps even stronger still."

I stayed silent, her words soaking in my head. Would that become of me in the future? Would I have to deal with more pain?

"It's best to be cautious, Sayuri," Hisoka said, "because no one knows who's an ally, or who's out to destroy lives in this life."

The next day upon my arrival to the clinic I saw Hageshi and Rin standing in front of the herb cabinet. As I came closer I noticed one of the jars wasn't there.

"Odd, isn't it?" Rin turned to me. "We seem to have a missing herb for today."

"Which one, Rin?" Iyasu asked.

"Ginseng. Why? I don't know." Hageshi's eyes narrowed and she whirled on Hisoka, who happened to have just walked in the room. "Did you do this, Nameless!?"

"Why would she want to cause trouble?" I asked, entering the conversation. "Nameless wouldn't want to soil her reputation."

"Nameless has no reputation, apprentice, or did you forget?" Rin said looking at me. "Even if she did have some sort of name for herself, it wouldn't do her good anyway." As she went to close the cabinet doors the red splotch on her hand made its appearance.

"Perhaps one of you used it yesterday and can't remember," Iyasu said.

"We had no patients yesterday," Hageshi said, as if to state a point. Both women stared at each other for a moment, then Iyasu sighed.

"I'll just send Han'ei a message, asking them to send us a jar of ginseng later today."

"That sounds good Iyasu-sama. Though I do wonder where that jar could have went." Rin nodded her head.

"You checked the full area of the clinic and the other rooms?"

"We have," Hageshi said. "We couldn't find anything."

"It's no matter. Let's just get this place ready for patients."

For the rest of the day we nurses waited with some patience for people to show. As I twiddled my thumbs and tapped my foot Hisoka went to stand by me. We watched Hageshi and Rin rush in and out of the Medical room as if a great wind blew behind them.

"Which one of them do you think took the jar?" she asked once Rin and Hageshi left the room.

"You're already pinning the blame on them, aren't you," I said with a snort. "We could have had a robber come in last night without us knowing."

"Iyasu always stays in the clinic after we all leave. She'd hear something like that if it ever happened."

We stayed silent as the day progressed in slow motion, no patients entering the Main room. Hageshi and Rin complained to each other about how this would affect their stocks and I decided to head to the Courtyard to get some fresh air.

Two crows cawed as they circled over the bamboo. I sat on the bench and tipped my head back, looking at the overcast sky. I thought about Akio and wondered where he was as I let my mind wander.

"Sayuri."

I jerked and looked at Iyasu, who made her way over to me.

"I hope I haven't disturbed you," she said as she sat on the bench.

"Oh, not at all, Iyasu-sama. I wanted to talk to you anyway."

"About what?"

"About Nameless. I want to know why Hageshi and Rin treat her wrong."

"I have told you that Nameless has a slow complex, right?"

"You have, but don't take this the wrong way." I felt the need to bow for a moment. "I just feel she doesn't deserve this life and I don't think her slow complex makes the other nurses bully her. I've spoken to her and she doesn't sound as bad as the others make her sound. She's respectful and kind."

Iyasu heaved a sigh. "I respect your concern for your fellow nurse, Sayuri. You have a good heart. However, I can't do anything to make Nameless fit in while she works here."

"Iyasu-sama, could you maybe release Hiso . . . I mean Nameless from apprenticeship? I see Rin and Hageshi put her down everyday and sometimes I just want to go over and stop them."

"Hmmm." Iyasu looked deep in thought, her mouth a line.

"Because she just looks miserable everyday when I see her. I just want to know if you could do anything for her. I think she'd benefit from a new life. She could start over again."

"Nameless never looked miserable in the first two years of her apprenticeship. She always seemed full of life around the other nurses. Then . . . I don't know what happened. The light shut off in her and now she schlepps around the clinic with the look of a beaten dog on her face. Hageshi and Rin don't care much for her anymore. What confuses me is how it all happened."

I knew the truth of Hisoka's situation but I zipped my lips and let Iyasu continue.

"Would you know anything? Have Rin and Hageshi said anything to you about Nameless?"

"They don't speak to me outside of ordering me around the clinic."

"I see." The elder woman stood. "Has Nameless told you anything?"

"She told me about how she wishes to get out and live again. I want to help her, Iyasu-sama, but I don't want to make you or Rin and Hageshi angry."

"I'll think on your words, Sayuri," Iyasu said after a long moment and I felt the small hope in my chest deflate. Of course her words meant she wouldn't think on them. I have come to think of Hisoka as a friend and if she couldn't have her freedom granted to her . . . she'd feel just as confined as me.

"That's all I ask," I said, giving her another bow. Iyasu walked out the Courtyard and I watched her go, biting my lower lip.

I must have dozed off, for I woke to Hisoka shaking my arm. "Sayuri, it's time for you to go. Korudo waits inside the Main Room."

The sky looked like the color of purple ink. I must have slept for longer than I realized.

"Did we receive any patients at all today, Hisoka?" I asked, standing from the bench.

"No, we've been as quiet as a garden snake. Hageshi and Rin aren't pleased."

I rubbed my eyes, following behind Hisoka. Upon seeing Korudo I saw a concealed angry look in his face.

"Come Sayuri. Let's go." He took my arm, leading me back to my cell.

The same thing happened for the next week. No patients showed to the clinic and nothing was done. It felt weird to me, not having anything to do. At least I wasn't stuck in my cell . . .

One morning, after Korudo dropped me off at the clinic, I saw darkened looks from Rin and Hageshi.

"Apprentice, we are displeased with you," Hageshi said, her voice tight.

"Why Hageshi-san?" I asked, confused.

"We have just heard a rumor while making our way to the clinic about a man who had died a week ago of a ginseng overdose. When we asked around, people said that he was treated by a skinny woman with long black hair and a sallow complexion."

The description fit my profile. I blinked. "How could I have used the ginseng if we hadn't received any patients last week?"

"The jar of ginseng went missing last week. Maybe, a few days before, you used it for the patient and didn't realize how much you used on him," Rin said.

"I'm not allowed to treat patients without supervision, Rin-san."

"I can understand if you wanted to try to treat someone on your own, but without consulting, me or Rin? What a disgrace." Hageshi shook her head.

"What would posses me do something like kill a patient with an overdose?"

"Perhaps 'Hisoka' persuaded you to cause some trouble for us," Rin said in a growl and I felt my eyes widen. "Oh don't give me that look. I've heard what you call Nameless by and I don't like it."

"Nameless stays nameless unless we say so, apprentice." Hageshi glowered at me. They both seemed angrier about my name for Hisoka than for my supposed killing.

"Wait until Iyasu-sama finds out about this," Rin said and I didn't fake the dread I felt. I knew the news would soon reach Korudo's ears. Perhaps that's why we haven't received any patients last week.

All through the day Hageshi and Rin tasked me with chores. 'Punishment chores,' Hageshi had said. 'Only Iyasu can punish you for real.'

When the dreaded moment of Korudo entering the clinic to take me back to my cell came I forced my gaze away from his. Not wanting to see any triumph. He had expected for me to fail.

"Korudo, sir. My sheer apologies on what happened not long ago." Iyasu bowed. "I understand that Sayuri here has caused some strife. You've heard the rumor?"

"I've heard the rumor, yes." The commander's eyes darkened. "I don't understand why Sayuri would do such a thing."

"I'll have to punish her for causing the death of a patient." The older woman turned to me. "I won't have her work here if she causes the death of people. We don't receive as much business as we used to anyway. For her to deepen the gap of trust is unacceptable to me. Sayuri is not allowed to work here anymore, Korudo-sama. I'm excluding her from apprenticeship."

"Before you jump to conclusions, why don't we state the facts." Korudo sounded too calm. "You have told me that Sayuri has been doing well as a nurse's apprentice, yes?"

"Yes, sir."

"Then by all means, why don't you have her learn about dosages? I figure the problem came about because she didn't know the proper amount to give the patient. Perhaps if she learned more about that, something like this wouldn't have happened. Why not have her stand off to the side and watch while procedures go on? One of man's greatest techniques for learning is watching. I refuse to let her lay about in her cell doing nothing but pining over what she did."

"I see, commander," Iyasu said.

"No, you don't see, because if you did you would've taught her all this long ago. You don't have to ostracize her because she made one small mistake."

"But to cause the death of a man—" "Sayuri made an accident, Iyasu. Must you try to argue with me? Sayuri will stay as an apprentice nurse and that's final!" Korudo interrupted, jaw clenched.

"All right, Korudo sir. I apologize for speaking against you," Iyasu said, not wanting to argue with him anymore. At this a smile came into Korudo's face.

"Good. Now Sayuri, if you'll come with me." Then he turned to the old woman. "Don't worry about punishment. I have that all sorted out for her." He began to take me out the clinic, Iyasu watching us go.

"I'm very disappointed in you, Sayuri. I expected better of you. Did you kill that man just to get taken out from apprenticeship?"

"No, Korudo. I had no part in this."

"First you'll address me as "Commander", understand? Second, if you weren't involved, then why did the man describe the nurse who took care of him as a long-haired woman with a pale complexion. Have you ever looked in a mirror? The description fits you perfect."

I refused to respond, keeping my jaw shut.

"Since this dreadful thing happened, I'm afraid your punishment won't feel pleasant." Korudo shook his head, as if in pity. "You did this to yourself."

He took me out to the village square where I saw Akio watching us, his expression stoic. I tried to flash him a glance but Korudo knocked me to the concrete, a smile now on his lips.

"Remember this?" he asked, drawing a long black whip from his belt, "because I do. It's been a while since this happened to you."

Later, as I lay in bed, my stomach and legs burning in pain, I heard the familiar tap-tap sound of Seishin outside my cell door. I turned to look at her and said in a hoarse voice, "I can't move, Seishin-chan. Korudo whipped my legs to the point where it hurts to even adjust myself on the bed."

"Why'd he do that to you?" she asked, angered.

"A man died a few days ago due to a ginseng overdose and I'm the suspected culprit."

"That's ridiculous." The girl let out a snort. "You wouldn't kill anyone even if you had the chance. What evidence do they have anyway?"

"People said that they described a long-haired woman with a sallow complexion as the man's nurse before he died. It seems to fit my description."

"So what happened? Did they kick you out of nursing."

"No, Korudo told the head nurse to keep me there and have me stand off to the side and watch procedures."

"Look Sayuri, you have to stop this now. You can't stick around here until you're a saggy old woman waiting to get freed. You have to escape now. It's okay if you have to repeat the past again."

"I wish I could escape, Seishin. I do . . ." A thought occurred to me in that moment of my next escape, interrupting me. I fell silent as a plan spread its roots in my head.

"Sayuri?" Seishin called after a moment, worry in her voice. I snapped from my thoughts and tried to stand.

"I've just thought of something right now, Seishin. Something that may help me."

"What is it?"

"I'll show you tomorrow night," I said and left it at that.

The next day, the somber atmosphere in the nursing clinic wafted all about as I watched Rin and Hageshi create poultices. Every once and a while they'd send me glares and tell me to leave their sight if they noticed me. I wandered about the clinic from the hallways to the Courtyard and back again. Hisoka and I stopped to chat if our paths crossed, but nothing eventful happened.

As I waited in the Main room for Korudo to come take me back to my cell, Iyasu entered and beckoned for me to come over to her.

"Sayuri, I must speak with you. It won't take long."

I nodded and followed behind her as we headed through the hallway to her room. The smell of incense blasted me as she closed her door.

"Look Sayuri, I understand you've done a fatal mistake. It happens sometimes. I feel reluctant to ostracize you because, as I've said in the beginning, I need more nurses to cover the clinic. I have twelve nurses and I think you've seen four of them in the time you apprenticed for me. Since Korudo took over Kagayaki I've had my hands full with caring for the slaves he or the other men abused, and the regular woes of the people. In order to keep us going, we need money. With the way things have planned out, I fear we might receive a financial shutout if no other patients come here."

"Iyasu-sama, I swear to the gods above that I didn't commit that crime. I haven't treated any patients on my own and I don't even know what to use ginseng for if a patient needs it."

"I understand Sayuri. You need not lie to me or the Jaakuna anymore."

"You don't understand! I haven't done a thing—" "—Sayuri, you will not argue with me on this topic. You will write a formal letter of apology to the family of the man and you will accompany them as they head to the man's funeral. It's the right thing to do and I'm sure you agree with me. You'll go, right?"

"Yes, ma'am." I bowed my head, knowing that I couldn't reason with her or anyone else anymore. Iyasu's features softened from the anger and a sympathetic smile now tugged her lips.

"I know how hard this feels. A horrible deed happened and you have to correct the wrongs the gods feel towards you. Now go Sayuri. Korudo has arrived to take you back to your cell."

As I left the room, incense still clung to my skin and clothes like grime. Anger whistled through me. I felt sick of accusations against me. I wondered how the plan that came to me last night would help me escape. I knew I had no allies outside of Kagayaki except for Seishin and . . .

I heard a small crash sound from down the hall, making me flinch. I raced to find the source, my ratty shoes slapping on the tatami mats. One door stood open and I burst into the room to see Hisoka cowering in a corner, Hageshi and Rin standing over her. There, a foot away, a strip of black hair lay on the floor. A strip of Hisoka's hair.

"Our apprentice did fine until you intervened," Hageshi said in a hiss. "Now she's just as corrupted as you!"

"Don't you ever learn from your mistakes?" Rin asked, raising her stained hand to strike Hisoka. "You'll never earn your name if you keep this up."

"Iyasu should ostracize you instead of our apprentice, Nameless."

"Stop!" I said, making the three women look at me. "Stop bullying her!"

"Apprentice, I think it would do you good to stay out of this," Rin said.

"You see Nameless? You corrupted her!" Hageshi grabbed Hisoka's hair.

"Hageshi and Rin! Stop harassing Hisoka and leave her alone! You've done this for far too long and I'm sick of it! You want Iyasu-sama to see this?!" I grabbed Hageshi's hand and wrenched Hisoka's hair from it.

"Don't worry Sayuri. I saw everything. You may leave," came Iyasu's calm voice. "I'll sort this out now."

I looked back at Hisoka and she flashed me a grateful smile with a small bow. Hageshi and Rin watched Iyasu come closer, nervous expressions on their faces.

"I won't stand for discrimination in my clinic. Perhaps that's another reason why people won't come here. They sense the dark spirits lingering in you women. Do you want us to lose money?" the old woman asked.

"No Iyasu-sama." Both women bowed low, guilty looks on their faces. This cued me to leave. I felt so tired of Iyasu,

Rin, and Hageshi and, as I left the room, I knew what I would do. I remembered seeing sheets of paper on one of the drawers in the Medical room and I headed there, feeling a tingle shoot through my veins.

Upon finding the paper and an ink pen, I snatched and hid them under my kimono's pocket. Korudo soon came into the room, his expression annoyed.

"Come on, Sayuri. I've waited at least ten minutes for you. What have you been doing? Now let's go." He grabbed my wrist and tugged me with him. "Don't think to cause anymore trouble. I won't let that go by so easy."

The banners flapped in the growing night sky, straining against the hooks that held them. The breeze felt pleasant after the tireless heat every afternoon. In the distance, I could see the hesitant outlines of people as they peered out their doors.

Once Korudo locked me into my cell and left, a mean smile on his face, I took out the paper and pen, beginning to write, the words burning in my head. Nothing else deterred me from my writing. My calligraphy looked horrendous, but it would have to do. As I finished and placed the pen down on the bed I read the letter to myself.

When Seishin came to talk to me later on in the night, I walked over to her. "I want you to take this."

"What's this?"

"A letter. I want you to take this to the village of Han'ei right now and give it to a man named Kotei. He must see this."

"What if I get caught on the way?" Seishin looked apprehensive.

"Seishin, you escaped Kagayaki two weeks ago and the Jaakuna still haven't found you. I don't think they'll search for you in the dead of night anyway."

"I don't know, Sayuri-san . . . I mean, you know I risk getting caught each time I come here to visit you."

"This'll ensure my freedom and yours. Please, you must do this for me."

"All right, I'll do it. Just for you," she assented and I handed her the folded paper.

"Thanks for helping me, Seishin-chan. You don't know what our friendship means to me."

"I told you I never leave a friend behind, Sayuri. I never lie," Seishin smiled and prepared to leave.

"Here, you need this," I said and handed her the map. She nodded and we bid each other goodbye. I watched her retreating form and hoped she'd reach Han'ei without trouble.

After the incident with Hisoka, my relationship with Rin and Hageshi worsened the next day. Both women now tormented me instead of Hisoka, ordering me to do tough tasks and degrading me.

"Look, here comes Hisoka's clone," Rin said as I entered the Medical room after my grueling chore. "Did you mess up the laundry today?"

"I tried my best to make it perfect," I said, giving her the batch of nursing aprons and towels. In traditional standards, women had to wash the aprons and towels in a different way from the other types of linen and cloth. In short, it took me a long time to get everything done and to Rin without dirtying them again. Hisoka told me that getting a cleaned nurse garment dirty again spelled bad luck.

"Sure you did," she said with a forced lilt as she wrenched the towels and aprons from my hand.

I tried asking Hisoka what happened to Hageshi and Rin after I left the other day. She looked like a bundle of energy and a smile lingered on her face as she saw me.

"Sayuri-sama, if you hadn't yelled for Hageshi and Rin to stop lat night, Iyasu-sama wouldn't have ever found out what those women do to me," she said before I opened my mouth.

"Why? What happened?"

"Iyasu took me aside after dismissing Hageshi and Rin and told me to explain to her what went on before. I told her about how they mistreated me for all those five years and how each night they come into my room to rip my hair from my scalp."

I couldn't help but feel relieved for her. "Did you tell Iyasu-sama about Rin's hand stain?"

"Nope." Hisoka smiled with a mischievous look. "I decided to let her figure that out on her own. Anyway, Iyasu and I kept talking and then she told me that I didn't have to work here anymore. 'If they have mistreated you, then I see no reason why you should linger here anymore, Hisoka.' That's what she said to me."

"She called you Hisoka?" I felt shocked. "That's my name for you."

"I know. Perhaps she saw you and me talking one day and she heard the name." Hisoka shrugged.

"At least you won't have to work here anymore, right?"

"Yeah. I feel so grateful to escape this life after so long. However, this wouldn't have happened if you never came here. You've helped me when no one else could. So thank you, Sayuri-sama. My friend." She surprised me further by giving me an embrace. I closed my eyes and couldn't stop the rush of emotion in me. The touch unlocked something in me, something I've hidden for so long.

As we drew back Hisoka cocked her head. "Sayuri? Why are you crying?"

"It's just that . . . no one's ever hugged me like that in so long." I wiped away the tears on my face, knowing I had just broken one of the mantra's I set for myself. However, I didn't care anymore. I felt more human than I ever did.

"Oh . . ." Hisoka's expression showed pity. "I'm sorry for making you cry." She gave me another embrace.

"No problem," I said, sniffling. "Don't blame yourself, Hisoka."

"I leave tomorrow . . . I still can't believe it," she said after I took a moment to clear my tears. I didn't want to show Rin, Hageshi, or Iyasu I had cried for any reason.

"You deserve it, Hisoka. You've struggled for a long time to fit in here."

"I know and now it all paid off for me. I won't have to worry about my hair getting pulled out anymore, that's for sure."

"Do you live here in Kagayaki, Hisoka?"

"No. I live farther north, up in the village of Zokusuru. I came south to look for a job and stick with it. I guess I'll have to start all over again up there." A light came on in her eyes and she looked at me, as if remembering something. "By the way, Sayuri. Did you speak to Iyasu about letting me go?"

"No, I guess she thought about it and decided to do the right thing."

Hisoka looked at me with a small smile and I knew she figured I had covered myself up just now. However she didn't reply to this and we spoke some more before Hageshi called for me.

"Good luck with them today, Sayuri-sama," Hisoka said.

"I'll need all the luck I can get. They've tormented me all day today."

"Exactly how I feel. Just multiply that by five years and you have me."

As I headed to the Main room to wait for Korudo Iyasu came over to me.

"Have you wrote the letter of condolence to that family last night?" she asked and I nodded, feeling terrible about lying.

"Yes, ma'am. I wrote the letter last night and gave it to them this morning before I came here. Korudo let me go there. The family forgave me for my mistake."

"Good. I feel glad you have repented yourself, Sayuri," she said just as Korudo came through the beads, looking bloated with egotism.

"Commander." Iyasu turned to Korudo. "The gods have accepted Sayuri once more. She has admitted her wrong doing and told me the family forgave her."

"What?" Korudo looked at me. "She did?"

"Yes, she told me now about it when I asked her. Don't you feel pleased?"

"Very. Now come along Sayuri. Time for your confinement."

Iyasu looked at him in bemusement. "If I may ask, Korudo sir, why must you confine her? She did well by letting the family forgive her."

"She's my slave, Iyasu. She must live in a cell or else she'll try to escape."

"Why haven't you told me this?" A disapproving look came into the older woman's eyes.

"Why do I have to? You shouldn't care about where your apprentices come from, Iyasu."

"Commander, I do not approve of slaves taking over my nursing clinic when another adequate person could use the job."

Her words stung. Korudo glowered at her.

"You should feel grateful I sent her here to work for you. Before that incident with the man she made you earn lots of money. We all know how you and your other nurses love those coins and paper bills."

The older woman fell silent.

"Come on, Sayuri. Let's leave this hag alone." Korudo grinned and tugged me along out the clinic.

"That was uncalled for, Korudo," I said. "Why'd you have to antagonize her like that?"

"What right does she have in questioning me? None. Even you break that rule as well, Sayuri."

"Don't involve me in this."

"I might as well, since you work for Iyasu and you help her earn money. Although," he said, "I suppose that won't happen now since you killed the man."

"Look Korudo. Who said the nurse who treated that man looked like me?" I asked, wanting to get the question out in the air.

"I did!" Korudo let out a cackle. At my confused expression he laughed harder. His body still heaved with chuckles long after he locked me in my cell and started walking out the building.

I lay on my bed, the loneliness hitting me hard as the night continued. I couldn't sleep, couldn't stop worrying about Seishin.

I clenched my fists as thoughts of everything I've done swirled in my head and I saw my future right in my grasp. I wept, chest heaving in a mute silence.

When Korudo came into the slave building to take me out to the clinic I felt liberated. The late summer sun felt glorious on my skin as we walked, a faint breeze stirring up the heat. Korudo walked, a scowl on his face. He stopped as we neared the clinic and, startled, I almost tripped.

"You always have to cause a problem, don't you," he said. "Not even Iyasu wants you anymore because of what I said about you."

"So why did you? Slip of the tongue, maybe?"

"I suppose I hadn't kept my guard up enough. My mistake there." Korudo sniffed in disdain. "Why must things always come up and destroy my plans?"

"The gods don't approve of you and your Jaakuna who kill men and enslave them for profit."

"The gods are fools, Sayuri. I believe fools cower and believe in beings who appear in folktales."

His blasphemous words made my breath catch.

"If the gods do exist, then why haven't they shown themselves? They must feel scared of mortals. What cowards." Korudo took a breath. "Now what should I have you do if Iyasu won't have you?"

"Could you let me say goodbye to the nurses?" I asked, wanting to see Hisoka off before she left.

"Why? They don't want you there . . ." His words were interrupted by Iyasu's voice: "Korudo! Where's my apprentice?"

I felt confused as his jaw clenched. The older woman came out the beads and saw us standing there.

"Commander, sir, what're you doing? Bring Sayuri in here."

He looked as though he contemplated refusing her, however he gave a huff and shoved me to Iyasu.

"What changed your view, Iyasu? Your endless greed perhaps? Then take the slave and have your business rot. See what I care." He stomped off, leaving Iyasu to shake her head at his retreating back.

"He acts like such a child at times, Sayuri. Does he give you a hard time as well?"

"He does, Iyasu-sama. He has for a long time."

"Korudo understands that part of our funds go to him. So if we have a few nurses short, he won't have money. Then again, neither will we."

"We don't receive patients anymore since the man died."

"True, but you must understand that Korudo depends on us as well to keep his Jaakuna alive and well. We may not receive regular patients, but the Jaakuna men still come." She led me into the clinic.

"Don't you hate the Jaakuna for taking over Kagayaki?" I asked.

"At times, yes. But they done anything drastic to make me loathe them. Though I wonder about the other villagers and why they never come out as they used to do."

"The villagers live in fear, Iyasu-sama," I said as we headed through the beads. "They fear Korudo will destroy this village just as he did with the others."

"How ridiculous." Iyasu paused in her steps as Hisoka entered the room with a small bow.

"Iyasu and Sayuri-sama," she said, giving me a smile.

"Have you packed everything?" Iyasu asked. "I don't want to find anything of yours and have to go looking for you."

"Don't worry. I made sure to make it seem as though I never worked here."

"Good luck out there, Hisoka," I said and my friend came over to embrace me one last time.

"I'll need all the luck I can," she said and Iyasu nodded, leaving to head to the Medical room. I didn't follow her and soon Hisoka and I stood alone.

"I heard the news last night? Sayuri, you're a slave?"

"Yes." I felt guilty all of a sudden. "Korudo captured me weeks ago and keeps me in a cell. He lets me out for this job."

"You poor thing," Hisoka said, shaking her head. "We live in a cruel world, Sayuri."

"We do and only good people can survive in it."

As we said our farewells I felt emotional once again. This time I kept a firm grip on myself and while Hisoka went through the beads I felt peace wash over me. I had achieved another goal.

Hageshi and Rin looked irritated when I came into the Medical room. An older nurse stood by, barking orders at them.

"Since Nameless left you two have to work extra hard to make Iyasu-sama happy," she said and Hageshi grumbled to herself.

The nurse noticed me and sent me a glare. "Oh look, it's the apprentice who made us lose our influx of money. How do you feel about that? Should we call you our next 'Nameless'?"

"This apprentice won't have to face Nameless's corruption anymore, now that she left the clinic. Can you believe Iyasu let her go after five long years? I can't." Rin looked steamed with anger.

"What I don't understand is why Nameless hadn't left a long time ago. You and Hageshi tormented her to the point where even I'd lose control if it was me, and that's saying a lot."

"She probably thought she looked better in Iyasu's eyes if she stayed," Hageshi said.

"Who knows? She's gone now and that's that," the other nurse said, huffing.

"What's going on here? Get to work instead of chatting like peasants," Iyasu said as she entered the Medical room.

"Yes, Iyasu-sama," all the women chorused.

"You, apprentice, come here," the nurse said as Rin and Hageshi went to create a fresh poultice. "What good can you do besides killing people?"

"I can assist with cleaning and creating salves," I said, speaking the truth.

"Right. Go clean these, then," she said and thrust towels at me. I rolled my eyes as she turned her back to bark another order at Rin. Nothing seemed to have changed since Hisoka left and I decided that nothing would.

While I cleaned the towels with the washboard I wished for company. Usually when I did these chores Hisoka hung around and talked to me. Now since she left I'd have to get used to silence.

I looked outside the open window and saw an overcast sky growing dark. Tension rose and as it did so, the hair on the back of my neck rose as well. I knew something bad would happen. Very soon.

Akio
Late August 1949

Akio stalked through Kagayaki, many questions brewing in his head. He glanced at the houses that stood vacant, the window curtains drawn and the doors locked. It made him wonder why the village people didn't brave walking outside in Kagayaki. He assumed Korudo had threatened the people not to interfere with his plans.

He thought about the words the runaway slave, Seishin, said to him a week before and he rubbed his eyes, feeling fatigued of everything. *Had she told me the truth?* he thought. As he walked he came across Korudo, looking dark with anger.

"Brother." He acknowledged Akio.

"Korudo, what ails you? You look enraged."

"Sayuri causes me more trouble each and everyday. Why must she act so difficult?"

"Maybe because you don't act strict enough with her. You do give her a certain liberty by letting her out of her cell to work."

"Why me though, Akio? Why me? I have to stay on top of everything and now I have to worry about Sayuri as well."

"And why would that affect you?" Akio arched an eyebrow. "Do you have a crush on her?"

"Crushes are for little girls, brother. You aren't helping."

"You need my help? Korudo the most hated man in all of Nagasaki had to stoop down low to ask for assistance?" Akio couldn't help chuckling.

"Don't mock me. You know father couldn't do what I've done in a span of two and a half years," Korudo said with a glare.

"Of course," Akio said, still chuckling, "of course." He wondered about why Korudo even bothered with Sayuri anymore. He figured by this time his brother would have grown tired of looking after a slave. Then again, he wondered why Korudo even wanted to capture her again for anyway.

"Korudo, if you feel sick of dealing with Sayuri, then why in the gods' name did you enslave her again? For ego?"

"For her to have escaped the old Jaakuna village as she had . . . No way would I let her go off Scott free. That's deplorable for me as the leader of the Jaakuna."

"Definitely for ego."

"This has nothing to do with my ego," Korudo said, although Akio knew his brother had just lied. The look in the his eyes betrayed him.

"Whatever you say." Akio inclined his head, then he gestured to the houses. "Why don't the people ever leave their houses? At least in the old village the people did come out into the sunlight. What changed here?"

Korudo smirked. "I threatened the villagers that if they got in my way, my men would kill them. The Kagayakians are such cowards, right? I sometimes wake in the morning and forget people still live in my village." He chuckled.

"Why would the villagers get in your way anyway? You have men deployed with physical hand weapons. They have nothing for their defense."

"That's just my point. I'm just making sure they won't try anything."

"You're insane. Insane." Akio shook his head.

"Sayuri said the same thing to me." Korudo's jaw set. "Why must everything remind me of her?"

"Because you have an obsession about her? You hover around Sayuri like a moth to a streetlamp. You always get in her way and change everything around so she doesn't raise a hand to you in rebellion. You want control over her, right? That's why you changed her job. Don't try to cover yourself this time, brother. It won't work."

"I have a brother who knows me better than I know myself." Korudo sighed.

Akio looked at his sibling, thinking about how he became such a hated man in the whole country. He compared himself to his vindictive and ambitious brother and wondered where he fit in. Akio never felt violent or determined to do much of anything and his mother was the same way. Yuki and Korudo had the same dream, to have their names recognized throughout the land, which led them to resort to violence and power.

Once more he thought back to what the runaway slave girl had said to him. His stomach began to hurt as he thought of how he treated Sayuri since he saw her again. Before the emotion flared to his face, Akio steeled his jaw and gazed at his brother. Korudo flashed a look at the nursing clinic and a small expression grew on his face for a moment. It looked like longing.

Akio remembered—as he saw this—seeing in Korudo's room a small slip of paper with writing on it. A poem. One that stated about the touch of a lily. It made him wonder what caused his brother to write those words.

Just as he readied himself to bring up the subject a loud crack sounded, making both men jump.

"What was that?" Korudo asked, looking about him. Akio shrugged.

"Maybe one of the slaves escaped."

"Impossible! All the slaves wouldn't have the power to make such a loud racket."

Another crash sounded and Akio ducked as he saw what looked like a bullet flying overhead.

Korudo blinked as another bullet whizzed past him. There, just entering the village, men marched, carrying rifles and wearing green military outfits. A fire soon started from off the side as the men shot bullets at a gas can. The flames licked the air.

"What now?" Korudo said in a dark tone as he stormed off to the men, unsheathing his sword, leaving Akio alone to decide what to do.

Sayuri
Late August 1949

A boom echo through the clinic from outside the village. From the window I saw a flash of orange and hurried over, seeing flames running through Kagayaki.

"What happened?" Rin asked, her eyes growing wide.

"Evacuate the clinic!" Iyasu yelled and Hageshi, Rin, the other nurses, and I followed her order. A blaze met our eyes as we exited through the beads. Flames licked all about and men in military outfits strutted about, shooting at the Jaakuna men. It confused me until I realized that these men may be from Kotei's army coming to help. Relief spawned everywhere in my body and I felt like crying from happiness.

Until a crack sounded as a bullet sailed into the nursing clinic, leaving a gaping hole.

"Everyone head to safety!" Iyasu said over the roar that started. "Don't worry about the clinic!" I followed behind Rin as we dashed through the village, bullets flying about us. The military men stood in view no matter where we looked. The sky grew darker, thunder rumbled, and heat lightning flashed.

As we neared an alleyway I felt hope that we'd get to shelter away from the madness. Rin turned to look at me just as hands grabbed my arms and dragged me. I bit my tongue and let loose a yelp, writhing to escape. Rin stood there, a helpless look on her expression and, out of the corner of my eye, I saw Korudo holding my arms.

"You had something to do with this!" He pulled me up by my hair. "You and your little slave friend planned this all along, didn't you?!"

His grip tightened and I whimpered, my eyes glazing over with tears from the pain.

"To think you could shame us Jaakuna again . . . you have nerve, Sayuri. You have nerve." His voice dropped to a dangerous tone.

Anger blazed in me. I gathered up my strength and spoke, "You have nerve, Korudo. You corrupted Akio and you have made our life miserable. You killed Yowai and his brother without any remorse. You destroyed villages across the whole span of Nagasaki just for your own pleasure. You're a cold, callous man, and I hope Kotei's army rips your Jaakuna to shreds tonight. You deserve it!"

"I deserve it?" Korudo barked out a mad laugh. "Since when did you receive this bravado? Before you acted like a sniveling, pitiful woman. Even two years ago you acted the same way." His eyes narrowed. "I get it. It's all just a ruse. A last resort to make me pity and trust you."

"Yes, that's right," I said. "All along I tricked you into thinking I became subdued. That facade no longer exists. I did have something to do with this, and now, you can't do anything to stop what I started.

"When my Jaakuna murder those men tonight I'll do with you as I please. You'll never see Akio or your little slave friend ever again, Sayuri."

The Jaakuna leader didn't flinch as a bullet ripped past us, hitting into a nearby wooden beam. Screams sounded as the people of Kagayaki flooded from their homes and fled from the onslaught.

"You want to know why I made your life miserable? I spoke to Akio two weeks ago and forced all the information out of him about you. He told me everything, from when he met you, to when you left him all alone to fend for himself. I found myself falling in love with you, Sayuri, but after hearing what you did to my brother I turned right around. I wanted you to feel the same pain you exacted onto Akio."

I said nothing, listening to Korudo as the truth spilled out into the open.

"You know that rumor about how you killed a man through a ginseng overdose? Well, that never happened. You hadn't treated a man with ginseng and killed him by accident. I made it all up, Sayuri," he said. My mouth gaped and I stared at him, in stone cold shock.

"And the real man who died? A slave. He displeased me and, in doing so, I killed him. The man gave me the perfect idea to get back at you for my brother. I created the rumor and spread it, tarnishing the trust the nurses and other people in Kagayaki had for you. Sure it cost me money, but the payoff of the nurses turning from you was a bigger accomplishment for me."

Anger settled in a haze in me and I gritted my teeth and balled my fist, ready to punch Korudo in the face. He laughed and pulled harder on my hair.

"Your road of causing me trouble ends now, Sayuri. You may have thought yourself clever by making these men come here today without my notice, but that doesn't change anything."

Two bullets sailed overhead as the fires raging the village entered my line of vision, hungry for sustenance to keep them going. Three of Kotei's men stepped over to us, guns cocked and loaded, ready to fire at will.

"If you try your hand at shooting me this woman will die," Korudo said with a cackle. "I bet you wouldn't want to hurt Sayuri here, so why don't you throw your weapons down now."

The men looked at each other, seeing the fire blazing closer and closer to me and Korudo. I willed them in my head not to follow his order. After a long moment they dropped their weapons to the ground and stood, looking at Korudo in unease.

"Good. Very good. I feel pleased you listened to me," he said, his tone silky. I watched as his expression flattened in an instant as he threw me into the nearby flames before I could react.

"Haha! Try saving her now you cowards!" I heard Korudo say. The pain of the flames ate at me and I screamed, feeling immense searing agony. All I could see behind my closed eyelids was red, blue, orange, and yellow as I writhed, trying to escape the flames. Everything hurt.

"This is for my brother, Sayuri! While you lay there and die I want you to regret the very moment you hurt him!" Korudo laughed. "Say hello to that coward Yowai for me when you see him."

I felt nothing but a burning pain and a release called to me as the pain lingered. Everything slowed. As I opened my eyes one last time I saw the outline of a tall man with a gun. He cocked it and blasted a bullet right into Korudo's skull. The Jaakuna leader collapsed to the floor without a sound, blood sizzling as it hit the flames.

Thank the gods, I thought as my conscious threatened to fade. Thank the gods . . .

Dear Kotei-sama,

Do you remember me, Sayuri, from when I visited Han'ei last? I need your help now, Kotei sir. The Jaakuna have captured me and stormed Kagayaki in the hopes of acquiring it for their own. They want to enslave all the people in Kagayaki and they don't mean to do so in light terms. As a person who experienced forced slavery, I wish for the unsuspecting Kagayakians not to fall to this fate.

I remembered what you said the last time we spoke about how I could count on you if I needed help. I remembered your kindness and knew you alone could answer my and the other people's plight. Once you get this letter don't reply back but instead come to Kagayaki and I'll see if I can somehow sneak out to speak with you.

Warm Regards,

Sayuri

Korudo
Early September 1949

Everything burned. Korudo opened his eyes to see a wall of darkness. He tried to squirm, to escape it at all costs, but he realized he couldn't move. It startled him to know a man like himself could balk at the inevitability of death. His stomach roiled, his body felt rigid, and his sight remained fixated on the darkness. Never did anything frighten him so about never breathing or seeing a beautiful world of boundless color again. Again and again he tried to move to some extent, to reassure himself that he wasn't in the final stages of life. However, he was and he knew his moment would soon come.

He thought of Sayuri . . . the woman he had combated with for so long. He loved and hated her, the conflicting emotions were what made him grow insane. To see her twitching in the flames unlocked some disgust in him at himself. When he felt the bullet sink into his brain from one of the army men, Korudo knew he deserved it. Now though, he felt endless fear for what would come to him next. He knew not if a second reality or world existed for him.

The Jaakuna commander couldn't hear anything, but he could still sense. Korudo sensed his body still lay on the burning ground, blood petering out it. As he came to terms, he thought about life and how an end happens. Sayuri brought him to his downfall and he had let it happen. Now Korudo knew why his brother loved her: she was righteous and just in the face of danger, thinking of others before herself. Sayuri was pure. Those qualities had always drawn Akio to them.

Korudo's vision returned to him, but no other emotion of life stirred in him except for bleakness and sorrow. For in his eyes, Kagayaki burned, a sheer mass of flames and soot surrounded him. His Jaakuna lay dead all around the flames and two men strode through the flames and picked up the limp body of Sayuri. Scent came back to him next, of sweet peas, as the men took her with them. And—through the gaps of the blazing fires—a true radiance became born again as the Jaakuna leader gave his last breath.

===

. . . .

Early September 1949

===

Blackness enveloped me and I felt certain I had died, my essence traveling up to the heavens. I couldn't hear, see, or feel anything. It all felt strange to me. I wondered if this happened to my mother, Yowai, and my other family members before they died as well. Silence abounded, as did the shadowy blackness.

I hoped Akio had gotten out of Kagayaki and I hoped Kotei could help restore those people back to order. I wondered about Seishin and whether she came back to Kagayaki alongside Kotei or if she went on the move to find a new home.

A small rush sounded and my conscious faded again. When I regained it again voices pierced through the haze and convoluted darkness. To me, they sounded like nurses . . .

". . . not much longer . . . heart rate too slow."

". . . needs more oxygen . . . more glucose."

Then, a different voice, more masculine sounding than the rest: "Sayuri . . . . don't die on me . . ."

===

Everything slammed back into me and I jerked awake in a bed with a gasp. The sights, scents, touch, and sounds overwhelmed me as I glanced about. People sat, nurses spooning food into their mouths and doctors administering injections to others.

"I'm . . . alive," I said, unable to believe it. How could I have survived? I looked down at my skin and yelped at what I saw. My skin looked like the color of a dark red apple and some parts peeled back, revealing bleeding scabs and raw skin. My fingernails looked charred and some didn't exist.

I felt my body shake and a nurse who noticed me awake hurried over and put a hand on me.

"Everything's all right. You're safe now. No need to look so worried," she said, her voice familiar.

"Hisoka?" I looked at her, my voice coming out as a hoarse whisper. "Is that you?"

"Sayuri, the gods have truly blessed you." Hisoka embraced me and I didn't mind as my skin screamed at the slight contact and pressure. "Everyone here felt convinced you wouldn't survive. When you first arrived you looked like you had a bomb dropped on you, all shriveled and small. I held faith, knowing you'd survive. If you can tolerate the torture of Rin and Hageshi, you can live through anything."

It hurt to move my face and my amused snort sounded half-hearted and choked. Hisoka stepped back and checked the IV needle in my arm.

"You work here now?" I asked, hating how my voice croaked.

"Yes, I work here in the Springheart Hospital of Nagasaki city."

"Nagasaki city?"

"Yes." Hisoka took my hand with care into her own. "We're in Nagasaki city. Two men carried you in here all the way from Kagayaki and urged for us to take you in and save you."

I reached to scratch an itch on my scalp and I paused, my eyes growing wide. I had no hair. It must have all burned off in the flames.

"Sayuri, would you like anything to drink or eat?" Hisoka asked and I shook my head, feeling sick. Bile rose in my throat and I lay back down, trying to hold it back and swallow it.

"Do you want some time alone or anything at all?" Hisoka had a look of pity on her face.

"Just talk to me . . . I feel lonely."

"I can chat for just a bit, Sayuri. Then I have to return to my other patients," she said, looking guilty.

"All right." I felt grateful to have some time to talk to my friend. "How long had I lay unconscious here?"

"For a month. During the whole time your body just lay as if in a comatose. You didn't blink or move. You breathed."

"What happened to those two men who carried me here? Did they leave?"

"In fact, they haven't. They come by every day just to see if you wake up and let them know you're fine. Those men came here so many times to the point where my fellow nurses and doctors feel sick of them." Hisoka laughed. "There are some good people out there in the world, Sayuri."

I was touched by the kindness of these two men. It made me wonder how they knew me.

"What about you? How did you get this job as a nurse here?"

"I traveled to my hometown and along the way I met a representative of this hospital. She noticed I had my nursing outfit in hand and asked me if I would like to work at the hospital. 'They needed fresh hands', she told me. I said yes, and when I realized it was *this* hospital, my jaw dropped. The most prestigious hospital in Nagasaki and I . . . have a job here. I still can't believe it."

"Good for you, Hisoka. You earned it," I said and she nodded.

"I suppose so. Everyone here acts supportive for me and it feels like such a change from the clinic back in Kagayaki, you know?"

"I know what you mean."

We chatted for a few more minutes until a doctor came over and asked me if I felt ready to receive visitors. I nodded and sank into the hospital bed, feeling the bristles of my burnt hair against my head. Again and again I looked at my fingernails and my peeling skin, my gaze lingering on them. My body had lacerations, burns, scars, and persistent whip lashes on its skin. Was it really my body and not just a swap?

As I closed my eyes I heard shuffling steps and I looked to see a tall man come over to me. At the sight of me, he cringed and his eyes pooled with sadness.

"Sayuri . . . how do you feel?" he asked, coming closer. I inhaled a long breath and shook my head, recognizing him.

"Terrible, Kotei-sama" I said and Han'ei's most loved man sighed and put a soft hand on my shoulder.

"If I and another man hadn't come get you out the flames when we did, you would have burnt to ashes."

My gaze once again flitted to my burns and nails. I didn't say a word.

"I've come here over and over, waiting for you to wake, just so I could thank you for informing me of the Jaakuna's conquest."

I looked at him, feeling mute.

"If you hadn't, I fear Kagayaki would have turned to them. I came just on time and my army killed those treacherous men. So thank you."

"No, thank you, for listening to me and saving my life along with the other people's lives." I gave him a solemn nod and a smile crossed his face.

"Anything to ensure the well-being of all people, Sayuri. That's what I do."

"I know," I said. "You're a good man, Kotei-sama."

We paused as another man walked over to us and stood by my bed, looking at me: Akio. Relief spawned in his eyes and I felt as though I hadn't seen him in years. He looked more mature and confident. I felt surprised not to see him wearing his Jaakuna attire.

"I'll leave you both to chat. I must return to Han'ei before my people believe something has befallen me," Kotei said, bowing, and I inclined my head, wincing somewhat at the pain.

"Thank you for waiting for me to wake," I said to him as he walked to the door. "I feel grateful to have heard some good news."

"The pleasure's mine, Sayuri." He flashed me another smile before heading out, leaving me alone with Akio.

"What happened after Kotei arrived and killed Korudo?" I asked him, clearing my throat of phlegm.

"I heard the sound of a gunshot and came over to see my brother dead on the floor and four army men pointing guns at me. I took off my armor and told I had no desire to kill them. I met Kotei then and we hoisted you from the flames. In the spur of the moment I remembered that Nagasaki city was close by Kagayaki and we hurried you there, heading to this hospital, hoping they'd take you. The Jaakuna who survived, Kotei's men captured. With Korudo dead they have no leader and they surrendered without hesitation."

"Why did you decide to switch sides again?"

"I switched because I couldn't stand it. I felt tired of concealing myself behind armor and a cold expression. It isn't who I am and it never will. I couldn't stand acting like someone different. It sickened me."

"Akio . . ." I looked at him, seeing a strange expression on his face.

"Plus I saw you burning in the flames, Sayuri. I couldn't stand there and watch you die. It would ruin me . . ."

"So what will you do now, Akio?" I asked feeling emotion struggle inside me. "Go looking for any of your other family members?"

"I made this decision as you lay unconscious. I'm going to stick by you and protect you. As I should have done in the beginning. I won't make the same mistake again."

Tears exited my eyes and I let them, feeling my heart begin to beat. Akio looked at me and I opened my arms. He came into them and embraced me with a gentle touch as I cried. We forgave me with this gesture as it lasted. Akio understood and knew my pain over leaving him behind. Both of us had changed just for each other, but now we could go back to how we remembered each other.

"Thank you, Akio," I said as we drew apart, my voice cracking. "Now I feel complete."

That night, as I lay in the hospital bed in pain I heard quiet footsteps come to my bed. A girl, and one I recognized.

"Seishin-chan!" I said and she grinned wide at my voice. Then she noticed my missing hair and burned skin and her smile faded.

"By the gods, Sayuri-sama. What happened to you?"

"I've had all my sins and doubts burned from me, Seishin. I feel reborn." I looked at the clock and noticed the time.

"Yep, I decided to come visit you after I saw Kotei walking back to Han'ei. I asked him where you were and he directed me to here. If you haven't noticed already," a smile returned to her face, "I'm visiting you at the exact time we used to meet when Korudo enslaved you."

"You're crazy, Seishin." I shook my head. "The doctors and nurses let you in at this hour?"

"Of course," she said. "I just told them I knew you and wanted to see you. I didn't think you'd look this bad."

"I know, I look horrible," I said and gave a laugh for the first time. It sounded raw and soft, like a child's voice when he or she begins to speak for the first time, and Seishin gave me a knowing smile.

"What?" I asked and she shook her head.

"Look in the mirror."

I did and I flinched at what I saw. It wasn't my appearance that struck me, the way my pale and bare face stared back at me. It was my mouth. It had turned upwards in the corners, just like a smile.

Even without any hair, eyelashes, or eyebrows, and even though my face looked like the moon to me, I felt drawn to stare, watching my smile grow on its own. Feelings washed over me, ones that I associated and knew they were from happiness.

I remembered what Seishin had said about me looking better with a smile on my face. I looked at the mirror and as the girl's words swirled in my head I knew the truth: Yes, I do look better with a smile on my face.

That night, when I fell asleep, Korudo and Kotei disappeared from my dream, leaving me with a wash of peace.

Sayuri
March 11th, 2011

The morning felt cool as I awoke, the sunlight streaming through the window. I looked over at my husband, seeing him still sleeping.

"Time to get up, dear," I said and he groaned, sitting up with a half-hearted stretch.

"Already? Feels like I just closed my eyes a mere second ago," he asked, groaning.

"I know, Akio. It all flies by too fast for our old selves."

"Sixty-six and sixty-seven years isn't that old yet, Sayuri." He made a soft amused snort. "You overestimate our ages, love."

I smiled and stood after giving him a soft peck on the cheek. My knee cried out as I shuffled to the window to open it and breathe in the air. Birds chirped in the restored trees and cars whipped down the roads, some blasting loud music.

"You have an agenda for breakfast?" Akio asked as he stood as well, reaching for his cane. I smirked as I studied myself in the mirror, seeing a mature women past her prime with permanent burned skin looking at me. I touched my lips, remembering so long ago when my lips lay flat and cold without any trace of a smile.

"I haven't gotten that far yet," I said and turned back to face him. My husband rubbed his cheek and came over to embrace me. "I can still remember what happened forty-five years ago when Kotei destroyed the Jaakuna and helped restore peace."

"Now we have a new life. We don't have to dwell on the past anymore," Akio said as we drew back and headed to the kitchen, me hobbling and him supporting me with a soft grip.

"True."

After breakfast I settled with heading out to the market to buy some needed items while Akio watched T.V. The weather felt warm and I sighed, rolling down the windows as I entered my car. Akio and I, after we married, headed to Yokohama on our honeymoon forty-eight years ago and, realizing how much we loved it there, decided to buy a house. We've lived here for ten years, happy without children. The people in Yokohama always had smiles on their faces and never seemed agitated.

The sun shone as I headed down to the market and parked in the lot. Most of the people there knew me and, as soon as they saw me, they waved me over to their vendors.

"Come buy this today Sayuri-sama!" one said as he beckoned me over.

"No, come buy from me. My food tastes better," another said.

"Buy my products and forget about those two," said another. "Mine have the best quality."

"Everyone, please," I laughed. "I'll have a chance to buy and look through your vendors, don't worry."

They all chuckled with me as I browsed and bought what I needed. The wind whispered through the small tents and clouds passed over the sun, continuing on their path. By the time I left, I had three bags full of fruits, ingredients for recipes, and in a separate bag, I bought myself a black kimono with a gorgeous golden flower design.

As I drove back home I thought about Seishin and Hisoka, making a reminder to call them and catch up with them.

The Pacific Ocean lapped against the shore as I drove over the bridge parallel to it. Mt. Fuji lay in the distance, her snowy peak visible today. It made me wonder if anyone tried to scale her in the past.

"Akio, I'm back from the market," I said as I entered the house. My husband jerked upright on the couch and I came over to him. "I bought some oranges as you asked."

"Good, I need to raise my vitamin C count before I have a deficiency," Akio said and I rolled my eyes.

"Don't feel so paranoid, dear. Your vitamin C count won't drop below average."

"Never hurts to be conscious," he said with a grunt and heaved himself off the couch. "What else did you get from the market? Did the people force you to buy anything?"

A soft laugh came from me as I said, "As always, Akio. You know I can't leave somewhere without buying anything. It doesn't matter if my friends at the market force me or not."

We shared a mischievous look as I emptied the bags onto the counter.

"What's that?" Akio asked as he noticed the kimono in my hand.

"Doesn't it look beautiful?" I opened it and showed him the front, the golden flowers outline shining in the light. "I saw it and just had to get it."

"Such a woman." My husband shook his head with a grin.

"Hey!" I pretend to look offended.

Akio chuckled. I loved the playful banter that went on between us. It made me feel young again, something I wished for as each year passed.

As I went to put the fruits and other food away in the fridge I received a terrible feeling that something would happen later. However, I didn't know what. I waved it off as nothing and headed into the bedroom to put my purse away in the bureau.

As the afternoon sun rolled around I turned on the news and was ready to change the channel after a bit until the weatherman's words stopped me.

"Over the course of the afternoon a massive thunderstorm with moderate winds and pelting rain will enter our atmosphere and linger well until tonight. Make sure to close your windows and stay inside for the day."

I looked outside to see the sun already shying away behind a cloud cover. Akio walked into the room and plopped onto the couch.

"Looks like rain," he said as he looked out the window and I nodded.

"The weatherman just said a thunderstorm would head our way and linger until nighttime."

"A minor annoyance."

The news began to cover events happening in America and I changed the channel. A low rumble sounded and I looked to see massive dark clouds heading to obscure the sun and brightness.

"Better close the windows now," Akio said as we both stood, "so we don't have to deal with a wet floor."

289

"Yes, these tatami mats try my patience when I clean them. They just never let go of any liquid they soak up." I headed to the nearby window and shut it while he went to shut the next one. The thunder boomed again as I headed into the kitchen to get a start on making dinner.

The clock read five forty-two as I boiled water in a pot, taking out the soy sauce and wasabi. As the sharp smells of my cooking rose into the air I heard Akio say from the other room, "Make sure not to put too much wasabi in tonight's dinner."

"I know," I said back with a small snort and shook my head. While I went to shut the flame off and let the mixed soy sauce sit the floor started to shake. I paused and my eyes widened as the tremors increased.

"Earthquake, a bad one!" Akio shouted as he came into the kitchen. We ran over to the doorway held on to it as the shaking grew in strength. The news didn't say anything about an earthquake happening today. Could it have just come about now?

The lights flickered once, twice, then remained off as plates and glasses teetered off the counter and smashed to the floor. The pot of simmering soy sauce and wasabi clattered to the tatami mats, splattering the liquid all about the floor.

"Well, there goes dinner," Akio said in a dry tone. I inhaled once and sighed. Once the rumbling ceased, I went over to clean the mess.

"Is the electric working?" I asked, taking a towel and wiping the mats, grimacing at the thought of the time I'd have to spend cleaning the mats. Akio shook his head, flicking the on and off switch for the lights in the kitchen.

"No good. We'll have to wait it out and hope for the best, I guess," he said, sitting on a kneeling cushion near me.

"It sure came upon us in a rush, that earthquake," I said and Akio nodded.

"It did. I wonder what caused it, anyway."

"Who knows? Things just happen and I go along with it."

I rubbed at the tatami mats, which already looked stained from the soy sauce. I huffed and added some water to the towel before continuing to get most of the liquid off the mats.

A large crash sounded outside and as Akio stood to look out the window, a sudden horror filled his expression.

"What is it, dear?" I asked, going over to him and he turned away from the window toward me. I came over and peered outside with a gasp to see water traveling straight for the house.

"Quick to the attic!" I said and we both hurried as fast as we could up the stairs, hearing them creak underfoot. I shut the door behind us and tried to calm my heaving breaths as Akio searched around the attic for something.

From downstairs I heard a crack and knew that the water entered our house. Then came the sound of rushing water and Akio and I retreated to the farthest corner of the attic, looking in concern at the door. We didn't move a muscle.

"I should have brought some supplies with us before we came up here," I said, feeling regret. "How will we have any nourishment? We might be up here for days now."

"It would've taken too much time to get food. I wouldn't want to have a surge of water slam you into the wall and drown you."

"Maybe," I said, hearing my stomach growl. "But how will we eat, dear?"

"We'll just have to go hungry tonight until this all settles down tomorrow."

Time sped and I knew hours must have passed for us in the gloom of the attic, but it all seemed to move in slow motion. Only when I yawned did I assume the hour had turned late. Akio searched through the attic, to no avail, for anything comfortable we could use to sleep with.

"The rain sounds stronger now. I can hear it from outside," Akio said as we lay down on the dusty boards, trying to get comfortable.

"Perhaps the worst of the storm arrived."

I couldn't stay asleep once I closed my eyes. Between my stomach's growling and my fears of more water tumbling into the house and destroying it, I continued to wake and hear Akio's soft snores.

When I could sleep after hours of tossing and turning, my dreams showcased dark twists on the events that just happened. In all of them Mt. Fuji rose from the black mist, safe and haughty in the distance.

I woke to something prodding my shoulder and my eyes opened to meet Akio's gaze.

"I just heard something. I'm going to go downstairs and check what happened."

"But Akio, what if the water's still coming into the house? I don't want you to get hurt!"

"Don't worry about me, love. I know nothing will happen. Just wait for me, all right?" he said as a loud bang sounded from downstairs.

"All right," I gave a nod and kissed him, trusting his word. He stood, stretched, and headed out the attic door. I clenched a fist, praying he'd come back okay.

I felt the need to pace as the minutes passed, my shoes slapping the wooden floor, my footsteps making them whine and creak. I paused when I heard the sound of heavy footsteps on the attic stairs, my body tensing, my breath catching.

"It's me, Sayuri," came Akio's voice and I sighed in relief.

"What took you so long? Did you get hurt?" The look in his eyes made me blink. "Akio?

"Dear . . . there's a person downstairs and, you're not going to believe this, but he's American."

"An American? How?" I asked. Memories of pain, fire, and explosions filled me and my past opened up to me like a book. I remembered my family, brutalized, my old home and village destroyed. All because of an atomic bomb the Americans dropped years ago. I clenched my fists.

"I don't know, but he waits downstairs."

"I recall the Americans caused nothing but pain and grief for us and everyone else in our past years. Akio, don't you remember the destruction and heartfelt from the atomic bomb?" I asked, anger lacing my words.

"Too well love. Too well. This American . . . he claimed he can bring us to safety in America where rehabilitation and medical care can help us recover" Akio said. Confusion reigned in me now.

"Why would the Americans want to help us? All they've done was destruction and merciless killing to us."

"I don't know Sayuri. I spoke with the man, who knows some Japanese. He said that seventy-five percent of Yokohama was destroyed by the tsunami yesterday. His leader authorized the relocation of all survivors to America for treatment and help."

I didn't say a word. How could the Americans turn around and act like our friends again?

"I can't think of another way to survive here now anyway. Everything's destroyed: houses, trees, cars, and signs. I looked outside the broken window and saw people who drowned in the water's surge. I think we should go with this American man. He might seem suspicious, but he's our one link to seeing some kind of normalcy again," Akio said and I sighed. My mind whirled with conflicting emotions. I knew Akio was right, but I also knew Americans couldn't be trusted.

"Do you trust him?" I asked, looking at him. Akio nodded and I knew I had no choice. If my husband found nothing wrong with this man, then I wouldn't either.

"Fine, then. We'll go with this man to America," I said and my husband took my hand as we walked out of the gloom of the attic. We descended the stairs together, a gasp ripping out of me from the coldness of the water as it touched me and the amount of wreckage in sight. The water came up midway to our calves as we walked through the kitchen, but it didn't stop us from continuing.

I forced myself not to pause as I saw a man with blonde hair and green eyes piercing my own. He stood in the doorway, his lips relaxed, but his expression impatient. Akio urged me onward if he sensed any hesitation in me and I clutched his hand tighter. The man wore military clothes.

Then came the sweet sounds of the birds outside, their songs filling the air. I felt hopeful despite the dismal setting. Perhaps I made the right decision after all.

And . . . as we neared the American man, his blonde hair waving in the slight breeze, I could smell sweet peas, the sweet smell enveloping me, clearing my mind, and freeing my heart of doubts.

Wakai raibu ka shinu

Epilogue

. . . That's my life. The pain, agony, sorrow, life-making decisions; all of it. All the people I have befriended, cared about, trusted, hated, and loved have changed me into the person I am today. The person who makes dinner for a husband who wouldn't have never met me if I hadn't survived the destruction. In a way . . . I miss those times when I traveled all over to find Akio and complete my life. In a way we created our future since our first meeting. It is human though, to yearn for different times . . .

Living in New York, the hustle and bustle of the most famed city in the world, makes me feel slow and undeveloped. I preferred the endless nature and spiritual quality of my home: Yokohama. Where people believe in working together to reach a goal. People felt more open to each other there. Here, no one seems to have time for anything. Rushing everywhere like bees in a hive. I tell Akio time and again about how, when we have recovered in full, we should return to Yokohama and start our lives anew. He'd just smile and nod, although I know he has grown to love New York and has no desire to leave.

Do I still feel resentful of the Americans now that I live in their nation? Somewhat . . . for they made me lose what I had clung onto when I was but a teenager and a young woman. However the destruction of the atomic bomb also showed me the reality of life outside of a fairy-tale world, a world some people live in throughout their whole lives. It makes me feel happy, the one emotion that had fleeted me since my plight in Nagasaki, to live in a place where one remnant of my past still exists to hold my hand and give me soft words of love.

And another remnant . . . barks with happiness, his black and cream colored fur brightening my day as he licks my and Akio's face in the morning. He eats more than his older ancestor did, but he's still the same dog—that much I know—with the same name.

Glossary

Name Translations:

Sayuri — Lily

Jaakuna — Malevolence/Evil

Akio — Glorious Man

Korudo — Cold

Yuki — Bravery

Katashi — Firmness

Maiko — Dancing child

Kimu — Gold

Hisoka — Reserved

Rabu — Love

O bachan — Grandma

Baunsu — Bounce

Seishin—Spirit

Kotei—Emperor

Rin—Severe

Isamu—Courage

Shinjitsu—Truth

Iyasu—Heal

Hageshi—Fierce

Dansei—Man

Yowai—Weak

Katsu—Victory

On'na—Woman

Kawa—River

Item, places, and food translations:

Ume—Peach

Izakaya—Tavern

Nikujaga Soup—A Japanese dish of meat, potatoes and onions stewed in sweet soy sauce, sometimes with corn and vegetables.

Gohei—a wooden wand decorated with two zigzagging paper streamers. Used in Shinto rituals.

Ichijiyu—Fig

Ume — Plum

Saba — Mackerel

Yakizakana — Grilled fish

Dashi — This soup forms the base for almost all of Japanese cooking.

Village name translations:

Han'ei — Prosperity

Dokutsu — Cave

Chinmoku — Silence

Kyroyoku — Strong

Hebi — Snake

Taka — Hawk

Kagayaki — Radiance

Zokusuru — Belong

Yujo — Friendship

Sayings translations:

Kawaii — Dear

Itadakimasu — I gratefully receive

Seisa-Style — Traditional Japanese kneeling position.

Arigato — Thank you

Oni no ie — Demon's House.

Wakai raibu ka shinu — Live or die young.

Haikei — Greetings

Common Honorifics

-san — Used in ordinary casual situations between two people, preferably strangers.

-sama — Used in the means of ultimate respect. Most use this honorific when speaking to someone of authority or extreme kindness.

-chan — Common honorific. Used when one person favors or likes another. Also used when speaking to children.